Praise for *Common So*

"Ms. Lorenz has blended a contemporary story with a paranormal flare that combines to create a fascinating story."

— Teresa, *Fallen Angel Reviews*

Rush in the Dark

"*Rush in the Dark* is a fantastic follow up to *Soul Bonds*."

– Ley, *Joyfully Reviewed*

Edward Unconditionally

"This is definitely not a story to be missed because the characters are so engaging that they will stay with you for a long time to come."

– Kimberley Spinney, *eCataromance*

"Fans will be over the moon at the introduction of one of her best characters yet, Edward Paul Beauregard III... It's a fantastic romance that blends madcap humor, memorable characters and scorching hot sex."

– Marame, *Rainbow Reviews*

"The action is fast, the emotions high, and the dialogue so funny, I had tears in my eyes..."

– *Literary Nymphs*

Loose Id®

ISBN: 978-1-60737-412-1
EDWARD UNCONDITIONALLY
Copyright © December 2009 by Lynn Lorenz
Originally released in e-book format in April 2009

Cover Art by April Martinez
Cover Layout and design by April Martinez

All rights reserved. Except for use of brief quotations in any review or critical article, the reproduction or utilization of this work in whole or in part in any form by any electronic, mechanical or other means, now known or hereafter invented, including xerography, photocopying and recording, or in any information storage or retrieval is forbidden without the prior written permission of Loose Id LLC, 870 Market St, Suite 1201, San Francisco CA 94102-2907. http://www.loose-id.com

DISCLAIMER: Many of the acts described in our BDSM/fetish titles can be dangerous. Please do not try any new sexual practice, whether it be fire, rope, or whip play, without the guidance of an experienced practitioner. Neither Loose Id nor its authors will be responsible for any loss, harm, injury or death resulting from use of the information contained in any of its titles.

This book is an original publication of Loose Id. Each individual story herein was previously published in e-book format only by Loose Id and is a work of fiction. Any similarity to actual persons, events or existing locations is entirely coincidental.

Printed in the U.S.A. by
Lightning Source, Inc.
1246 Heil Quaker Blvd
La Vergne TN 37086
www.lightningsource.com

EDWARD UNCONDITIONALLY
COMMON POWERS 3

Lynn Lorenz

Chapter One

"Well, Winston. What do you think about Texas?" Edward drawled in his soft Georgia accent as he cast a sidelong glance at his best friend and constant companion.

Winston, a six-year-old English bulldog, didn't answer. He was far too busy hanging over the edge of the passenger door, his face in the wind, pink tongue lolling from the side of his gaping mouth, as Edward drove down the rural blacktop at sixty-five miles per hour.

"We're definitely not in Georgia anymore." Edward sighed. "I've never seen so much livestock in all my life." He shuddered. Another field of black cows dotted the rolling hills. "Although, I've always wanted a brown and white cowhide Louis Quatorze chair. It would be *très chic, n'est-ce pas?*"

Winston eyed him sadly.

"The only good thing about Texas is the cowboys. I do love me some cowboy." Edward gave a low, "yum yum yum," and wiggled his eyebrows at Winston.

Winston favored him with a soft *woof,* then returned to flying his tongue in the wind.

"You like them too, huh? Maybe you'll find a cow dog."

Woof.

"Honestly, you'd probably have better luck out here than I would."

Edward picked up the map he'd folded, laid it on the steering wheel of his Miata, and glanced at it. Spring Lake had been circled in red, and the road they were on had been highlighted in yellow.

Who'd ever heard of a Farm to Market Road? He'd exited I-10 westbound and turned south onto the two-lane road, all the while wondering where the market was or if he'd come to the farm by following the road to its end.

The idea of being on a farm gave him the heebie-jeebies. He was so *not* a *Country Living* kind of guy. More like *Metropolitan Design*. Sleek leather, minimalistic window treatments, grass-mat flooring. No livestock in the house.

Not lace curtains, tacky multicolored chintz, and those god-awful oval rugs from the fifties. *So* Lucy and Desi move to Connecticut.

He shuddered again.

But duty called. Well, not exactly duty, but his mother, Lillian. When Lillian Rawlings Beauregard bellowed, Edward Paul Beauregard, the Third, answered with a controlled, if tight-lipped, "yes, Mother."

And if Edward valued his trust fund, and he did, he did what he was told. He gave a silent but respectful, "fuck you," to his late father for requiring Edward to reach forty before he inherited. As if at thirty, or now at thirty-five, Edward didn't know what he wanted to do with his life or that he'd outgrow being gay. Never mind that he'd never finished college or that he'd had numerous careers, each one more exciting than the last.

Who made the stupid rule that you had to do one thing for your entire life? Or even for a few years? Life was meant to be lived, not to wallow in a rut.

He'd be the first to admit he'd led an unconventional life. A wild life, even. Scads of parties, beaucoup champagne, madcap friends, overseas adventures, and numerous lovers. For his father, that was right where it had begun and ended.

Edward's lovers.

Like his latest debacle. No, he didn't always pick the best men. Okay, he *never* picked the best men.

"Can I help it if I'm drawn like a moth to the flame whenever there's a bad boy within reaching distance?" he asked Winston.

Woof.

Edward glanced at his dog. "You did *not* just roll your eyes at me."

Woof.

"Since when have you started channeling my father?"

Woof.

Edward gave a long-suffering sigh.

With the gay half of Atlanta buzzing over Edward's latest spectacular breakup, and oh yes, they *always* had to be spectacular—this time in the middle of the dance floor at this season's gay black-tie ball—Edward needed a quiet place to lick his wounds. Hurt and embarrassed, Edward had crushed his slice of seven-layer chocolate Doberge cake in that cheating bastard Derek's face, whom Edward had taken into his heart and into his condo.

Secretly relieved to get out of town, Edward had made his excuses for the rest of the social season, packed his matching Louis Vuitton travel bags, and hopped in the convertible. Then he drove to Houston from Atlanta, with instructions from his mother to visit his grandmother and find out what was ailing her.

And heal her.

* * *

Chief of Police Jack Whittaker had the mother of all headaches. Again.

Sitting in his white unmarked patrol car, he rubbed his forehead as he leaned back against the headrest. He'd almost run off the side of the road when his vision blurred.

"Shit." This was the third time in the last two weeks. Whatever was kicking his ass was getting worse, not better. Now his vision was being affected.

Fear crawled into his belly and scratched at his insides. A blind man couldn't be a cop, much less chief of police, and he was nowhere near old enough to retire. Hell, he wasn't even forty-five yet.

Jack glanced at his reflection in the rearview mirror. Deep blue eyes. Deeper lines around them. A touch of gray at his temples.

There was no getting past it: he looked older.

"It ain't the years, boy, it's the miles."

He'd seen a hell of a lot of miles, for damn sure.

Jack blinked, his vision cleared, but the headache pounded on. Opening his glove box, he pulled out a bottle of extra-strength pain relievers, popped two, and chased them down with a swig of cold black coffee.

He wouldn't be sitting out on this road if he didn't have so many men out with the flu. Having them come in and work their shifts had only spread it faster through the ranks. But whatever Jack had, it wasn't the flu.

On days like today, he hated his job.

When he'd pulled over, he'd been on his way back to the station at Spring Lake from a vandalism call that had turned out to be nothing more than a high school prank. Not to mention, this afternoon he had a budget meeting with the mayor.

As he'd sat there, the road had been as empty as his stomach. He put the cruiser into gear and checked for traffic in his rearview. A car appeared over the hill. His heart kicked up a notch, that familiar rush of the chase grabbing his gut. He waited, watching it eat up the road.

As the bright red Miata convertible passed him, its wind trail rocked his car. The guy had to be doing sixty—maybe sixty-five. In a forty-five.

With a growl, Jack flicked on his lights, hit his siren, slammed his foot on the gas, and fishtailed onto the road in pursuit.

* * *

"Hell and damnation!" Edward flicked his gaze to the rearview mirror.

A large white car with blue and red flashing lights followed him, and he could hear the wail of a siren. For a moment, he thought about not stopping but decided Texas wasn't the place to try to elude the cops. Didn't they use cattle prods here?

"You don't think that's the welcoming committee, do you?"

Woof.

"I didn't think so." Edward slowed down and eased off the road as far as he could without going into a ditch big enough to eat a Buick.

He reached over, picked up his jacket, and fished out his wallet. Taking his proof of insurance and the registration papers from the glove box, he sat back and waited, his fingers drumming rhythmically on the wheel.

"You don't think Barney Fife was using gaydar, do you?" Edward chuckled as he watched the cop car pull behind him.

Winston scratched at the door.

"You need to go walksies, Winston?"

Woof.

Edward grabbed Winston's leash, dug under the red bandanna that decorated Winston's neck, and clipped the end to a leather collar. Getting out, Edward pulled on the leash, and Winston hopped down.

A deep, irritated voice came out of the air. "Driver. Get *back* in your vehicle."

Edward waved at the cop to let him know it was all right and walked around the car with Winston. "Pay no attention to that man behind the curtain, Winston," he intoned as the dog, head down, nose in action, sniffed his way along the grass at the side of the road.

"I said get back in your car. That's an order."

Good Lord, there was no need to get pissy about it.

Edward called over his shoulder as the dog pulled him farther away, "My ID is on the seat if you need it. I just need to walk my dog."

* * *

"No. No. No," Jack muttered. This was *not* happening to him. He'd given that guy a direct order, and he wasn't used to being disobeyed. Jack shook his head, and the motion started the pounding again.

"Fuck!" He opened the car door, got out, slid his hat on his head, and put his hand on the butt of his semiautomatic. There was no way in hell he was going to take this crap from some… He stopped, doing a double take at the young man and his dog.

"What the—" he muttered under his breath.

The man and the dog wore matching red bandannas tied around their necks. Jack blinked. The dog, one of those ugly-as-hell bulldogs, waddled down the side of the road. Immense balls swung with every step as he pulled his master after him like a cowboy holding on to a stubborn cow headed for the barn.

His owner wore the tightest dark blue jeans Jack had ever seen cover a man's behind. His ice blue shirt was Western cut, but the piping had brown leather fringe. At least, Jack thought it was leather.

"Oh my God." Jack held back a snicker. Was this guy for real?

Jack headed to the car, leaned over the door, and picked up the packet of papers.

"Get over here. Now," Jack ordered as he looked at each form. After checking the name, Jack tossed the registration on the seat. It matched the name on the insurance card, which he added to the pile.

He picked up the leather wallet. Soft, supple, it reeked of Italy and money. He had no idea how much it cost, but it was probably more than he'd spend on a good leather jacket. Looking up, he watched the driver approach and come around the car with the dog pulling hard on the leash and growling.

Jack looked at the dog and frowned, then up to the man's face. Early thirties, five feet ten inches, short black hair, and deep brown eyes that stopped Jack in his tracks.

The growling grew closer, louder, then white-hot pain erupted as the dog chomped down on Jack's ankle and shook his leg like a...well, like a dog with a bone.

"What the fuck!" Jack jumped back, dropped the wallet, and drew his weapon.

"No! Don't hurt Winston!" the guy yelled, lunged forward, and grabbed Jack's weapon arm.

Jack's mind screamed *ambush*, and his adrenaline kicked into overdrive. He hopped backward as he jerked his arm away from the man and tried to kick the dog off his leg at the same time. Everyone was growling, and everyone had a piece of him.

"Let go of me!" Jack shouted. "Stop it, or the gun might go off!"

"Don't shoot!" The man's grip tightened on his arm, now more frantic than before. Jack flexed his bicep and pulled the guy into him, his gun pointed at the sky.

Through gritted teeth, Jack said, "If you let me go right now and get this mutt off me, I won't shoot you both." They weren't quite chest to chest; the guy was shorter than Jack by a good four inches. Jack wanted to kill the son of a bitch right then and there. Then the damned dog.

"Promise?" Breathy and soft, that one word shivered down Jack's spine and held him in its grip.

"I promise." He had no idea why he was making promises to this man. He didn't have to promise a damn thing; he was the law.

The man let go and stepped away just as the dog shook Jack again, its massive head snapping from side to side. Jack hopped backward and his arms pinwheeled in the air. He lost his footing, went down on his side, hit his head on the ground, and a new wave of pain erupted as his elbow jammed down on the blacktop.

The gun went off.

The front tire on the car hissed and flattened.

Someone screamed.

The man grabbed the dog, cooed to it, and Jack felt the dog's teeth release his leg.

No one was going to believe this. Thank God his patrol car wasn't one of the ones that had the new dash video cameras and that this moment wouldn't be captured. And shared among all his men for them to laugh at him.

If it were up to him, no one would know about this either.

Standing over Jack with the dog in his arms, the man looked down at him. The bulldog's tongue licked around its mouth as if savoring the taste of Jack's flesh and blood, looking very pleased with itself.

From his spot on the ground, Jack said, "You're lucky I didn't shoot *you*."

He shoved his gun back into the holster and pushed himself up to sitting. After pulling up his leg, he rolled up his cuff, pushed down his black sock, and examined the bite. Two puncture wounds just above his ankle leaked blood, his pants were shredded, and his dignity was shot to hell.

Would it be murder? First degree or manslaughter? How much time would he have to do?

"I'm going to have to impound your dog. He doesn't have a tag." Jack grabbed his hat and shoved it back on.

"You can't do that!" The man clutched his dog to him and stepped back. "Winston can't go to jail."

"Yes, I can. I'm the fucking chief of police. I can do anything I fucking want to. And if you give me any more lip, I'll toss you in a cell and throw away the fucking key." Jack pushed to his feet. "Now, put the dog back in your car."

Finally, the guy did what Jack told him to do. The dog hopped in, and as the man shut the Miata's door, he murmured to the dog, "Stay right there, Winston."

Woof.

Jack glared at the dog, then said, "Now, hands on the car and spread your legs."

"What?"

Jack grabbed the man's arm and spun him around. "I said, spread your legs," he growled as a flash of power and control shot through his body. Uh-uh. Not good.

"But I hardly know you. I'm really not that kind of guy," he drawled over his shoulder.

As the bulldog kept his eyes on Jack, probably looking for a chance to bite again, Jack slid his hands over the guy's back, hips, and down his legs, lingering on firm muscles, absorbing the heat of the younger man's body. "Anything you want to declare?"

"Just my sexuality, Officer."

"That's chief of police." Unfortunately, he was clean. Jack had hoped he'd find something on the dude, just to add to the list of charges. "Put your hands behind your back." Jack pulled out his cuffs.

"What?"

"I said, 'Put your hands behind your back.'"

"Am I under arrest?" This time the younger man did as he was told. Jack slapped the handcuffs over his wrists and then walked him by the arm over to his patrol car.

"This is for your protection and mine. I'll take them off if everything checks out."

"Promise?"

Jack caught a flicker of fear in his brown eyes; then it was gone. Jack didn't answer. Instead, he said, "Stay here; don't move." Jack leaned him against the bumper.

Sliding behind the wheel, he picked up the radio and took a deep breath. The man had made him so mad Jack had lost his professionalism, lost his control, and had cursed. Not cool.

Christ, Jack had been so rattled, he hadn't followed procedure. For all Jack knew, he could be wanted in three states. That shirt alone should get the guy arrested.

He stole a look at his prisoner, decided it was time to pull himself together and act like the cop he was, put down the mic, and got out of the car. He strode over to the Miata and picked up the driver's license and wallet lying on the ground, then gathered up the other papers.

Jack stared at it. "Edward Paul Beauregard the Third? Are you joking?"

"No." The man stood straighter.

"The Third?" Who puts that on their license? Senior, junior, maybe, but the little III behind the name seemed so pretentious.

"Yes. I'm Edward Beauregard, of the Atlanta Beauregards," he drawled, as if it should mean something to Jack.

"Well, Mr. Beauregard, I'm going to call in your license and see if you need to be sitting in the back with that crazed mutt of yours." Sitting in the car again, he picked up the mic and read off the numbers to his dispatcher. If it came back positive, he'd put the guy in the back of the car. With his damn dog.

"He's not a crazed mutt. He's registered." Beauregard tilted his nose upward.

"Registered as a lethal weapon?"

"Lethal weapon. Cute. I had no idea sheriffs were *so* funny."

Jack let the sheriff comment slide. "Does he always attack people?"

The man looked Jack up and down, then purred, "Like me, I guess he can't resist a man in uniform."

Jack stared at Beauregard, opened his mouth to respond, but before he could put his big foot in, dispatch came back. "He's clean. No record. No warrants."

"See." He gave an exasperated shrug. "I'm not a criminal escaping justice."

How the hell was Jack going to explain this?

"Jesus, give me strength," he muttered, his finger on the button.

"Come back, Chief? What'd you say?" his dispatcher replied.

"Dispatch a tow truck to mile thirteen on FM 123 and pick up a red Miata. Have them take it to Smith's to have the tire fixed."

"Everything all right, sir?" The voice crackled back at him.

"Just peachy-damn-keen." He slammed the receiver on the hook, leaned back against the headrest, and closed his eyes.

His head pounded, he'd been dog bit, and he'd lost a fight with the gayest man he'd ever seen in his life.

Jack groaned.

"Officer, are you all right?"

Jack stared into the man's worried face as he looked through the windshield.

"Against my better judgment, I'm going to release you." He fought the urge to shoot someone, including himself. Instead, he got out of the car and opened the rear door, then uncuffed Beauregard.

"Put the dog in, sir."

"But…" The man bit his bottom lip, full and pink. Men shouldn't have such plump lips; there should be a law. And he certainly should *not* be noticing such things.

"Now." Too tired to argue, Jack stared him down.

He nodded, got the dog from his car, and led him back to the cruiser. "Get in, Winston. Don't worry. I'll get you a lawyer."

The dog hopped in, climbed onto the seat, and sat back. His owner fastened the seat belt over the dog's broad chest, gently closed the door, and stared through the window at the beast.

"You're not going to hurt him, are you?"

Jack looked down into brown eyes surrounded by thick lashes that matched the younger man's short black hair.

For some reason Jack *absolutely* did not want to explore, he softened his tone. "You'll have to prove he's had his shots, see the judge, and pay a fine. But no, I'm not going to hurt him." That would be up to their animal control officer, if it went that far. "Get your stuff from the car. You're coming with me until I get this all straightened out."

Jack watched as that incredibly firm ass walked back to the car, opened the trunk, and pulled out a suitcase and a duffel bag. He'd seen a set of bags like those in the mall in San Antonio, at one of the upscale shops. Leather, maybe, and if the guy's wallet was any indication, they probably cost more than Jack made in a month. Maybe two months.

The young man shut the trunk and then came back to the patrol car. Placing the luggage on the ground in front of Jack as if *he* were supposed to stow them away, the man turned and went back to the wounded Miata. The familiar smell of leather came from the bags, reminding Jack of saddles and tack. Heady. Manly.

They didn't seem to match the man. At all. Maybe they were borrowed.

The dog's owner leaned over the door, giving Jack another eyeful of ass, then scooped up a worn brown leather jacket and returned.

He pointed to his bags. "Those need to go in the trunk, Officer."

"I'm the chief of police," Jack gritted out.

"Of course you are," he said, then walked to the passenger side, opened the door, and slid into the seat with nary a by-your-leave.

"Jesus." Jack looked up at the sky. "Don't give me strength. I'd just kill him with my bare hands." Then he picked up the bags and put them in the trunk of the cruiser.

Chapter Two

Jack drove to town in a steaming silence. His ankle had beaten out his head for the grand prize of pain as it throbbed with every movement. In the backseat, the dog rode peacefully, no frothing at the mouth, no wild barking, as if he'd ridden in the back of a cop car his whole life. And wearing a seat belt, for God's sake. He'd never seen a dog wear a seat belt.

Beside Jack, the stranger stared out the window at the scenery.

Not one word of apology for Jack's bite.

Jack snatched up the mic again. "I'm bringing someone in."

"What's your ETA?"

"Ten minutes." He hung up the mic.

Jack cleared his throat. "So, what are you doing in Spring Lake?"

"Spring Lake? Why, I thought I was in Hooterville," the guy drawled.

The comment set Jack's teeth on edge. He hated being thought of as a hick cop. "Look, I don't care if you're from fucking New York City, Spring Lake is not…"

"Relax, Sheriff." Beauregard grinned at him. "Besides, I thought all you country boys were easygoing and laid-back."

"Normally, with decent folks, that's the truth," Jack shot back.

Beauregard stiffened. "And I'm indecent. Why? Because I'm gay?"

"I didn't say that—"

"There are laws against discrimination, you know," Beauregard snapped.

"I know, it's my duty to uphold—"

"Because if you treat me any less than you would any other run-of-the-mill *straight* criminal, I'll get a lawyer, and you and Hooterville will *never* hear the end of it." His voice rose and quivered with emotion.

Jack restrained himself from pulling his gun again by clutching the steering wheel until his knuckles turned white. His head regained the lead as it passed his ankle in the quarter-mile stretch of the pain derby.

Why did this kind of shit always happen to him? Why couldn't one of the other men have caught this, like his new officer, Brian Russell? He was gay, living in Spring Lake with his life partner, rancher Rush Weston.

"Oh, I promise to treat you the same as any of our *regular* criminals." Jack fought to keep his voice civil.

"Well, I should hope so." Beauregard gave him a curt nod and turned away.

Did the guy have to have the last word?

"Don't worry," Jack added.

"I won't."

Yep. The last word.

* * *

Jack gritted his teeth and stared straight ahead as he drove down Main Street to the station. He prayed no one would be in the parking lot when he pulled in, and he could slip the dog and Beauregard in unnoticed. The fewer questions, the better.

He pulled through the gates, drove to the spot marked CHIEF OF POLICE, and parked.

"Hey, does the chief know you're parking in his spot?" Beauregard asked.

"I told you. I'm the chief," Jack replied, barely keeping his temper in check. Throwing the guy in a jail cell and forgetting about him for a few days was looking better and better. Maybe he could get his hands on a cattle prod.

Except for the personal cars of the officers on duty, the dispatcher, and Jack's secretary, the place looked empty. Before anyone else showed up, he got out and opened the back door.

The dog sat on the seat, panting. The plastic seat was covered in dozens of shiny droplets of dog drool. Someone was going to have to clean that up, and Jack had a sinking feeling who that would be.

Beauregard got out, came around to Jack, leaned down, and peered in. "Winston? Are you all right?"

Woof.

With a loud sigh, he reached in, took the leash, and led the dog out of the car.

"He's going to need some water. He's very upset." Beauregard looked down at his pet and frowned. The dog sat on the blacktop and grinned up at Jack.

"He doesn't look upset to me." Jack glared back at the dog.

"Well, he is. You don't know Winston as well as I do."

"And I hope I never do." Jack shut the door. "Let's go, Roy Rogers." Dale Evans was more like it.

"Roy Rogers? What do you mean by that?" Beauregard's eyebrows rose.

Jack motioned to the man's clothing and thickened up his Texas twang. "Why, you look like you're fixin' to go to one of them there Yankee fancy-dress parties, pretending to be a cowboy 'n' such."

Beauregard's eyes narrowed. "I'll have you know this shirt is the *height* of Dallas Western fashion."

"Dallas, huh? Figures." Jack led the way to the station's back door. He pulled it open and waited as the dog and his owner entered.

"What's wrong with Dallas?" The guy actually sounded a little worried.

"Well, that's *north* Texas. We don't hold with their ways here in *south* Texas." Jack gave the guy his serious "I mean business" face as he walked down the hall to his office.

"I didn't know that."

Jack stopped, leaned in, and lowered his voice. "Well, I'll bet you didn't know that down here in *south* Texas, a man could get his ass kicked for wearing a shirt with that much fringe on it."

Beauregard looked down at his shirt and ran a well-manicured nail across the breast pocket's fringe. "Too much fringe?"

"Hell, yeah. But don't worry, cowboy. Uh, you don't have any more of those shirts, do you?" Jack raised an eyebrow at Beauregard and kept walking.

"Nooo…" He sounded unsure, or afraid to admit he had more.

"That's good. Folks around here do hate fringe." Jack shook his head as if it were a pity people took such a dislike to fringe.

Beauregard's eyes narrowed and he stopped. "Sure it's just the fringe they hate?"

Jack looked Beauregard up and down.

"I sure hope so." And for some reason, he did.

His secretary, Kristen, looked up as he entered the main office.

"Dear Lord, Chief. What happened to you?" Kristen stood, her hand at her mouth, and stared at his leg.

He looked down. He'd left a small trail of blood on the linoleum floor. "Damn. I had a little"—he glared at Beauregard—"accident."

"Do I need to call the doctor?" She picked up the phone.

"No, just get me the first-aid kit. I'll take care of it."

"Right away, sir. I'll clean this up too." She put the phone down and vanished into the back hall where the lunchroom and bathroom were located.

"You." Jack pointed to Beauregard and crooked his finger. "Follow me."

"To the ends of the earth," Beauregard cooed.

Jack entered his office, tossed his hat on the desk, and fell into his chair.

What a hell of a day.

Beauregard came in after him and shut the door. The dog sat by his feet and looked up at his owner as if awaiting orders.

If the dog attacked again, this time Jack *was* going to shoot.

"Now that you've got me alone, what are you going to do with me?" Beauregard asked. His voice was low and seductive, but the way his gaze darted around the room gave him away. Jack could almost smell the fear on him. Or maybe it was his cologne. Probably it was the dog.

"I fill out some forms, you sign them, and I lock up your dog."

"Lock him up? Here?"

Jack looked at the younger man. After bringing the dog in, Jack realized they didn't have a facility at the station to hold an animal. "I'll have to call the vet and see if he's got a cage free."

"A cage? Winston can't go into a cage." He shook his head and pulled tighter on the leash, tugging the dog closer to his leg.

"And why not? He's a dog." Jack rubbed his eyes, and the pounding lessened.

"Because he's claustrophobic."

Jack dropped his hand from his eyes and stared at Beauregard. "Claustrophobic?"

"That's right."

"The dog?"

"Winston."

Jack grimaced. "Winston is claustrophobic." Okay, now he'd heard everything.

"Yes. He was traumatized in a tragic cage incident when he was a puppy, and he's never gotten over it. Have you, Winston?" he cooed.

Woof.

"Quit yanking my chain, Beauregard."

"I'm serious. If you put Winston in a cage and anything happens to him after I warned you not to, I'm going to own Spring Lake." Beauregard looked dead serious, and from what Jack had seen, he had the money to back up his threat.

Jack sat back and sighed. "You must really love that dog."

"He's very important to me." Beauregard looked down at his dog, and when he looked back at Jack, his brown eyes looked dark and liquid. "Don't put him in a cage. Please."

Jack ran his hands over his face. Why him? He was a good guy. Kept the peace, upheld the law, went to church on Sunday, and was kind to old ladies and children.

He picked up the phone, flipped through his Rolodex, and found the vet's number.

"Can I speak to Dr. Martin? It's Chief Whittaker." Jack held on as music played in his ear.

"Martin here."

"Doc? It's Jack."

"How are you, Chief?"

"Doing fine. Listen, I have a problem. Got a dog I need to have impounded, but his owner says he's claustrophobic and can't go into a cage. Is that possible?"

"Well, sure, Jack. Some dogs can die due to the stress of being caged," the doctor confirmed.

"Die, huh?" Jack glanced at Beauregard who was hanging on to every word.

"They go into shock, or panic and have heart attacks."

"What do you suggest? The dog bit someone, and he has to be kept until we can confirm he's had all his shots."

"What is his behavior like now?"

Jack shrugged. "Well, he's just sitting there."

"Any more attacks since the first one?"

"No."

"Does he look vicious?"

Jack leaned over the desk and stared at the dog. It had lain down and was licking its paws clean, no doubt of Jack's blood. "No."

"Well, perhaps there were special circumstances that led to the attack. Was he provoked?"

Jack didn't want to explain the incident. Not to the vet. Not to anyone, for that matter. "No, he wasn't. Just walked up and bit the guy."

"Well, he doesn't sound dangerous. Just find someone to keep him while you investigate."

"I don't suppose you could—"

"No can do. Sorry." The vet chuckled.

"Right. Thanks, Doc." Jack hung up and settled back in his chair.

"See? I told you," Beauregard gloated.

Jack sighed. "Okay. No cage."

"Can't you release him in my care?"

"No. You're just passing through town. I need him here where I can get to him if I need him." Like if we have to kill him, cut off his head, and then test for rabies. Jesus, more than anything, Jack didn't want it to go that far. Those shots were killers. He rubbed his hand over his belly just thinking about them.

"I'm not passing through. I'm here for a visit." Beauregard's face lit up.

"A visit? With who?"

"My grandmother. Mrs. Olivia Rawlings."

"Olivia Rawlings?" Jack sat up. Far as he knew, Miss Olivia didn't have any family.

Beauregard smiled. "That's right, Sheriff."

"It's Chief of Police Jack Whittaker. I work for the city. The sheriff works for the county, and it's an elected—"

Beauregard cut him off. "Well, can he stay with her?"

Jack was trapped. "Okay. I'll fill out these forms, and you call Olivia and set it up. Do you need a phone?" He stood, walked to the file cabinet, fished for the proper forms, and pulled them out.

"No, I have my cell." Edward slumped into one of the two chairs that sat in front of Jack's desk and made the call. This was the absolute worst pickle he'd ever been in. Worse because it wasn't just him, it was Winston.

He had no idea what had come over Winston. Sure, the chief looked good enough to bite, in an older, distinguished kind of way, but still.

He ran a shaking hand through his hair and searched his list for his grandmother's number, then hit Send.

"Hello?" A strong female voice came over the line. He didn't recognize it except at some instinctual level deep inside. He hadn't spoken to her since he was sixteen.

"Meemaw? It's Edward." He glanced at the rugged cop on the other side of the desk. Jack was so *not* his type. He was older, for one thing. Edward *never* dated older men. For another, he was *not* a bad boy. Far from it. And he certainly wasn't gay.

So why had he been flirting with the cop?

"Edward? Edward who?" She sounded suspicious.

"Your grandson, Meemaw. Edward. Your daughter Lillian's son." Edward bent over his legs, crossed at the knee, and stared at Winston. The dog was handling this like a trooper, stretched out on his back, four paws in the air, asleep.

"Edward!" Her voice sounded warm and welcoming. It hit Edward's heart and filled a spot there he never knew was empty. "It's been ages, child."

"I know." Edward sighed.

"Where are you?"

"That's just the thing. I'm here in Spring Lake." Edward gave a little laugh, fully aware that Whittaker's blue eyes were on him. It made him uncomfortable, as if he were being measured and found lacking. It was the same look his father had given him so many times.

"You are! Well, come on over right now."

"I can't. I'm at the sher—the police station. Winston's gotten into some trouble."

"Winston? Do I know him?"

"No, Meemaw. Winston is my dog. He bit someone, and he's being impounded."

"A dog. Your dog bit someone. Who? Do I know them?" She sounded quite excited.

Edward mumbled into the phone, "The chief of police."

There was a long silence on the end of the phone.

Laughter burst across the line. Edward had to hold the phone away from his ear. Whittaker looked up at him, one eyebrow raised. Edward reached down and scratched Winston's belly to avoid the cop's intense gaze.

"Oh my Lord, Edward. You haven't changed a bit. Still the same imp that found a million ways to get into trouble."

"That's me." Edward sighed. "Can I bring Winston to your house? He can't go in a cage; he's claustrophobic."

"Oh, I'm sorry, child. I'm allergic to cats and dogs. My throat closes right up. But you're welcome to stay with me, of course." Edward slumped in his seat. Winston was out. Now what would he do?

"Thank you, Meemaw. I'm here to see you anyway."

"Well, get that dog thing settled and come on by. I'll get the guest room ready for you."

"Yes, Meemaw. See you soon." Edward closed the phone and slipped it back into his pocket. He stared at Winston for a long time.

The solution came to him in a heartbeat.

Edward straightened. "She can't take Winston. She's allergic to dogs." He stared into Whittaker's deep blue eyes, and their gazes locked for what seemed a very long time. Edward had to remember to breathe. When he did, he took a deep breath and then let it out. There was only one way out of this.

"Will you take Winston, Chief Whittaker?"

Chapter Three

"Are you out of your mind?" Jack bellowed. He slammed his hands flat on the desk, and everything bounced. "That animal bit me!"

"I know. But I don't know anyone else." Edward leaned forward, hands on the desk.

"You don't know me! Tie him to the fence outside. Lock him in a car; he seems to be happy there." Jack waved his hand at the window.

"I can't leave him outside. He's not an outside dog. And I'm not tying him like some animal to the fence." Edward glared at Jack as if even suggesting such a thing was barbaric.

"He *is* an animal. *All* dogs are outside dogs."

"Not Winston."

"Have you looked at him lately? Looks like a dog to me." Jack glared at the subject in question. He'd curled up next to Jack's desk as if he'd slept there his whole life.

"Winston is more than a dog to me." Edward bit his lip again. "Didn't you ever have a dog?"

Jack froze. Aw shit, Beauregard had to go there. Had to fight dirty.

"Well?"

"Yeah. I had a dog. When I was a kid." Jack frowned.

"Then you must understand how I feel about him." Edward lowered his voice. "Please. He's my...best friend."

Jack looked from the man to the dog. Yeah. He knew about dogs. When he was a kid, Rascal, a beagle, had been his best friend, his only friend. And when, at sixteen, Jack had run away from what could only loosely be called home, he'd taken nothing but a duffel bag and that dog.

Jack ran his hand through his hair.

"I can't believe I'm doing this."

"Thank you!" Edward smiled, and his face lit up. In that moment, Jack could see the man's youth, hope, and genuine thanks. It transformed his face and made him look, not handsome, but beautiful. Younger than the midthirties he was.

Jack held out his hand to stop Beauregard from coming around the desk to hug him. "But this is just until the confirmation of his shots comes through and the judge releases him."

"I understand." The relief on Beauregard's handsome face was evident.

Jack sat down and rubbed his palms against his eyes. They felt like they were pushing out of his head.

"Hey, are you all right?" Beauregard's soft voice and Georgia drawl stopped Jack.

"Just a headache."

"I can help you with that, you know."

Jack looked up. "I have some pain relievers." He pulled open his drawer, pulled out a bottle, and shook them as if the medicine would ward off Beauregard.

"That just masks the problem. I can heal you."

"Heal me? Like some faith healer?" Jack sat back and cocked his head at the younger man. Could this day get any stranger?

"Maybe 'heal' was the wrong word. But I can take the pain away."

"How?" Jack narrowed his eyes at him.

"Massage. I'm trained in massage therapy."

That would mean Beauregard would have to touch him. "Uh-uh. No way."

"It won't hurt, and it won't take but a minute."

"No. Thanks, but no." Jack shook his head. It felt like his brain was a small metal ball and his skull was the pinball machine. Right now, TILT should be flashing in the air over his head.

Just then, as if to save him, Kristen knocked on the door and opened it. "I have the first-aid kit, sir." She came in, placed it on his desk, stared from one man to the other, then at the dog. "You need anything else?"

"No, Kristen. Thanks."

She nodded and left, pulling the door closed behind her.

Jack reached for the kit, opened it, and pulled out what he needed to treat the bite.

"I can do that for you," the man offered.

More touching. "No, thanks. I think you've done quite enough as it is. You're free to go."

"I'd love to, but...you shot my car, remember?"

Had he already begun to block the memory? "Okay, let me call one of my men, get him to take you to the garage. The car should be fixed by now. Then you can go on to Olivia's." And get out of Jack's hair.

Beauregard stood. "First, I need to tell you about Winston."

"Tell me what?" Jack narrowed his eyes and braced himself.

"Just a few things. First, you can't leave him outside at night. Promise me."

More promises? "Okay."

"Second, he only eats Mighty Dog Stew. It's in a can. His favorite is liver and egg. He hates the hamburger and cheese flavor. No table scraps; he's on a diet."

"A diet. Uh-huh." Jack listened with all the intent of forgetting every word of the man's instructions.

"Third, he likes to take a walk just before bedtime. At least fifteen minutes long. And you have to walk him, not just let him out. He needs the exercise."

"Right." Jack's patience had just about reached the end of its rope.

"Four. He likes to sleep by my feet in bed."

The rope hit its end with a resounding *twang*. "No."

"What?"

"I said no. I'm not sleeping with a dog in my bed." He hadn't shared his bed with a dog since he was a teenager. Hadn't shared it with anyone since then, for that matter.

"Why? Doesn't your wife like dogs?" Beauregard snapped.

"I'm not married."

"Your girlfriend?"

"No girlfriend."

"Oh." Beauregard's eyebrows rose.

The men stared at each other, and Jack felt the snap, crackle, and pop that arced between them. No fucking way.

He jerked open another drawer, pulled out a ticket pad, slammed it on the desk, and began writing.

He tore off the first sheet. "First, this is your speeding ticket. Going sixty in a forty-five." Tossed it across the table to Beauregard. The paper soared through the air, then landed near Beauregard's hand.

Scribbled again. "Second, this is your ticket for having an unlicensed dog in city limits." Again the paper floated to the other side of the desk.

"Third. This one is my favorite." He took his time writing it out. "This one is for assault on an officer, namely me, by that animal of yours." He ripped it out and added it to the stack.

"You're joking, right?" Beauregard picked them up and looked through them.

"No, I'm not joking. You have thirty days to pay the fines or appear in court with a lawyer." Jack pulled out his cell phone, searched for Brian Russell's cell number, and hit Send.

"Brian? It's Whittaker. Can you swing by the station? I need you to pick someone up and take him to Smith's Garage for me. Great." He closed the phone and stared across at Beauregard. "Your ride will be here in five minutes. Now get out of my office."

Beauregard stood. "Can I say good-bye to Winston?"

Jack nodded.

The young man went around the desk to where Winston lay sleeping, and knelt down.

"Hey, boy." The dog woke and tried to crawl into his lap. "The nice chief is going to let you stay with him for a few days, okay?"

Woof.

"Be good for him. I'll come and visit you soon, I promise." Then he leaned down, kissed the dog on the head, and got a quick swipe of the dog's tongue on his cheek. He stood, gathered the tickets, and shoved them into his wallet.

"Take care of my dog, Jack." Those deep brown eyes penetrated Jack with a look that demanded a promise. What was it with this guy and promises?

"I promise, Mr. Beauregard."

"I'll hold you to it." Again with the last word.

Beauregard walked to the door, turned, and gave Jack a quick smile. "My name is Edward." Then he slipped through the door and shut it softly behind him.

Alone, Jack ran his hands through his hair. He felt a gentle nudge against his leg, and he jerked back, his chair rolling against the wall with a sharp thud.

Winston looked up at him, his hindquarters shaking with what passed for a wag.

"Oh, no. Don't give me that look. You bit me." Jack shook his head.

Winston squirmed between Jack's legs and the corner of the desk and curled up underneath it next to Jack's feet.

Uh-uh. No fucking way.

"Get out from there."

The dog didn't move.

"Now, Winston. Right now. Move." Jack snapped his fingers at the animal.

Winston rolled over on his back, rear legs splayed, front paws bent, mouth open, tongue lolling, and fell asleep.

Jack didn't know which one was worse, the dog or his master.

Both of them refused to obey him.

Both of them drove him to violence.

Both of them made him so mad he could spit.

But if he had to choose which one was the biggest pain in the ass?

It would be Beauregard. Hands down.

Edward Paul Beauregard the Third.

Chapter Four

Edward sat on a wooden chair against the wall of the reception area and draped his jacket over his lap. Blinking to clear his eyes, he refused to think of the worst case. That would be too much to stand, and he had nearly fallen apart in Jack's office. He already had a good idea what Chief of Police Jack Whittaker thought of him. Edward didn't intend to give credence to the "emotional fag" stereotype by crying. Beauregards were made of sterner stuff.

He'd never been separated from Winston, except on a few overnights, for almost six years. Now, Winston's life was on the line, and Edward swore he'd do whatever it took to free his best friend.

Edward didn't think Jack would hurt Winston, but if there was one thing he'd picked up from the chief of police in their too-brief time together, it was that Jack Whittaker upheld the law, no matter what the law decreed.

Even if it said a little dog had to die.

Jack's secretary gave him a smile, then went back to her work, whatever it was one did when one worked for a chief of police. The main office was large, nondescript, and her desk sat like an ugly brown metal guard outside Jack's office. At the other end was another hall that led to the back where he supposed the criminals were kept. The place smelled of cinder block, Lysol, and the cloying gardenia scent Kristen wore.

"What's down that hall?" he asked.

Kristen looked up. "That's the muster room and the cells. If you need the bathroom, it's the first door on the left." She pointed and gave him another smile.

Edward smiled back at her, and time ticked on.

"So," she said. "I like your shirt. It's pretty."

Pretty? He paid one hundred and fifty dollars at a trendy Dallas shop, and all he got was "pretty"? Not fabulous. Not stunning. Not, "it goes so well with your eyes"?

"Thanks. Not too much fringe?" Edward ran his finger along the chocolate brown strings, enjoying the way the suede felt on his skin. Satin sheets trimmed in this fringe would be just the thing. He could have them made back in Atlanta. It would be like swimming in chocolate. Delicious.

She looked at it, then shrugged. "Maybe for a man's shirt. I've never seen a man's shirt with that much fringe on it. Mother-of-pearl snap buttons, maybe, but not fringe."

"Oh." Maybe Jack hadn't been joking. Maybe he looked like a fool in this shirt, instead of hot as sin, but it had looked so good in the mirror at the store, setting off his dark hair and eyes. Even that cute young salesman had said so.

"Now I've seen women's shirts with fringe. Lots of those, especially for parties and such. But men, no." She shook her head. "Where'd you get it?"

"In Dallas."

"Oh. Dallas." She sniffed. "I suppose for Dallas it's all right."

"Have you ever been to Dallas?" Edward had no idea why he was extending the conversation, at least, no idea he wanted to confess to.

"Yep. Every year for the Texas State Fair. You?"

"Just a few days ago, on my way here."

"Oh." She went back to her typing.

"My grandmother is Olivia Rawlings." Never hurts to name-drop.

"Miss Olivia?" Her eyes brightened, and she gave him an even bigger smile. Seems the name worked. "Everybody knows her. I didn't know she had any family."

"My mother is her daughter," Edward enlightened her.

"Funny, she never talks about any family." Now, she narrowed her eyes. "You sure you're kin to her?"

"Yes." Edward frowned. If his grandmother hadn't mentioned him, that was her right. Still, it stung.

She lowered her head again and typed.

"How long has *he* been chief?" Edward tilted his head at Jack's office door, no longer able to resist asking about the ruggedly handsome cop, and the real reason he'd kept talking to the young woman.

"The last five years." Her eyes never left the screen.

"He's kind of young for such an important position, isn't he?" He hadn't missed the sprinkling of gray in the chief's hair that made him look distinguished. And sexy.

"Youngest chief we've ever had." She nodded, and the conversation came to a standstill.

What else could he ask without looking obvious? He already knew the man wasn't married and didn't have a girlfriend, and asking if he had a boyfriend would be the height of indiscretion.

Just then, the outer door opened and a drop-dead gorgeous cop sauntered in. Edward had to keep his teeth together to keep his jaw from dropping.

"Hi, Kristen," the officer greeted the secretary.

"Hi, Brian." She jerked her head at Edward, and he sat up straighter. "He's the one."

The cop turned to Edward, raised his eyebrows, and gave him a nod of hello.

"You need a ride to the garage?"

Edward's first thought was to say, *Yes, I'm the one. Me. Me. Me*, and throw himself into the man's arms, but instead he stood and held out his hand. "Yes. Edward Beauregard." Hell and damnation, if he'd known they grew them so big and good-looking here in Spring Lake, he would have come to visit his grandmother sooner.

But did they all have to be cops? And straight? What *was* a boy to do?

The cop shook his hand. "Officer Brian Russell. Well, come along, and I'll drop you off." He headed for the door.

"See you later, alligator," Edward quipped at Kristen.

"After a while, crocodile," she shot back. They laughed and Edward trailed behind Brian out the door, enjoying the way the cop's ass looked in those black uniform pants. The officer led the way to a marked patrol car, opened the passenger door, and then headed around to the driver's side. Edward got in, buckled up, and sat back.

"Had some car trouble?"

"Your chief shot my tire." He probably shouldn't have said that.

The officer turned and stared at him. "How did that happen?"

"It was after my dog bit him," Edward mumbled as he adjusted his bandanna.

"Your dog bit him?" He put the car in gear and pulled out of the lot.

"After he stopped me for speeding." Edward rolled his eyes.

"So. You're a dangerous criminal, huh?" Brian chuckled.

"That's me." Edward sighed and stared out the window.

"What's up?" The cop sounded concerned. It was probably something he'd learned in cop school, or wherever they teach that sort of stuff, but his soft voice drew Edward in.

He turned in his seat to look the guy in the eyes, and it all came out in a rush, "I've had a horrible day. My dog bit Jack, and now he's being held until I can prove he doesn't have rabies, and Jack's going to keep him for me because my grandmother is allergic, and Winston is claustrophobic and can't stay in a cage or a cell or be tied outside to the fence like some wild animal—" Edward took a breath, but the cop interrupted by holding up his hand.

"Whoa! Slow down."

Edward exhaled. This was just another fine mess he'd gotten himself into. No. He'd gotten Winston into this mess. Hell and damnation, maybe his father had been right about the trust fund after all. Right about what a self-absorbed—

"Look. I'm sure whatever happened, Chief Whittaker will handle it with fairness and respect. Your dog, that's Winston?"

"Yes."

"The chief stopped you for speeding, and the dog bit him?"

"Right. I don't know why Winston did it. He's never bitten anyone before. Ever."

"Okay. And the dog can't go into the kennel, so the chief is going to hold on to him for you, right?" The officer spoke as he drove down a main street lined with businesses and stores.

"That's right. Do you think he'll treat Winston okay?"

"Of course. Chief Whittaker is one of the most decent men I know. If he says your dog is safe, then he's safe."

Edward let out his breath in a long exhale. "Thanks. I thought so; I just wanted to hear someone else say it." He smiled at the cop.

"You're not from around here, are you?"

"No. How could you tell?"

"Well, other than knowing most of the people who live here, the shirt was a dead giveaway." Brian, the hot cop, chuckled again. Besides his good looks, Brian had a way of putting Edward at ease. Edward couldn't help but like him.

Edward winced. "I know. Too much fringe."

He nodded. "And your accent. Georgia?"

"Atlanta." Edward nodded.

"What brings you to Spring Lake?"

"I'm visiting my grandmother, Olivia Rawlings."

"I didn't know she had any family."

"So I hear." Edward frowned. "I'm a big secret."

"Is it because you're gay?"

Edward turned to the officer. "No. She had a falling out years ago with my father. How did you know I was gay?"

"You're joking, right?"

Edward waved his hand down his chest. "The shirt?"

"That, and since I'm gay, it's easy for me to spot another gay man. And you don't exactly hide it, you know."

"You're gay? Get back, Loretta." Edward slapped his thigh.

"Gay and taken." The officer held up his left hand to show a solid platinum band.

"Of course. Just my luck." Edward sighed and sat back. "What about Jack?"

"What about him?" Russell asked warily.

"He wouldn't by any chance be gay too?" Edward turned and looked out the window, not positive if he wanted to know. It didn't matter anyway; Jack was *not* his type. Repeat. Not his type.

"Here's the garage, Mr. Beauregard." The cop pulled up in front of the door and waited for Edward to get out.

"Thank you, Officer Russell." Edward leaned down and smiled at him. "Nice to meet you."

"Same here. See you around." Russell gave him a salute and pulled away, leaving Edward's question about Jack unanswered.

Edward slung his jacket over his shoulder and went inside the shop's office.

Behind the counter, a young man in a blue work shirt with the name PHIL embroidered above the pocket looked up. His eyes widened as his gaze traveled up and down Edward.

"Can I help you?" he asked, trying to keep a straight face.

Anger prickled Edward's skin as he read the man's expression. This guy was going to give him a hard time. He braced himself and walked to the counter.

"Yes. I came to pick up the red Miata. The tire was flat."

"Oh, right. Hold on." Phil stepped to a door that led to the service bays, opened it, and leaned out. "Is the Miata ready?"

Someone called back something, and Phil stepped out where Edward couldn't hear him, then came back in.

"It's done." He stole several glances at Edward as he worked with the papers.

Edward leaned against the counter and tried to see what the man was doing.

"That's one hundred and seventy-one dollars and fifty-seven cents."

"Is that for a new tire?" Edward asked.

"Yep. And the tow. Couldn't fix the old tire. You can't fix two holes in the sidewalls. How'd you manage to do that?"

Edward just shrugged. He definitely wasn't telling this jerk.

Just then another man, older and covered in grease stains, came through the bay door. "This the guy?" He had JIMMY embroidered over his pocket. With the grease on his clothes and his hands, Edward figured him for the mechanic. As the man stared at him, Edward's stomach started a slow slide down to the bottom, where fear waited.

"Yep. That's him." The younger man stepped back, not bothering to hide his sneer.

"Un-fucking-be-liev-able. Well, aren't you pretty?" He gave a low whistle as he shook his head. "I wouldn't have believed it if I hadn't seen it."

Edward glared at Phil. "Is my car ready or not?" The office felt too small, and the urge to bolt washed over him, but he locked his knees and stood firm.

"It's ready. What's your hurry?" Jimmy asked.

Edward hadn't been in a hurry; he just wanted to avoid any more trouble. He'd certainly met his quota for today. Okay, for the next year. Besides, the next time he saw the police chief, he didn't want to be wearing a set of shiny new handcuffs. Or sporting a lovely black plastic body bag.

He placed his credit card on the counter and pushed it at the young man, but the older man snatched it up. "Edward P. Beauregard *I-I-I*. What's that mean?"

"May I speak with the manager?" Edward kept his lips tight, he'd dealt with people like this ever since he'd come out.

The guy from the front desk stepped up. "Let me have that, Jimmy." He took the card from the man, wiped it clean, and ran it through the machine. "Better get back to work."

Jimmy returned to the garage but stopped in the doorway and turned back. "I swear. Ever since those two faggots took up residence here, the place is swarming with them. Spring Lake is going to be the next San Fran-fucking-cisco, if you ask me."

How did three gay men make a swarm? Was that like a herd of elephants or a school of fish? Shouldn't it be something like a quorum of queers or a gaggle of gays?

The young man snickered and held out the receipt and the credit card. Edward signed them, handed him the yellow copy, and held out his hand, palm up. "My keys?"

"In the car. Jimmy'll bring it out for you."

Edward nodded and left the office. Jimmy gunned the motor and backed out of the closest bay, cut the wheel hard, and nearly hit Edward as he came to a brake-squealing stop.

Curbing his anger, Edward set his face to neutral and walked around to the driver's side, doing his best "manly" walk. Hey, he could do butch if he had to.

Jimmy got out and held the door open, as if being polite, but Edward knew better. People like these two men wore thin veils of civility over the senseless hatred that boiled underneath, and when that hatred erupted, someone usually got hurt. Or killed.

Edward got in, and Jimmy shut the door. Still holding on to the door, Jimmy leaned over, his cigarette-laced breath puffed against the side of Edward's face as he growled, "I hope you don't plan on hanging around here for long, Mr. *I-I-I.* This is a God-fearing town, and we don't need any more of you faggots settling here, for damn sure."

Edward knew arguing or even trying to reason with people like Jimmy and Phil was a waste of time and energy. Despite the fear and anger that warred inside him, he remained silent, which seemed to piss off the asshole even more.

"Just keep your hands to yourself, faggot. We catch you with any of our boys, we'll hang you by your dick from the nearest tree."

Looking straight ahead, Edward put the car into gear and hit the gas. The mechanic jumped back, cursed at him, and gave him the finger. Heart pounding, Edward pulled out of the drive and into the street without a clue as to where he was going. All he could think about was to get as far away from the garage as possible.

Once free, Edward slowed down, and the tension in his shoulders eased. He could see the billboard... *Spring Lake: The next San Francisco.* He laughed. Not without the hills, the marina, and the Castro District.

How paranoid could some God-fearing people be? Did they really think he was going to start trolling outside the junior high school, enticing young boys into wickedness, sin, and manis and pedis with candy and video games?

Hell and damnation. He was a homosexual, not a pedophile. They were *not* synonymous. The thought of touching a child was as abhorrent to him as it would be to anyone else.

He drove a few more blocks, spotted a coffee shop, and pulled into their drive-through. After he ordered a latte, he got out the map and studied it as he waited. He was on the main street, and from there, he traced the route to his grandmother's house.

He paid, got his drink, and pulled out.

"Over the river and through the snow, to grandmother's house we go," he sang, off-key, then sighed and looked at the empty seat beside him.

It wasn't the same without Winston.

Chapter Five

After seeing to his wounds, Jack rolled back to his desk. His foot bumped the dog. He pushed back and looked down. The animal was dead asleep, the tip of his long tongue stuck out of his mouth between his front teeth as if giving Jack a permanent raspberry.

This was ridiculous. How on earth did he get stuck babysitting a dog?

Right. He'd promised Edward. No. He would not refer to Edward as Edward. Mr. Beauregard or Beauregard, but *not* Edward.

His stomach rumbled. His head pounded and his ankle ached. Jack popped two more painkillers and dry-swallowed them.

Kristen knocked, opened the door, and stuck her head in. "Chief?"

"Yes?"

"You've got the meeting with the mayor in thirty minutes, remember?"

Jack sighed and stood up. "I don't suppose you'd go in my place?"

She cocked an eyebrow at him.

"Right. Best be going. Maybe I can grab a burger on the way there." He grabbed his hat and came around the desk to take the file Kristen held out to him.

Behind him, he heard the patter of nails on linoleum. Winston, dragging his leash, trotted up to him and sat.

"Oh no. I've got a meeting. You have to stay here." Jack shook his head.

Woof.

"I don't care, you're not coming."

"Chief? When you talk to him, does he answer you?" Kristen's eyes were all scrunched up as she fought to keep her lips straight.

"No, of course he doesn't talk." Now Edward—Beauregard—had him doing it. Kristen stepped out of the office. Jack followed and closed the door before the dog could get out.

Woof. Woof. Woof.

Kristen raised her eyebrows and looked at the door, then at Jack. "Oh no, is right. I'm not sitting here all afternoon listening to that dog bark. And I'm not cleaning up any doggy messes."

"But I can't take him with me to see the mayor."

Woof. Woof. Woof. Woof.

"Why not? You said you'd watch him, didn't you?" Kristen had her hands on her hips.

"Yes, but…"

Woof. Woof. Woof. Woof. Woof.

"Take him, or I'm taking the day off. With pay." She raised her voice to be heard over the barking as she went for her purse behind her desk.

"No, wait!" He held up his hands in submission. "I'll take him." Jack went to the door, opened it, and out trotted Winston. Jack bent down, snatched up his leash, and frowned at the animal. "Okay, Winston. Best behavior, right?"

Woof.

Jack hoped that meant "yes" in dog talk, not "just wait until I bite you again." He pulled on the leash and headed down the hall to the parking lot. Winston dragged him straight to his car.

Hell, maybe the dog was smarter than he looked, because he sure was one ugly dog. His nose was smashed in, his jowls hung, and he snorted when he breathed. A small patch of light brown covered one eye, but other than that, the dog was white. And that tail. A dog should have a proper tail.

Jack opened the back door, but the dog just sat there. "You got in before. In, Winston." Jack snapped his fingers, jerked on the leash, but the dog wouldn't budge. He could pick the animal up, but that was getting closer than he was prepared to be. Once bitten, twice shy.

Winston stood and pulled him around the car. Christ, the dog was strong. They reached the passenger side, and the dog sat at the front door.

"Oh, no. You are *not* sitting in the front seat with me." Jack folded his arms across his chest, determined to make a stand, but a glance at his watch told him he was just wasting precious time.

With a growl of his own, Jack opened the door. Winston jumped in and settled into the seat. Jack shut the door, went around the car, and got in. He pulled out of the lot, and headed toward city hall. There was a burger fast-food place on the way there and fifteen minutes left to get it, eat it, and be in the mayor's office.

He stopped at the order board. "One burger, all the way, and a coffee, black."

Woof.

Jack looked at Winston. "Ed—" Shit. He gave up. "Edward said no table scraps. You're on a diet."

Woof.

"Add a burger, plain." Jack rubbed his temple. This took the cake. Ordering fast food for a dog.

"Will that be all?"

"That's it."

"Five oh three. Pull to the first window to pay."

Jack pulled up, paid the young lady, got his receipt, and pulled up to the second window for the food. Winston leaned across Jack's body, sniffing the air. Then he put his paws on Jack's leg and strained toward the window. Christ, even though the dog was small, he weighed a ton.

"Get off me, Winston," Jack growled and pushed him back with his elbow.

The manager of the restaurant grinned at him. "Cute dog, Chief. Is he new on the force?"

"No," Jack replied. He took the bag and the coffee, nodded, and pulled away. He sat the coffee in the holder. "Now, sit there and be good." He took a burger out of the bag, opened the paper, and put it on the seat next to the dog. The animal lay down and began eating.

Jack opened his sandwich and ate it in about four bites, washing the last bite down with a sip of coffee. He hadn't realized how hungry he was until he'd smelled the food. They pulled up to city hall and he parked, then watched Winston lick the paper wrapper spotless, slobbering all over the seat.

Jack had two minutes left.

Chapter Six

Edward pulled up outside a small Craftsman cottage and parked. It was white, with a lovely garden that bordered the porch on either side. He checked the address with the one stenciled on the top step of the porch and got out.

He stomach danced, and he tried to shake it off, but it'd been a long time since he'd seen his grandmother. He should have changed his shirt, but it was too late now. Would she recognize him? Would he recognize her?

He walked down the brick path to the wooden steps and up to the front door. Pushing the bell, he gave his bangs a final brush with his fingers, then stepped back.

A few moments later, a vaguely familiar woman with short gray hair opened the door. "Edward! I'd recognize you anywhere!" She gave him a quick hug.

Her warm smile helped to settle his stomach, and he nodded. "Meemaw?" He slipped into the name he'd called her as a child.

"It's been a long time. Come in." She stepped back and pulled his arm.

Edward stepped into the living room, and the aroma of just-baked cookies filled his nose. "Oatmeal raisin?"

"That used to be your favorite, if I remember." She led him to the couch. On the coffee table was a plate filled with cookies.

"They still are," he replied as he reached for one and took a bite, unable to stop himself. It was a little piece of heaven. "Mmm. Is that just a hint of ginger?"

"Why, yes, it is. Most people don't recognize it." She sat down and patted the cushion next to her.

"I have a sensitive palate," he mumbled around a mouthful of cookie as he sat. "These are wonderful. Just like I remember them." It was funny, but until he'd taken a bite, he'd completely forgotten that she'd made those cookies for him whenever he'd visited her with his parents.

"Glad you still like them. Now, Edward. What brings you to Spring Lake?" She sat back and watched him with sharp brown eyes.

Unsure whether he should spill the beans about his mission, he shrugged and went with his second reason for visiting. "I needed to get away, Meemaw. Things in Atlanta...well, I needed a change."

"Edward. Are you in trouble with the law in Atlanta too?" Her eyes smiled at him, and he felt that she'd love him even if he had been a wanted man. For Edward, that was a rare thing.

"No. Nothing like that." He sighed. "It's more along the line of an affair gone bad."

"Ohh." She nodded. "Had your heart broken?" She reached out and put a comforting hand on his leg.

"Worse. I was dumped in the middle of the biggest social event of the year. Right in front of *everyone*," he whispered. The mortification of it still hung on him like cheap knock-off cologne.

She nodded again. "That must have been awful."

"You have *no* idea." He rolled his eyes. "I just couldn't stand the phone calls from so-called friends pretending to be sympathetic but just wanting to hear all the sordid details."

"The 'I told you so's'?" she added.

"Yes. But no one ever told me." He shook his head and took another cookie.

"You wouldn't have listened, would you?"

He stared at her, cookie in his mouth; then he took a bite, chewed, and swallowed. "No, I don't think I would have."

"You were in love."

"At least I thought I was. I thought he—" Edward froze and looked up at his grandmother. Hell and damnation, he'd just outed himself to her.

"You thought he loved you, right?" She smiled at him, her eyes holding love and acceptance.

"Yes." He hung his head, so ashamed that he'd been played for a fool. Again. "I don't seem to pick the right men," he confessed.

"I was like that. Always the wrong man." She leaned closer to tell her secret. "For me, it was bad boys." She waved her hand in front of her face. "Oh my Lord, I did love bad boys. High school dropouts. Carnie workers. Rodeo cowboys. The kind of man that would make your head spin with danger and excitement, get you in nothing but trouble, and then be gone the next week." She laughed.

Edward sat up. "Me too, Meemaw. Bad boys." He rolled his eyes. "Guess it runs in the family." He loved finding that there was more in common between them than blood.

She chuckled, picked up a cookie, and took a bite. "These *are* good. Now, don't you worry, child, you stay here as long as you need to. I've got the guest room all ready." She reached into the pocket of her jeans and pulled out a key. "Here's the key to the house. You come and go as you please. No curfew." She winked.

"Meemaw!" Edward put his hand to his mouth in mock shock. "You're joking, right? I'm gay; you do realize that?" He took the key and slipped it onto his key ring.

"So?"

"There are no gays in Hooterville."

"Sure there are. Rush Weston and his partner, I think you call it? They live here."

"That must be the cop I met, Brian Russell."

"That's him. Such a nice man. I was so glad to see Rush finally find someone who makes him happy. Besides them, there's no telling who's hiding what around here. I have a few ideas of my own about that list, but they'd scandalize the town." She laughed and slapped her leg.

Edward sat back and observed his grandmother. His family had only visited occasionally. He'd been a teen the last time he'd seen her, and not very interested in spending time with her, so wrapped up in his own set of worries, his fights with his dad, and with the dreaded realization that he liked boys, not girls.

She hadn't attended the funeral, either.

She'd certainly surprised him. He'd never expected to be able to sit with his grandmother and talk to her about being gay. Even his mother never spoke so openly, only with vague references to his "friends" and "dates." And his father? When pigs fly.

"Wow. You blow me away, Meemaw." He threw his arms around her, they hugged, and he was glad that her grip on him was just as strong as his on her. "Thank you." Tears burned his eyes. Right now, he needed someone to understand him, not to judge or condemn him or to call him a gullible fool.

She gave him a final pat on the shoulder. "Now. Tell me all about your run-in with the local law."

Edward sat back, picked up another cookie, and told her all about meeting Jack.

* * *

Jack looked at the dog and faced his next problem. If he left the dog in the car, it would be just his luck that someone would report it.

DOG LEFT IN POLICE CHIEF'S CAR TO DIE

PETA ASKS FOR CHIEF'S RESIGNATION

Headlines like those he couldn't afford, not if he wanted to keep his job, and he'd worked too damn hard to blow it now over some rich guy's mutt.

He grabbed the leash. "Come on, Winston. You're with me." He got out and Winston followed. As he walked up the sidewalk to the main doors, Winston stopped, lifted a stubby back leg, and generously watered the flowers that lined the paved brick walk. A passing woman glared at Jack and the dog, telling him with narrowed eyes and a frown that she didn't approve of their pit stop.

Winston finished, then grinned up at her as he happily scraped his back legs on the grass, sending clods flying. She turned the full force of her glare on Jack, and he could feel the heat rise in his cheeks. *Shit.* Damn dog.

"Come, Winston." Jack yanked on the lead, and Winston waddled after him. At the double door to the building, Jack hesitated.

DOG BITES MAYOR

CHIEF OF POLICE FIRED

Could the headline be worse? Either way, he was screwed. If he ever got his hands on Edward P. Beauregard the Third, for putting him in this mess, he'd gladly do life.

Jack would just make sure the dog didn't get too close to His Honor, that's all.

"I have a meeting with the mayor," Jack informed the secretary. She looked over her glasses, down her long, narrow nose at the dog, and he watched as her eyebrows rose.

"I have you down, but your friend isn't listed." Her pursed lips twisted in a smile. "I'll tell the mayor you're here." She picked up the phone, pressed a button, and spoke, "Chief Whittaker and his friend are here to see you."

Jack rolled his eyes, and she winked at him. "I don't know, sir." She looked up at Jack. "What's your friend's name?"

"Winston."

"Winston, sir." A pause as she looked at the dog. "Yes, *just* like Churchill. Yes, sir." She put the phone down. "You can go in."

Jack nodded to her and pushed through the mahogany door with the seal of the city on it.

His longtime friend, William Lansing, sat behind a large cherry desk and glanced up from his paperwork. A huge map of the city covered the wall behind him.

"Hello, Bill."

"Hello, Jack. Who's your friend?" Bill Lansing pointed to the dog as he came around the desk and shook Jack's hand. "New recruit? Is he a new item in your budget?"

"No. He's impounded."

"Impounded? A desperate criminal, eh? It's good to know you're keeping the town safe. What did he do? Rob the savings and loan?" Bill, always quick to needle Jack, chuckled as he sat in one of the black leather wingback chairs in front of his desk. Jack sat in the other. Winston curled up at Jack's feet.

"He bit me."

Bill's dark eyebrows shot up, and he fixed Jack with warm brown eyes. "Bit you? So you're keeping him close, in case he tries to escape?" He chuckled.

"Actually, I stopped his owner on a speeding charge, and the dog attacked me."

"He attacked you. You're kidding, right?"

Why did everyone say that? "No. He bit my ankle." Jack frowned at the dog. "Anyway, he can't be caged, and his owner is a flight risk. He's just visiting in town. I wanted to make sure the dog had his shots before I let him go. Just in case. You know...rabies."

Both men looked at the dog and rubbed their stomachs.

"Until then, he's with me."

"I understand, but can't you lock him in a cell or something?"

"No. The owner has made it clear that if anything happens to his dog, he's going to sue the city."

"Is he serious?" Bill leaned forward, all laughter gone from his eyes.

"Dead. He's very attached to the dog. And from what I can tell, he has the money and lawyers to back it. He's Olivia Rawlings's grandson." That was putting it mildly. The man's affection for the dog bordered on the fanatic. If that red bandanna the dog wore was any indication, Edward probably had little outfits for Winston to wear. Christ, the man was so gay it was embarrassing.

"Olivia?" Bill blew a soft whistle. "She's got big money."

"So does her grandson, it seems. He's one of the Atlanta Beauregards," Jack added in an imitation of Edward's soft accent.

Bill nodded as if it meant something to him. "I knew the rest of the family had moved away. Tons of money. Oil and gas leases."

Jack hadn't known that. So, Edward had money. Much more than Jack would ever have, no doubt. Why did that bother him? Hell, it just rankled him when someone didn't have to work hard for what they had, when it just got handed to them on a silver platter. Jack had worked damned hard for every scrap he'd ever had from the time he was sixteen.

"Well, I guess, if you put it that way, you're doing this city a service. Do whatever you have to do to keep this guy from suing us. We can't afford it."

"Sure." Jack wondered just "whatever" might entail. Or how far he'd have to go?

"He doesn't look dangerous. In fact, he looks expensive. Dogs like that can cost thousands of dollars. Come here, boy." Bill leaned down and called to the dog.

Too slow, Jack tried to reel the dog in on his leash, but the little bulldog was quicker. Winston's head popped up off his paws, and he trotted over to the mayor, his hindquarters wagging in greeting. Winston sat at the mayor's feet without a single growl. All tongue and no teeth.

"I can't believe he bit you. What did you do to him?" Bill cocked an eyebrow.

Jack watched as the bulldog rolled over on his back and let Bill scratch his chest.

"Nothing. He just walked up and bit me."

Great. Even the mayor was charmed by the damn dog. Wait until Bill met Edward. What would he say then? To give Bill credit, he didn't blink an eye when Jack had told him about hiring Brian Russell, an openly gay man, as an officer on the town's small force. And in the twenty-or-so years they'd been friends, Bill had never made any remarks about gays. Not that they'd had many conversations about gays, but Bill wasn't the kind of man who held bigoted beliefs. At least Jack didn't think he did.

"Not this good boy." Bill gave the dog a final pat and then straightened.

Jack sighed. "Hard to believe." Winston came back to Jack's chair and lay down.

At last, they stopped talking about the damned dog and got down to the reason for the meeting: this year's budget for the police department.

Jack pulled out his papers, gave Bill a copy, and they got down to their discussion.

Chapter Seven

"Well, first thing Monday, you'll just have to get the vet to fax Winston's certificate of health to the police." Olivia patted Edward's knee.

"Of course. Nothing is going to keep me from getting him back, Meemaw. I just don't know what I'm going to do with him once I do get him back." He gave her a halfhearted smile.

"I feel so bad about that. Really. And if there were any way I could let him stay here in the house, I would."

"I know. I suppose I'll just get a room at that motel up on the interstate. I can make the drive to and from Spring Lake to visit you each day. It's less than half an hour."

"Hell, I used to drive all the way to San Antonio just for lunch. These days, my doctor has forbidden me to drive at all." She shrugged but didn't explain any further. Edward figured if she didn't share, he shouldn't ask, but it was a perfect opening and he took it.

"How *are* you feeling, Meemaw?" She looked trim and fit in her blue jeans, white cotton shirt, and loafers, but there was a slight cast of shadow under her eyes.

"Well, for an old broad, I'm doing damn fine." Her eyes sparkled when she laughed. "But like anyone my age, I could complain. But I don't. Can't stand to listen to those old biddies around here talking about their aches and pains." She shook her head and then winked at him. "I'd rather hear about who's fooling around with who."

Edward gasped. "Not here in Hooterville? With all these God-fearing decent folks?" He couldn't resist taking a dig at the locals.

"Why not? Small towns are just as bad as big towns. Worse. Why, there are skeletons buried all over this county, child. Got a few out back myself." She winked.

"Do tell?" Edward leaned closer. "One of those bad boys of yours? A nosy neighbor, maybe?"

She laughed. "Maybe."

"I can believe it too."

"Edward." She grew serious. "What do you think about the chief of police? Jack Whittaker seems to have made an impression on you." Her eyebrow rose as she pinned him with a brown gaze so similar to his own.

"Jack?" Hell and damnation, he couldn't help but smile when he said the man's name.

"You know him well enough to call him by his first name?" She cocked an eyebrow upward.

"Well, I let him keep my dog, didn't I? I wouldn't let just *anyone* do that." Edward could do coy as well as any ingenue.

"He's a good-looking man." A mischievous light flickered in his grandmother's eyes as she fished for information.

"He is." No point in denying that; everyone could see Jack Whittaker was handsome.

"He's been alone for a long time."

"Has he?" Edward feigned disinterest. "I wonder why."

Her brow furrowed. "I know he didn't grow up here. I'm not sure where he's from." Her gaze got fuzzy as her words faded.

Edward kept quiet and let her think. He wanted desperately to know what she knew about the man, but pushing her would let her know just how desperate he was.

"There was an engagement."

"Oh?" Edward slouched.

"But it fell through."

"Oh." He sat up. That could mean anything.

"It was called off right before the wedding. She wasn't local. Some girl he'd met in college, I think." She shrugged. "All I know was Jack was in his early twenties, out of college, and newly hired with the police. Handsome as the devil, even then. Everyone says it broke his heart so bad, he's never let anyone close again."

Edward could just see Jack, as tanned as he was now, but younger, less serious. Maybe he'd even smiled more back then. Before he could blink, Edward had fashioned a story. Jack, unaware of his inclinations, gets all the way to the altar before facing the truth and calling off the wedding.

Bride seen fleeing the church. Parents in an uproar. Guests stunned.

It *could* have happened that way.

Twenty years ago, some gay men would have gotten married and stayed in the closet.

Maybe Jack was still in the closet.

Maybe Jack longed to come out.

Maybe Jack just needed a little push.

* * *

What Jack really needed was to go home, take a hot shower, and get his foot up. The throbbing had returned as his pain meds ran out. Maybe a cold beer would help his head, because it was still pounding.

The meeting with the mayor had gone well, and Winston hadn't bitten anyone, especially Jack.

He straightened the papers on his desk and shut off his computer, then stood and scooped up his hat.

"Winston, we're going home early today. I'm beat." Jack leaned down, clipped the leash to the dog's collar, and they headed for the door.

"Kristen, I'm going home. If anyone needs me, call my cell. But only if it's an emergency, okay?"

"Sure, Chief. You look tired. Get some rest." Kristen smiled at him and then went back to work.

Jack led Winston out of the building and to his cruiser. This time, he didn't bother to argue about where the dog sat. Winston hopped into the front seat, and Jack went around to the driver's side and got in. He rubbed his eyes with the palms of his hands, pressing into his temples with his thumb. It offered a little relief from the pain, but only as long as he kept up the pressure.

He put the car in gear and pulled out of the parking lot. His house was only about fifteen minutes away, where the main road veered south, past the edge of town. He liked it there. Minimal noise, few neighbors, and light traffic.

Pulling into his drive, he felt the quiet pride that coming home always gave him. The house was solid, well built, and had plenty of room. He'd saved years on a small-town cop's salary to get the down payment to buy it. And he'd spent most of his free time and money fixing it up. It was a hell of a long way from the piece-of-shit trailer he'd grown up in outside of San Antonio.

Here he could be himself, away from the pressure of the job and everyone's expectations of him. It might be lonely off and on, but he'd gotten used to it over the years. Alone was good. Alone was comfortable. Alone didn't hurt anymore.

"We're home, Winston," he announced. Winston whined and scratched at the door. Jack got out and let the dog out of the car, then bent down and unclipped the leash.

"Go ahead, boy. Check it out."

He leaned against the car as Winston, nose to the ground, trotted around the half-acre front yard. Jack took time to observe the animal. Low to the ground, the dog was solid, not fat, with a broad, deep chest, sleek, short white fur, and a massive head. Those dark brown eyes held an intelligence Jack hadn't noticed in most dogs he'd seen.

Winston was so ugly he was cute.

"Come here, boy."

Winston didn't respond. That wouldn't do. It bugged Jack when someone didn't listen to him or obey him. It was a sign of disrespect. But he could fix that.

"You need some training." Jack went inside, opened the fridge, and pulled out some cold cuts. Taking a few slices, he tore them up and put them in a small baggie, then went back outside just as Winston watered Jack's azalea bushes.

Jack pulled out a small piece of meat. "Come, Winston." He held the food in his hand so that the dog could see it.

Winston trotted over to him, and Jack gave him the treat.

"Good boy."

He let the dog wander off several times and repeated the command and awarded with the treat when Winston obeyed. By the fourth time, he could call Winston and the animal would come to him without seeing the meat.

Satisfied with his progress, Jack gave the dog the last of the treats, rubbed him behind the ears, and praised him. Together, they went inside.

Jack put a bowl of water on the floor, and Winston went right to it. His long tongue lapped the liquid and drops flew, splattering Jack's pristine white cabinets. Then, as Winston walked the bowl across the slate tiles, water splashed all over the kitchen floor. Jack got out a dish towel, wiped up the mess, and put it underneath the bowl to absorb the water spillage and keep it in place.

That done, Jack headed to his room to undress and take a hot shower. He stripped down, tossed his uniform into the hamper for his dry cleaning, his T-shirt and briefs into the hamper for washing, then leaned into the double shower stall and turned on the water. When he could see the steam rise behind the glass blocks, he stepped under the overhead spray and just let the water beat on his back and shoulders as he leaned against the tile wall. His tension eased, but his headache stayed with him, making it impossible for him to relax.

Maybe he should go into Houston and see a doctor. The last thing he wanted to do was admit he was sick. Which kind of doctor would he see? What kinds of tests would they run? Hell, maybe he'd just go to one of those acupuncturists. He'd read they could knock out pain with a few well-placed needles.

Maybe he just needed to get laid.

He looked down at his cock. It had been unresponsive ever since the headaches started. In his condition, trying to have sex would be a waste of time. And the very last thing Jack ever wanted was to be embarrassed. Not getting it up in front of someone, even a stranger, would be mortifying.

Jack sighed and squeezed shampoo into his hands, worked it through his hair, and then rinsed it out. Shutting off the water, he opened the glass door and stepped onto the rug to catch the water that dripped off his body. Then he wrapped a towel around his waist, avoiding looking in the mirror, and went into his bedroom.

Winston sat on the floor next to the bed, waiting for him.

"Hey, buddy."

Woof.

Jack tossed off the towel, took some sweats and a T-shirt from a dresser drawer, and put them on. "Let's get some dinner."

They trod back down the hall to the kitchen, and Jack took up his station at the fridge. Not much to choose from since it was the end of the week.

He pulled out a small pan of frozen lasagna. "This looks good. Of course, I'm sure it's not what you're used to with Edward P. Beauregard the Third, but around here, it's simple eats." He put the pan in the microwave oven, punched in the time, and hit Start.

Woof.

Jack got a beer from the fridge, sat at the wooden kitchen table, propped his foot up on a chair, and waited for the microwave to *ding*. He held the bottle to his forehead, leaning into it, letting the cold freeze his pain away.

If he couldn't shake this headache, it was going to be another long night.

* * *

"Edward. Get your bags and I'll show you to your room." Olivia stood.

"Sure." Edward stood, then slapped his head with the heel of his hand. "Hell and damnation. I forgot my bags."

"Where are they?"

"I left them in Jack's cruiser." He sat back down.

"Call him and ask him to drop them off."

"Meemaw, I can't do that. I've asked so much of him already." Edward bit his bottom lip. "I'll just go and get them from him at the station." He'd get to see Winston again; that would be good. He should stop at the market and pick up the dog food too.

"Okay." She picked up the glasses and plate of cookies and headed into the kitchen. "You've got your key. Just let yourself in when you get back."

"Are you sure?" Edward went to the door. "Will you still be up?"

"I go to bed early and wake up early these days." She came out of the kitchen and walked up to him as he stood at the door. "If I don't see you, have a good night, and I'll see you in the morning." She leaned up, he offered his cheek, and she kissed it.

He kissed her cheek in return. "Good night, Meemaw. I'm so glad I came."

"Me too, child." She patted his cheek and then headed down the hall. "Your room is the one right here." She stopped by the first door. "The next is the guest bath."

"Thanks." He nodded, then slipped out the front door, pulling it shut behind him, then locking it.

Edward got in the Miata, backed out of the drive, and headed into town.

At the police station, he parked and went inside.

Kristen looked up from her work. "You again?"

He propped his hip on the edge of her desk. "Yes. Did you miss me?"

She laughed, pushed him off, and shook her head. "No."

"Is Jack here?"

"No, he's gone for the day. Can I help you with anything?"

"Well, I left my bags in the trunk of his police car."

"In the cruiser?" She frowned. "He takes that car home. Sorry. If it were here, I'd get your bags for you."

"Great." Edward sighed. "Where does he live? I'll just go and get them."

Kristen stared at him as if making up her mind to give him this valuable piece of information. Her mind made up in Edward's favor, she tore off a sheet from a notepad and scribbled on it, then handed it to him. "You take the left when the road splits. He's about five miles down the road. The house sits all by itself; you can't miss it."

"Thanks." Edward smiled and left Kristen to her work.

* * *

Jack scooped half the lasagna onto his plate, put the other half on a plate for Winston, and placed it on the floor. The dog wasted no time in digging in. Jack sat at the table, picked up his fork, and attacked his food with much less enthusiasm than the dog. Since this headache, his appetite had fallen off, and most of the time he didn't feel like eating.

The silence was broken only by the scrape of Jack's fork and Winston's chomping and snorting. Christ, the dog was the noisiest eater he'd ever heard. And sloppy. Buried in the lasagna, Winston's face was covered in red sauce, and the plate danced across the floor as the dog licked it clean.

"Good, huh? Glad you liked it." Jack smiled at the dog. Winston lay down, noisily licking his muzzle and cleaning his paws. "You're like a cat, you know? Only sloppier and louder. Cleaning yourself up all the time." He chuckled.

Winston ignored the insult.

Jack got up, picked up Winston's plate, washed both plates, and put them in the rack to dry. He went into the living room, sat in the recliner, and pulled the lever to recline.

Feet in the air, the pain in his ankle lessened, but his head still pounded.

Jack turned on the TV and flicked around the stations. Found a documentary about Antarctica and settled back to watch. After about ten minutes, his vision blurred again, and he rubbed his eyes to clear it.

"Shit." This was getting scary. He looked around the room, trying to focus on anything, but it was all a blur of colors and shapes. Getting up, he made his way to the kitchen sink and splashed water into his eyes.

Still blurry.

Fear, asleep in the pit of his stomach, woke and began clawing its way out.

His doorbell rang.

"What the hell?" Jack dried off his face. Of all the times for someone to drop by, it had to be now, when he could barely see. In the hall, he misjudged the space and slammed his bare foot into the small table that held his keys. "Shit!"

The doorbell rang again.

"I'm coming! Hold your horses." He limped to the door and jerked it open.

A man stood in the doorway. Jack blinked, trying to focus, but the man's face was in shadow. "Who is it?"

"Don't tell me you forgot about me that fast? Why, I'm crushed," a soft voice drawled.

"Edward?" Shit. He did not need this. Not right now. "What do you want?" he barked.

The man jerked back, as if Jack's hard words had a physical effect.

Winston came out of the kitchen at a trot.

Woof. Woof.

"There's my boy!" Edward knelt, and Winston tried to climb into his lap. The dog licked him once, then struggled to get down. Edward gave him a scratch behind the ears and stood.

"Are you all right, Jack?" Without being asked, Edward stepped inside. "You don't look good."

Jack leaned back against the wall as Edward barged past. "I've just got a headache, that's all."

"Must be one hell of a headache. The same one from earlier today?"

"Yeah. It's a bitch." Jack walked back into the living room and sat. Edward followed. "Why are you here? Checking on your dog?" Just then, Jack noticed Edward carried a brown paper bag. "What's that?"

"I figured you wouldn't stop at the store and get Winston his dog food, so I did it myself."

"You came all this way to bring me dog food?"

"No. I came all this way to bring *Winston* dog food," Edward corrected. "I came to see *you* because you've still got my bags in the trunk of the cruiser." He walked into the kitchen and put the bag on the counter.

"Shit. I forgot about that." Jack sat on the couch.

"Me too." Edward came back into the living room and sat on the coffee table in front of Jack, their knees just inches apart. He stared into Jack's face. "You don't look good. You're squinting. Are you having trouble seeing?"

"Go away, Edward." Jack did not need this. He hadn't planned to let anyone know about this weakness. "I can deal with it myself."

Edward sat back and crossed his arms. "Oh yes, I can see how well you're dealing with it. Have you seen a doctor?"

"No, and I'm not going to." Jack shook his head, then grimaced as the pain throbbed. He didn't want Edward to be concerned for him. Didn't want Edward to become involved in his life at all.

"Jack. Let me help you. I can make the pain go away."

"No. I don't believe in any of that touchy-feely shit."

"Are you scared to let me touch you?"

Jack sat back, lips a thin line, forehead creased. His resolve wavered under the weight of his pain.

"I'm only going to touch you with my thumb." Edward held up his thumb. "See? Nothing else. If I touch you, it doesn't make you gay, you know. It's not contagious." Edward didn't hide his hurt, in his voice or in his dark eyes, and something deep inside Jack tugged hard.

"I know it's not. I just don't like anyone touching me." Jack frowned at the young man across from him. Did he really think he could make this pain stop?

"You've just gone too long without being touched. It's really quite nice, you know, if the right person does it." Edward smiled.

Jack rubbed his eyes. He didn't want to think about Edward touching him, but what if he *could* take the pain away? Right now, he'd let monkeys dance on his back if the pain would just stop.

"Okay. But just your thumb." That should be safe enough.

Edward slapped his thighs. "Good." Jack watched as Edward rubbed his thumb against his forefinger and his middle finger, as if smearing oil over them. "It's going to be warm at first and gradually heat up." He moved so that his knees were between Jack's knees, but not touching.

Jack nodded.

"Close your eyes."

"No."

Edward sighed. "I'm not going to do anything to you. Can't you *just* trust me?"

Jack blinked, and for a moment, his vision cleared. Deep brown eyes that hid nothing looked back at him. They were open and honest and incredibly beautiful.

He wanted to trust Edward, if only to be rid of the pain. God knew Edward had trusted him with his dog and had trusted all Jack's promises.

Damn sure he didn't want to dissect his reasons, Jack let go.

"I trust you." Jack shut his eyes.

Chapter Eight

"Breathe normally." Jack let his breathing slow as he tried to relax.

Edward touched Jack's brow, ran his thumb over it, leaving a streak of warmth behind. Jack had to keep from shuddering. The touch repeated, and just that brief stroking eased Jack. The pad of Edward's thumb pressed under Jack's eyebrow, near the bridge of his nose, and as the pressure increased, the warmth became heat.

The throbbing lessened. As if it were being pulled out of him, the pain in his head condensed, grew smaller, more localized. It drained through the spot under his eye and into Edward's thumb. But that was nuts, right?

Jack's breathing eased as the pain faded.

Faded.

Gone.

Edward gasped. "Hell and…"

Edward's thumb slipped away and scraped down Jack's cheek. Jack opened his eyes.

Body rigid, Edward's head was thrown back, his corded throat worked as if he couldn't get enough air, his features contorted as the seizure racked his body. With another horrible gurgle, he slumped to the side as his body did a slow-motion slide off the coffee table. Jack grabbed Edward's arm and the back of his neck, and eased him to the floor between the couch and the table.

Kneeling beside the unconscious man, Jack shoved the table out of the way.

"Edward." Jack tapped him on the cheek. "Edward."

No response. He lowered his face to Edward's. He wasn't breathing. Shit.

He felt for a pulse on Edward's neck. Nothing.

Desperate, he moved his fingers along the indentation in Edward's throat, searching for a pulse, any pulse. The touch was intimate yet clinical. He pressed harder.

"Come on, Edward. Stay with me, baby." Jack's heart hammered so hard, he didn't know if he felt his own pulse or Edward's, but after what seemed like too damn long, a pulse thumped softly against his fingertips.

Jack's body shook with relief.

"Edward. Wake up." Another light tap on Edward's contorted face.

Jack sat back, unsure what to do. He looked up at the phone on the kitchen wall. He should call an ambulance, but he couldn't bring himself to leave Edward's side. Glancing down at him, Jack watched the lines of pain smooth out, the creases in Edward's brow fade, and his body relax.

Edward's face transformed. Like a little brat who'd fallen asleep, all the mischievousness, all the impish delight, all the precociousness, transformed into an angelic facade.

He stared down at the young man, struck again by Edward's beauty. Not handsome or rugged, as a man should be. Edward had beauty and grace, like some creature of immense worth, delicate, vulnerable. His features were fine, his lashes too long for a man's, his lips full and plump.

Without thinking, Jack brushed his finger over Edward's lips. So soft. So smooth.

Edward's cheek showed just a hint of five o'clock shadow. Jack cupped Edward's face, the light stubble a soft roughness against his palm. Edward's hair, coal black, thick, tempted Jack.

Everything about this man tempted Jack.

Jack never gave into temptation. Never. That meant giving up control, and Jack needed control like he needed air.

What would Edward's hair feel like as it slipped between Jack's fingers?

Jack ran his hand through Edward's bangs, pushing them off his face. It was as if he'd run a silk scarf, fine and soft, through his fingers.

He let his hand fall away and rest on his thigh. Leaning over, he was unable to take his eyes off Edward's lips. They begged to be kissed.

Edward's eyes fluttered. "Jack?" he whispered as his eyes opened. He gazed up into Jack's face, bent over his.

"Shit, Edward. You scared me half to death." Jack exhaled and sat back, putting distance between him and temptation.

"Sorry." Edward sat up with a groan, rubbing his forehead. "It's not usually like that."

"What the hell just happened?" Jack stared at Edward.

Edward raised his hand and touched Jack's cheek. His fingers were still warm against Jack's skin, and Jack had to fight not to lean into Edward's touch meant to comfort him.

"I didn't mean to scare you." Edward's hand stayed there, building heat beneath it. Their gazes locked.

Jack could feel the blood pounding in his throat and his dick. Shit. Of all the times for his cock to come to life, it had to be now? Fuck, it felt so good to know he was still able to get it up. Matching pulse beats told Jack he'd be in deep trouble if he let this go on.

"Jack." Edward's dark eyes, large and liquid, focused on Jack's lips.

Jack pulled away. "I want answers, Edward. What happened?"

"Are you feeling better?"

"Yes. And I want to know why." Jack got up and sat on the recliner.

Edward rolled his shoulders, gave Jack an unsteady smile, then pushed himself up and onto the couch. "I told you. I healed you." He raked his fingers through his hair to straighten it.

"Does that happen every time?" Jack narrowed his eyes at Edward.

Edward sighed. "No." Jack caught the slight tremble in Edward's hands. He tried to steady them by rubbing them against his thighs.

"Then why now? What was different?" Jack leaned forward, his hands clasped between his knees to keep from reaching out to Edward.

Edward sat back, closed his eyes, and bit his lip. "Whatever was wrong with you was serious. More so than I thought."

"Serious? What do you mean? Why did you faint?"

"Faint? Is that what happened?" Edward gave a nervous laugh and rubbed the back of his neck. "I'm not sure, but if I had to make a guess, I'd say maybe an embolism." He shrugged.

Jack sat back. "Shit. No way." He ran a hand through his hair, feeling his head as if he could locate the problem inside his skull. "What happened to it?"

"This is the hard part to explain. I'm not sure I can, and I'm not sure that you'll believe me if I do." Edward tucked one leg under the other and sat back. He'd never tried the truth before; most of the time he explained it away as the wonders of massage. Somehow, he knew Jack wouldn't fall for that. Jack would demand more.

"Try me."

"I'm able to absorb...illness, I suppose. Transfer it from a person to myself. Then my body absorbs it, displaces it, or dispels it, I've never figured out which."

Jack stared at him. "You're crazy."

"I told you."

"It's some sort of mind trick. Like a placebo. People can't just take pain or an illness away. Not normal people." Jack stared at him.

Edward made a short laugh. "In case you haven't noticed, I'm not like everyone else. Take this shirt, for starters." He held out his arms to demonstrate, trying to ease the tension between them.

Jack, tight-lipped, stared at him. Edward winced at the disbelief on his face. What did Edward expect? He was surprised Jack hadn't called him crazy and thrown him out of the house.

"Does your head hurt? Can you see now?" Edward waved his hand at Jack, feeling very tired. More drained than he'd ever felt before.

"How did you know I couldn't see?"

Edward stared down at his hands in his lap. "When I took your pain, I went blind. Then I...fainted." He raised his eyes to catch Jack's gaze. He'd done more than just faint, but he wasn't ready to deal with that yet.

"Shit. Holy shit." Jack ran his hand over his face. "This is too fucking much."

"It's okay if you don't believe me." He shrugged. "I didn't expect you to."

"I don't know why, but I do. Christ, maybe *I'm* the one who's crazy."

There was a long silence between the men.

Unable to control himself, Edward whispered, "Were you going to kiss me?"

Jack jerked his head up. "No. Hell, no."

"Uh-huh. But you touched me, didn't you?" He should let it drop, but he couldn't.

Jack bolted out of the recliner. "You need to go. Let me get the keys, and I'll get your bags for you." He headed to the door.

Hurt and anger warred in Edward as he followed Jack, grabbed his arm, and spun him around. "I felt you. Touching me."

"I was just trying to see if you were alive."

"Bullshit." Edward didn't release him.

Jack jerked away. "Let me go."

"You want me." Why did Edward always have to push? He knew he should leave it alone, but he just couldn't stop himself, even knowing that it might drive Jack away.

In one quick move, Jack twisted Edward's arm behind his back and shoved him face-first into the front door. He slammed his hand over Edward's, trapping it against the door, and leaned against Edward's back. It was rough and violent and the most erotic thing Edward had ever felt. Hell and damnation, he'd popped a boner at the manhandling, and his dick pressed with delicious pain into the wooden door.

What the hell was he doing? He'd lost it, but goddamn it felt good to force himself on Edward, show him who was in control. Edward had this innocent wildness, this need to be tended. He needed someone to show him the way, and Jack needed to be the one who conquered him.

But it was impossible.

Edward was so incredibly *wrong*.

Resting his forehead on the door next to Edward's face, he said, "I'm not gay, Edward. Leave me alone." His ragged breath puffed Edward's hair.

Edward didn't say a word, just pushed his ass back into Jack's groin and uttered the sweetest little moan Jack had ever heard. Christ, it took every ounce of control Jack had not to press back, to keep his prick from leaping at the taunt.

Why did Edward stir him up so? Push him to the edge of reason and control? Make him feel? Jack hadn't felt anything in so long, and he wasn't ready or willing to start now. And even if he were, it sure as hell wouldn't be with Edward. Jack had been so careful not to put himself in such a weak position, by cutting himself off from everyone who could hurt him or drag him down the slope to the trash pile he'd climbed out of.

Losing control with Edward would put him in danger of losing everything he'd worked so hard for his whole life, and he was never going to sink to that level again.

"Please." Eyes closed, Jack knocked his forehead against the door. "I'm the chief of police. I'm *not* gay. I am *not* interested in you," he whispered. It was the only way.

Edward stilled beneath him. "Let me go."

Jack stepped back and released Edward's arm. Blushing, Edward rubbed his shoulder.

"Did I hurt you?" Jack asked.

"Only my pride," Edward drawled. "It's a wonder I have any left." He stepped away from the door, opened it, and rushed out.

After a few quick breaths, Jack regained control and reined in the feelings that threatened to betray him. Then he followed Edward to the patrol car. Edward waited at the trunk, looking out at the street, his back to Jack. Jack unlocked the patrol car, lifted the two bags out, and placed them at Edward's side.

Without looking at Jack, Edward picked them up and headed to his car. He tossed them in the backseat, opened the door, and slipped behind the wheel.

"I hope you can forgive me," Edward said quietly. "I seem to have made a fool of myself." He started the car and drove off, leaving Jack with a new ache.

This time, it wasn't in Jack's head.

Chapter Nine

Jack shut the door and leaned against it.

Winston sat in the hallway and whined at him.

"Sorry. He had to leave without saying good-bye."

Woof.

Jack slid down the door to a squat and gave Winston the command to come. The dog trotted up to him, his big, goofy jowls and wide mouth grinning at him. Jack scratched behind Winston's stubby ears as the dog snuggled up to him, working his way into Jack's heart.

The last thing Jack wanted to do was think about what just happened. The crushed look on Edward's face and the hurt in his eyes. The way he wouldn't even look at Jack. And Jack definitely didn't want to think about how crappy that had made him feel inside.

Shit. What had Edward expected him to do? From the moment they'd first met, Edward had done nothing but push Jack, and this time he'd gone too far. It was Edward's fault. Someone was bound to get hurt.

And Jack had sworn a long time ago, it would never be him.

Unwilling to keep hashing it over in his mind, Jack pushed up and went to the kitchen, got some cold cuts, ripped them up, and put them on a plate. Then he went back to the living room.

"Winston. Come."

Winston waddled over.

"Sit." Jack held up a piece of meat and pushed down on Winston's rump.

The dog sat.

"Good boy." Jack fed him the treat.

After thirty minutes, Jack had Winston sitting and lying down. Tomorrow he'd work on Stay and Heel. The dog was smart and a quick learner. He couldn't understand why Edward had never trained the animal.

But that was just like Edward. Out of control. Rash. Impulsive.

Everything Jack found irritating and weak. Everything that Jack had eliminated from himself, like a surgeon with a scalpel, cutting away weakness, leaving only strength.

But Edward wore it like a soft velvet cloak that wrapped his emotions, his vulnerability, and his tenderness around his lithe, hard body. It tugged on Jack's protective nature, made Jack quiet his voice and step easy around the younger man.

Right up to the point when Edward had just made Jack so damn crazy he'd lashed out.

Before any more thoughts of Edward swamped him, Jack went to the kitchen and took the last beer. Winston padded after him, right on his heels. Sitting on the table was the bag Edward had brought. Jack reached inside and pulled out half a dozen cans of dog food. A bag of dog treats. Organic treats? Who the hell ever heard of organic dog treats? He rolled his eyes.

Reached in, and his hand hit something else. He peered in and smiled.

Jack pulled out a six-pack of Shiner Bock and set it on the table.

He looked down at Winston. "How the hell did he know it was my favorite? Did you tell him?" Jack chuckled.

It had been a sweet gesture. From a sweet man.

Woof.

"Lucky guess, huh?" Jack put them in the fridge; then he opened a can of dog food and put it in a bowl.

While Winston chowed down, Jack finished his beer. It wasn't late, but he was beat. Jack went to his bedroom, stripped down, and climbed under the covers.

Winston jumped up onto the bed, circled his wagons, then lay down at Jack's feet.

Jack was too tired to chase him off. He closed his eyes and added Off to the list of commands he'd teach the dog over the weekend.

No pain. Not a single twinge. He was tired, but not hurting. Christ, he'd lived with the pain for weeks and now, just like that, it was gone. In a weird way, he missed it.

He rolled over and tried not to think about it.

Edward had taken his pain. But it wasn't just that, and Jack knew it.

Edward had saved his life.

Whatever he'd taken from Jack could have killed Edward, and for a moment, Jack would have sworn Edward had died, but that couldn't be.

Whatever it had been, it had been meant to kill Jack.

Christ. Would it have happened tonight? Would he have died in his sleep? Just dropped dead?

How long would it have taken someone to notice he hadn't shown up for work? He was going to be off all weekend. Jack shivered at the thought of being found dead days later. He'd seen those bodies before, bloated, distorted, and reeking. For the first time in years, the desolation of being alone rocked him.

Morbid thoughts were useless. He hadn't died. He was fine. No sense in getting all bent out of shape over something that hadn't even happened. It was just too damn close for comfort, like knowing he'd missed taking a bullet, or he'd stopped at an intersection just as an eighteen-wheeler barreled through.

Fuck. It was the "your life flashes before your eyes" kind of scary.

* * *

Edward pulled onto the highway. His hands clutched the steering wheel, and he refused to acknowledge the water standing in his eyes by wiping it away. Between his terror at what had happened when he'd taken Jack's pain, and Jack's rejection of Edward's stupid advances, his stomach rebelled.

He pulled over, jumped out of the car, and ran to the side of the road. Falling to his hands and knees, he threw up into the grass, his stomach heaving until long past empty. Finished, he spit, wiped his mouth with his sleeve, and got to his feet, clinging to the side of the car. He staggered around to the open door, then slumped into the seat and leaned back against the headrest.

He'd only wanted to help Jack, to help the man he'd been drawn to as if Jack held all the answers to all Edward's questions.

He'd thought Jack just had a headache. Maybe even a sinus infection. Something easy, simple, like all the other times he'd used his power. He hadn't been prepared for what he'd found, not for what had come rushing at him through their connection.

Hot, blinding agony wrapped in a pulsing fireball.

How the hell had Jack stood it all this time?

And when Edward had opened his eyes—utter darkness. A desolation that had left him like a lost child, crying in the dark for comfort. Had Jack felt that too, or was that something only Edward had felt?

Then the explosion hit, and he'd lost consciousness.

Edward took several deep breaths, inhaling and expelling air, until the trembling stopped and he'd regained some control.

He'd almost died. Maybe, for a second, he did. He wasn't sure of anything. Whatever had been inside Jack's head burst after it had entered Edward. His gift, and his life, both of which he'd always used so cavalierly, had almost been taken from him. He'd saved Jack's life, of that he was sure, but he'd come close to losing his own, and that terrified him.

Never again.

And speaking of never again... He'd done it again. Made a fool of himself by throwing himself at Jack, only to be rejected. Had he been out of his mind? A man like Jack wouldn't want him. Jack was a man's man. A Texas lawman. He was John Fucking Wayne, for God's sake.

At least this time, it hadn't been in public.

Just a private humiliation.

His face burned as he relived Jack's voice, whispering so hoarsely in his ear, searing him from the inside out. He closed his eyes and could feel the weight of the bigger man pressed into him. The heat of Jack's hard body. Jack's scent. Jack's breath. Jack's hand on top of his. Edward had had an erection as Jack trapped Edward between his body and the hard wooden door.

Edward would have dropped his jeans and let Jack fuck him at that moment.

Now, Edward just wanted to run away, like he'd run from Atlanta and all his problems there.

He snorted and rolled his eyes. If he kept doing that, eventually he'd run out of places to hide. With his track record of failure, he stood a pretty good chance of finding himself in Timbuktu, and Lord knew, he did not look good in khaki.

He could run, but he couldn't hide. Not from himself.

He needed to face facts. Get a grip on his life and come to some understanding.

There was something wrong with him.

Edward flipped down the visor and opened the mirror. He studied his reflection by the glow of the small light. Stared into his own watery eyes, searching for signs.

It must be some internal failure. A design flaw. Something down at the cellular level that rendered him unlovable, that sent out some sort of homing beacon to the wrong sort of men and lit up the big sign on his back that said, BREAK MY HEART. As if he were some perpetual victim, caught in a never-ending loop of bad choices, bad mistakes, and bad lovers.

Except Jack wasn't the wrong sort of man. He was a good man. Honest, sincere, trustworthy, and in control. Everything Edward had never been attracted to, had always sneered at, only now it turned him on. This must be some kind of cosmic karma.

Because, to add insult to injury, Jack wasn't gay.

Edward sighed.

He was falling in love with a man who wasn't gay.

Talk about your hell and damnation.

* * *

Jack flopped onto his back, and his hand brushed his half-hard cock. He grunted. That hadn't happened since the pain started. Hard to get it up when you're in agony. Unless you're into that sort of thing, and Jack wasn't. Just plain, old-fashioned, vanilla self-gratification for him. Nothing he couldn't control, nothing to get excited about. Nothing to involve his emotions.

After weeks of not jacking off, he needed some relief. Jack leaned over, pulled open the drawer on his nightstand, and took out a small bottle of baby oil. No way would he be caught buying sex lube or one of those massage creams guaranteed to make your dick tingle. Not even online. The only computer he had access to was the one on his desk at work, and he'd never risk putting anything but business on that.

But baby oil? Everyone bought that stuff.

Jack guarded his privacy. It was necessary in a small town where everyone knew everything about each other, and what they didn't know, they were more than willing to speculate about.

The last thing he needed, as chief of police, was to not be respected, to be made the town laughingstock, or to have his personal life subject to gossip and speculation.

He'd never be in that position again. The object of ridicule, ashamed of who he was, where he'd come from. Poor white trailer-park trash, with a couple of drunks for parents. The kid no one wanted to hang with or even sit next to in school.

The best thing he'd ever done was run away and start a new life when he was sixteen. At eighteen, he'd changed his name to escape any attempt his lousy excuse for parents might make to find him and drag him back.

He had no regrets about leaving or cutting them out of his life. They were toxic, like cancer. Without them putting him down, eating away at his self-confidence, telling him he was no better than they were, he'd made something of himself, and he was damned proud of it. So what if it came with a cost. Everything worth fighting for did.

Just like he'd fought so hard to be the best cop he could be. That had gotten him noticed and moved up the ranks, until he'd been offered the job as the youngest chief of police this town had ever had. Another reason he could hold his head up with pride.

He dripped some oil into his palm, rubbed his hands together, and fisted his dick. After a few strokes, he still wasn't hard. The fire smoldered but didn't seem to catch. Jack reached for his balls, slicked them up, and squeezed, pulled, and rolled them in his hand. It felt good, but tonight it wasn't enough.

Frustrated, he rolled onto his side, his hand still working up and down his prick. He'd forgotten about Winston until the dog growled at being jostled.

"Get lost, buddy." Winston hopped off the bed and trotted out of the room.

The dog had probably seen plenty of Edward's jack-off sessions, maybe even Edward and his lovers going at it, but he wasn't going to watch Jack.

Did Edward have a lover back in Atlanta? Of course he did; the man was gorgeous. So if he did, why all the flirting?

And why the fuck was Jack thinking about Edward's lovers, his flirting, and his whacking off? And getting irritated by it? Irritated or jealous?

No no no.

He stopped, emptied his mind, and added more oil to his hand. Then he began the process again with the same result. A half-limp dick.

What the hell was wrong with him tonight? He usually had his routine down pat. The same jerk-off session, a couple of times a week, for the last God-knew-how-many years. He knew just how he had to touch himself, just how hard, how fast, where.

It was as if his rhythm was off, and he couldn't find the right beat.

He closed his eyes and let his mind wander, but like an arrow, it flew straight back to Edward. Jack's cock swelled in his grip. "Oh shit." He moaned.

No fucking way.

The younger man had made him lose control tonight, and Jack had struck out in violence, grabbed Edward, and thrown him against the door. Jack had reveled in the rush of adrenaline and dominance, of letting Edward know that Jack could handle him any way Jack wanted to, if he felt like it.

And Edward had surrendered, made that dick-hardening little moan.

Jack slipped his hand over the tip of his prick, his thumb smeared precum over its head. He hissed his pleasure, and his eyes shuttered. Thrusting his hips, his dick slid through his hand, a poor substitute for the tightness and heat he craved.

For a moment tonight, he'd had Edward pinned beneath him. He'd pressed into that tight little ass as he assured Edward he wasn't gay and didn't want him.

Christ, he got so fucking hard just thinking about Edward. Okay, so what if he was attracted to Edward? Attraction was merely that, attraction. Not need, not want. Not, for Christ's sake, love.

Those things were too dangerous, opened a man up to weakness. Jack had given them up a long time ago when life had picked him up by the throat, shook him until his teeth rattled, and then tossed him aside, broken and bitter.

Thoughts, on the other hand, were safe. Merely fantasy. People thought about things they'd never do in real life all the time to get turned on. And Jack was definitely turned on. More than he'd been in a very long time.

His eyes closed as he pictured Edward's smaller body beneath his. Jack's hips jerked as his stroke faltered. He pulled on his cock, hard and fast, as the need in his body built. Bowstring taut, his body vibrated, but release eluded him.

Growling, Jack rolled onto his back, one hand on his dick, the other rubbing the tender flesh beneath his balls, a placed he'd discovered on his body that usually sent him over the edge. Close, his orgasm built in his balls, but it slipped away again.

With a cry of frustration, he sat up, knocked the pillows off the bed, and knelt facing the headboard. He clutched the top rail as he jerked off with frantic motions. Slammed one hand against the wall above the bed as he rocked his hips back and forth, sliding his dick in the tight grip of his other hand, striving for release. Begging his body to let go and fucking let him come.

"Oh, Christ," he gasped as he gave in to the knowledge and awareness.

He'd wanted to fuck Edward against that door. Use his dick as a battering ram in Edward's tight, hot ass. And it would be so fucking tight, he just knew it. And scorching hot, so hot it'd burn him like a brand.

As his cock thrust, hitting the wood, it left smears of precum, evidence of the dangerous truth.

Jack slapped the wall harder as the head of his penis banged against the headboard, against Edward's ass. The pain was so sweet. So fucking sweet.

Jack reached the cliff, raced toward it, and then hung on the edge for what seemed the longest moment of his life.

"Oh fuck, Edward," he whispered and plunged over the edge.

His balls tightened, and with a final thrust and cry, he sat back on his heels and came. Jack watched as streams of cum hit the headboard, his dick pulsing. Christ, he thought he'd never stop shooting spunk, stop his body's shuddering, but at last, he came up empty.

White ropes of jism dripped down the dark-stained mahogany like raindrops on a windshield.

Groaning, he fell backward. His heart pounded like a son of a bitch, his shaft hypersensitive to the slightest touch, and its head ached from being battered.

Shit. He'd never jerked off like that before, with so much anger, passion, and primal need. So out of control.

He waited until his breathing eased, then rolled out of bed, wet a cloth, and cleaned off his headboard. Then he put the pillows back, climbed in, and pulled the covers up to his waist.

It was just a fantasy and didn't mean a goddamned thing.

Chapter Ten

Edward unlocked the door to his grandmother's house with his new key and quietly stepped inside. All he wanted was to take his bags, go to his room, and get under the covers. And never come out.

How in the world could he face Jack again?

He'd just have to pretend as if nothing had happened. And it was the truth, nothing happened. Damn it.

At least, not on Jack's part. But Edward had gone out on that fragile limb, exposed his emotions, and had been knocked off it. Really, he had to stop doing that.

Confidence shattered, he undressed, brushed his teeth, and put on his pajamas. Tonight he needed the black silk pair. Slipping on the loose pants, he took a moment to enjoy the way the pure silk caressed his skin. This pair had always made him feel better. He knew about comfort food, but for him, texture soothed his soul. Food he could take or leave, and he'd never been one for drugs or alcohol, just the occasional glass of white wine with dinner.

As he buttoned up the shirt, he stared at his reflection in the bathroom mirror. He looked awful. Too pale, for one thing. He leaned closer to the mirror. Were those crow's feet at the corners of his eyes? When did *that* happen? Thirty had been bad enough, but thirty-five sucked.

What would his life be like at forty?

Too fucking depressing to think about.

He left the bathroom and went back to his room, thinking about his immediate problem.

If he didn't get that proof of vaccination, he might lose Winston. Edward slumped onto the bed. If that happened, he'd have no one. Well, no one who mattered. No one who'd love him just because he was Edward.

Happy when Edward got home, Winston always barked and raced around Edward's legs until he got the attention he demanded. Edward felt Winston's love in the boundless exuberance the little dog always greeted him with.

Through thick and thin, over the last six years, while lovers had promised him their love, had lied and cheated, or used him for his money like Derek, Winston had been there for him.

Winston never lied to him. Never promised him anything other than he'd always be happy to see him, always be waiting. He'd always been faithful and steadfast. As long as he had Winston, Edward wasn't really alone and unloved.

The room seemed emptier without the little dog. Edward missed feeling the weight of the dog near his feet and tucking his cold toes under Winston's warmth. He even missed Winston's snoring.

Crawling under the covers, Edward stroked the silk shirt over his belly, soothing himself. It was something he'd done since childhood whenever he'd been upset. He'd hidden the compulsive behavior from everyone, especially his father, as he moved into his teens, but he'd had the same velvet pillow for years. Alone at night, as his fears and worries loomed in the dark, he'd clutch it to his chest and pet it until he'd fallen asleep.

It was so quiet. He got out of bed, went to the light switch, and flicked on the overhead fan, just to have some noise to break the silence. His fears didn't cry out so loudly then. His mother's sighs of exasperation signaling her disappointment were muffled. His father's voice not near as sharp and ridiculing.

He could barely hear Jack whispering, "*I'm not gay, Edward. Leave me alone.*"

How could Edward have been so wrong? He'd thought he'd seen a heated flicker of interest in the police chief's sexy blue eyes. And Jack *had* touched his lips with his fingertip and had cupped his check. Edward was positive he'd felt those tender caresses, that they hadn't been in his head. Or had they?

No. A blast of sexual attraction and mutual desire *had* passed between them. He'd certainly felt that enough to recognize it. Too many times. And when Jack had thrown him against the door? Hell and damnation.

In Atlanta, the gay scene was filled with willing partners, just not filled with willing life partners. Edward had long since grown tired of casual or anonymous sex and had started looking for that special someone to share the rest of his life. Someone whom he loved and who would love him back.

Was that too much to ask?

It seemed to be.

Edward rolled over and closed his eyes. His body felt battered. Whatever had happened to him at Jack's left him feeling as if he'd been run over by a UPS truck, without the hunky driver in those cute shorts.

Okay, time to end the pity party. He only allowed just so many such thoughts per night, and he was over his quota. That's what had made those damn crow's feet around his eyes. Worry. Self-doubt. And not enough moisturizer.

Edward sighed. He had a bigger problem to deal with than the lack of a love life.

How was he going to heal his grandmother when he was too terrified to try his power again?

* * *

Edward woke the next morning after a restless night. None of his problems had been solved, and the rosy morning light streaming through the blinds on the window didn't make them look any better.

Since he doubted Hooterville had a gym, he decided to take his act on the road and go for a run.

He didn't bother with the shower, no point if he was going to come back all hot and sweaty, so he just pulled on his jockstrap, slipped into a pair of running shorts, a T-shirt, socks, and his trainers.

Olivia was having coffee at the table as he came into the kitchen.

"I'm going for a quick run, Meemaw. Do you mind?"

"Not at all, child. Go have your run. I'll have breakfast ready when you get back." She smiled at him over what looked like the local paper. The Hooterville *Gazette* couldn't have been more than a dozen pages long.

"Don't go out of your way for me. I'm just a coffee and cereal kind of guy."

"Cereal? I'm not sure I have any." She frowned. "I can make you eggs and bacon, though."

Oh God, that would be decadence itself. He rarely splurged on breakfast, and especially not bacon or sausage. He'd have to stop at that market again and pick up a box of Cheerios. He knew they wouldn't carry the organic cereal that he usually bought.

"Well, I suppose I could let you talk me into it." He winked. "Just this once."

"Watching your weight?" She eyed him up and down. "In my opinion, you could stand to gain a few pounds, Edward."

Soaking wet, Edward didn't weight more than one hundred and sixty, and at five-ten, he kept most of it tight and taut. Most of his lovers had truly appreciated his efforts.

"What? And ruin this fabulous body?" He struck a few poses, showing off his muscles like a weight lifter.

She laughed at his antics and waved him off. "Get going. I'll see you when you get back."

Edward gave her a kiss on the cheek and headed for the door.

Outside, he went through his stretches and then started jogging in place to warm up. Once he felt ready, he took off down the block.

Pounding down the pavement, Edward came to the main street and turned the corner. He passed all sorts of shops and stores that hadn't opened yet. The little town was still asleep. The morning was cool, traffic nonexistent, and clean country air filled his lungs. He loved running in the early morning when he could just let go of everything, concentrate on his feet hitting the concrete, his even breathing, and keeping his pace steady.

So unlike his wreck of a life.

He never took Winston running. The dog was just too short-legged and became too exhausted to go far. But Edward loved it, loved stretching his legs, loved doing short sprints toward the end, then slowing down as he finished and walked the last few blocks to cool down.

He'd focused on the sidewalk ahead of him and never noticed he was coming up to Smith's Garage until he was right on top of it.

"Hey, look who it is!" A voice called out. "Looking good, princess!"

Edward looked around, saw where he was, and stumbled. He went down, his knee hit the ground, and he threw his hands out to keep his head from hitting.

Laughter echoed in the empty street. After pushing up the garage doors, Phil and Jimmy slapped each other on the back as they whistled and catcalled at him.

Gritting his teeth against the pain and his anger, Edward checked his knee and wiped off the blood that ran from the deep cut with his T-shirt. His palms were scraped but not bleeding. His knee and his pride had taken the brunt of the fall. He pushed off the ground and brushed off his legs.

Jimmy started toward him, a sneer on his already greasy face. Did he come to work that way or did he apply the grease once there?

Edward stepped back and looked up and down the street. His knee screamed at him, but fear screamed louder. This was not the place or the time for a confrontation, and Jimmy had "gonna kick your fag ass" written all over him.

Edward turned and jogged away, praying Jimmy was too lazy or out of shape to follow.

"Hey, come back, princess! We've got your Prince Charming right here!" Only Jimmy's taunts chased him down the block. Edward didn't slow down until he'd gone three blocks, and then he came to a limping halt.

Bent over, he struggled to catch his breath. Blood ran down his shin and soaked his sock. Running home was out of the question. The few blocks he'd traveled had only aggravated the cut and made the bleeding worse.

If only his power worked for him. He could take away other people's pain but couldn't do a damn thing for himself. What kind of power was that?

Edward began walking. Actually, it was more of a step, limp, hop, step, limp, hop. It would take him forever to make it back to the house. There were still six blocks to go before he turned on Olivia's street and then another six blocks or so to her house.

He'd covered another block when a horn sounded and someone called his name. Edward dunked his head, as if whoever it was wouldn't recognize or see him, but since the guy had used his name, and since there was no way he could limp fast enough, he stopped.

A huge black truck pulled to the curb.

Instead of Jimmy or Phil, a handsome cowboy, complete with black cowboy hat, hung out the window. Edward glanced over at him. He didn't recognize him, but he wished he did. Then another man leaned over and waved.

"Mr. Beauregard? It's Brian Russell. From yesterday? I gave you a ride to pick up your car?" The big cop, dressed in a red T-shirt, smiled at him.

Edward limped over to the truck. "Hi. Fancy meeting you here."

"I'd like to introduce my partner, Rush Weston. Rush, this is Edward Beauregard, from Atlanta. He's visiting Olivia." They shook hands through the window of the cab.

"Nice to meet you." Edward smiled at the happy couple. Lucky boys.

"What happened to your leg?" Rush asked, adjusting his Stetson.

Edward cast a glance down the street. "I was concentrating on my running and someone called out to me, and I tripped and fell." He shrugged. He didn't intend to tell anyone about the men at the garage. That would only stir things up. Discretion was definitely the better part of valor here in homophobic Hooterville.

"It looks like you could use a ride home," Rush drawled. "Hop in." He jerked his head at other side of the truck.

Brian was already opening his door. "Get in here. I insist."

"Okay. Thanks, I really appreciate it. I left Olivia thinking I'd only be gone for about a half hour. I don't want her worrying about me." He climbed in as Brian scooted over next to Rush. Edward didn't miss Brian's claiming hand on Rush's leg, or the way Rush's arm wrapped around Brian's shoulders.

See, it did happen for some men. Why not him?

"Do you know where Olivia lives?" Edward asked Rush as he pulled away from the curb.

"Sure. Been here all my life, and she's been here longer. 'Course, she used to live on the old ranch, but about fifteen years ago she moved into town."

"I didn't know that, babe. I thought she'd been there forever." Brian laughed. "I've only been here for about six months myself, Edward. Can I call you Edward?"

"Sure. As long as I can call you Brian and Rush."

"It's a deal." Brian nodded. "So, are you going to stay long?"

"For a while. I have to get Winston back. That should be on Monday; then I have to move to the hotel up on the interstate, and I still have some business to take care of with my grandmother."

Rush turned to Brian. "Winston? That the dog that bit your boss?"

Brian chuckled. "Yes. Jack wanted to keep it quiet, but by the afternoon, thanks to Kristen, the story had spread to just about everyone on the force."

Edward groaned and rubbed a hand over his face. "I didn't mean to cause Jack so much trouble. It's bad enough my dog bit him."

"Jack, huh?" Rush raised an eyebrow. "Not Chief Whittaker?"

Edward blushed.

Brian told Rush, "Edward asked me if Jack was gay."

The fire in Edward's face burned all the way to the roots of his hair. He had no idea what to say, so he just sat still and waited for the moment to pass and the topic of conversation to change.

"That's an interesting question, Edward." Rush grinned. "Any reason why you'd think so?" The cowboy sure wasn't giving Edward any answers, just more questions.

Edward bit his bottom lip, unsure what to say.

The men waited.

"Okay. You know, when a guy looks at you like he wants to gobble you up? Like he hasn't eaten in days and you're bananas Foster?"

"Uh-huh," Rush said.

"You got that look from *Jack*?" Brian asked as one eyebrow rose.

"I think so. When we first met on the side of the road. After my dog bit him. And again in his office, right before he threw me out."

Rush let out a low whistle. "Well, I never knew it, that's for damn sure. Of course, I was pretty deep in the closet myself until I met Brian and found a damn good reason to come out. Maybe Jack's in there too. What do you think, darlin'? You work with him every day."

"No way." Brian shook his head. "I've never seen the man do or say anything that even hinted at being gay. Sorry, Edward."

"That's okay. I must be nuts to think…" Edward sighed.

"To think what?" Brian urged him to finish.

"To think a man like Jack Whittaker would want someone like me." Edward ran his hand through his hair and stared out the window. It *was* nuts.

"What's wrong with you?" Rush asked. "From what I see, you've got a lot going for you. Especially that cute butt of yours."

"Thanks." Edward grinned as Brian elbowed his partner.

"You're not supposed to be checking out other men," Brian growled.

"I'm all yours, darlin', but a man can still look." Rush laughed and ruffled Brian's hair, then gave him a peck on the cheek.

Edward shrugged. "Thanks for noticing my ass. I just wish Jack had noticed it too. What I meant was, I'm nothing like Jack. He's all male and alpha and strict and sexy and…" He exhaled. "Not gay. He told me so."

"You asked?" Brian sat back.

"No." Edward sighed. "This is so embarrassing. Please promise me you won't mention a word of this to anybody, especially Jack."

Brian held up his hand as if taking the oath in court. "I promise."

"Me too," added Rush.

"I sort of came on to him. I'd been flirting with him since the stop, but last night at his house—"

"Wait. You were at Jack's house?" Brian interrupted.

"Yes. I went there to bring Winston some dog food. Anyway, I came on to him. I thought...I felt...he... Anyway, it doesn't matter. He told me to leave him alone and that he wasn't gay. I was so mortified."

The men nodded their understanding.

"I'm usually right when it comes to these things. But this time I was *so* wrong."

Edward caught the look that passed between Rush and Brian, but they said nothing more until Rush pulled up in front of Olivia's.

Rush spoke as Edward got out. "We're having some friends over on Wednesday evening. Why don't you join us?"

"That's a great idea, babe," Brian chimed in. "Come out to the ranch, Edward."

"How sweet of you! I'd love to. Is it a real ranch?" Edward wasn't sure about going to a ranch or what he'd find there. He had a vision of trying to drive the Miata through a herd of cows. What if there was a stampede? In those old westerns, the cattle always charged right over a cliff.

"Yep. Got horses and cattle."

"But no cliffs, right?" Edward asked.

"No. No cliffs. Most of our land is pasture, woods, and rolling hills." Rush tilted his head as if pondering the question and its meaning.

"That sounds nice," Edward said.

"I'll call you later to give you directions. Give me your cell number," Brian said. They swapped numbers, and then Edward thanked them and limped up the path to the front door as the two men drove off.

Despite his run-ins with the jerks at the garage, most of the people he'd met here had been very nice and welcoming. Of course, he hadn't met more than a handful of people, but so far, Hooterville was shaping up nicely.

Chapter Eleven

Edward expected to smell bacon or sausage cooking when he came in, but only the light scent of lavender caught his nose. Had he been gone too long, and she'd given up on him?

"Meemaw?" he called out. No answer.

He went to the kitchen. The paper and her coffee cup sat on the table as if she'd just gotten up and walked off. He turned around and went to the hall, passed his room and the guest bath, and went straight to her room.

Edward knocked softy on the door. "Meemaw? Are you all right?" After no answer, he opened it and peeked in.

Olivia lay stretched out on the bed, her arm slung over her eyes.

"Meemaw?" Edward's stomach dropped. She was so still. So small on the queen-size bed.

He went to her side and bent over. Taking her hand, he petted the back of it.

"Meemaw? Are you okay?" Thank God, it was warm.

Her eyes fluttered and opened. They looked dazed as she searched his face.

"Edward? You're back." She sighed. "I'm sorry about breakfast, but I had a bad spell."

"I don't care about that. Did you fall? Are you hurt?" He looked her up and down but didn't see any sign of bruises or cuts. "Should I call your doctor?"

"No." She shook her head. "I just get weak and have to lie down." She tried to get up. "I'll get your breakfast now."

"You will not!" Edward put his hand on her shoulder and pushed her back gently. "I'm a big boy. I can fend for myself. How about I fix you something?"

She patted his hand. "No, thanks. I need to rest, and after one of these spells, I can't touch food for a while. Go take care of yourself, child."

Edward frowned. "Maybe I'll just get cleaned up and come sit with you."

She smiled. "That would be nice; I'd like that."

"Be right back." Edward left, hurried to his room, gathered some clothes, and headed to the bathroom. After a quick shower, he skipped shaving and fussing with his hair, and then tackled the cut on his knee. Once he'd cleaned and bandaged it, he dressed and went back to Olivia's room.

She was sleeping. Edward slipped into a chair near the bed and watched her. Even, shallow breaths made her chest rise and fall in a steady rhythm. That was good. When she felt better, he'd ask her about the spells.

The area around her eyes looked sunken, her skin pale, papery, and almost transparent. She looked terribly old, and Edward was struck by her mortality. She'd seemed so alive just this morning. What had reduced her to this in just one short hour?

Whatever it was, Edward wasn't sure he wanted to tackle it. Not until he understood exactly what "it" was. He needed to speak to her doctor.

If she had one.

Surely, she'd been to see a physician about these attacks? His mother ran to the doctor for every ache and pain, real or imagined. But old people were funny sometimes. She'd already said she hated complaining and listening to other old people talk about their illnesses. Did she hate it so much she hadn't gone?

That he'd have to forge ahead, into a situation he knew nothing about, and try to use his power to heal her, terrified him.

Like he had with Jack.

He stared at the woman he'd come to love in just two short days. She'd loved him from the first moment he'd entered her house. Had loved him all along. Edward knew that. He'd felt it in his bones. And in response to that love, he loved her back. She'd accepted him without hesitation. Without snide remarks or suggestions about how he could change or improve himself because he wasn't good enough.

He'd been good enough for her just as he was.

She was his grandmother, and he barely knew her, yet he loved her fiercely.

But did he love her enough?

* * *

Jack stared at the empty shelves of his refrigerator. The six-pack of Shiner was nestled in the door tray. Over the last day or so, he'd fed most of his food to Winston during their training sessions. Jack would have to go to the store and do some shopping if he wanted to eat this week.

Winston, on the other hand, had the dog food that Edward had brought him.

Shutting the fridge door, Jack straightened and looked down at the little bulldog.

"Well, buddy. Looks like we're going out for lunch."

Woof.

"I could go shopping, but I don't really feel like it." Actually, he hated it. Of the few things that got to him about being alone, shopping for groceries was at the top of his list. There was nothing worse than pushing a half-empty cart down the aisle, picking up beer, chips, cans of soup, and frozen TV dinners.

Nothing said "single and alone" quite like that.

He'd thought after all these years of cooking for himself that he would have become a great chef. But that was so wrong. He'd burn water if given a chance.

Emptying soup into a bowl and microwaving it was the extent of his culinary skills. Sure, he could fry an egg and some bacon. Make toast. Nuke a potato.

But fashion a delicious meal from scratch?

No way. He'd long since gotten tired of throwing away burned, overcooked, or just plain bad-tasting food.

Maybe he'd pick up some steaks and chops. Fire up the grill. He didn't suck at cooking meat over a fire, but for most men that was innate. Something that still lingered in all male genes. A throwback from the time of cavemen.

Fire good.

He chuckled and picked up Winston's leash. "Come on, buddy. Let's go to the drive-through. We'll get a couple of chicken dinners with all the fixings."

Woof.

The dog danced around his legs, his tongue hanging out of the side of his wide mouth, dark eyes shining.

Jack hooked him up and they left.

Winston trotted over to the cruiser.

"No, buddy. I don't drive that on my days off. Personal time. Personal car." Jack led him over to his gray Silverado. It was old but paid for, and in Jack's book, that was just fine. He'd never been one of those guys who waited for the newest model to come out so he could trade in the old. He didn't see any sense in paying never-ending car notes.

The old girl didn't have any of the newer fancy gadgets, like a CD player or places to plug in one of those iPods or a cell phone. She was just a good, old-fashioned, American-made, pick-'em-up truck, with all the dents, scraped paint, and road dirt to prove it.

He opened the door, and Winston tried to climb up. His front feet reached the running board, but his back legs couldn't make it. The dog hung, one back leg searching for purchase, as he struggled to get inside.

"Too short, huh?"

Forgetting to worry that the animal might bite him again, Jack leaned down and picked the dog up. Winston was compact, but Christ, the dog had the density of a small planet. He stilled in Jack's arms as he lifted him, then scampered onto the bench seat and trotted over to the passenger side.

Jack got in and started the truck. Winston leaned on the door, pressed his face and flat nose against the window, leaving ugly smears of dog drool and tongue prints that blurred the glass.

Woof. Woof.

"I get the message." He hit the window control, and Winston's window rolled down. The dog hung over the side, ready to go.

Jack backed out of his drive and headed to town.

Once on Main Street, he slowed as he approached Olivia Rawlings's street.

Plenty of time for a quick cruise around town. Check out things. Roll through the neighborhood.

Hitting the turn indicator, he made the turn. He cruised down the street to her house and pulled to the side. He noted the little red Miata, its top still down, parked in her driveway. Under the carport sat her old blue Cadillac Eldorado. From the dust, it looked as if it had been parked there for ages.

He couldn't remember the last time he'd seen her driving it. He always thought she'd be driving that car around to all her meetings, to shop in San Antonio, and out to the old ranch, until the day she died.

Maybe he should look in on her. Pay her a visit. She might be ill.

He had his hand on the keys when he froze.

Who the hell was he kidding?

Cursing himself, he threw the gear stick into drive and pulled away from the curb.

Was he that pathetic he had to make up some lame excuse just to see Edward again?

Fuck no. Edward was the last person he needed to see.

What he *needed* was for Edward to finish whatever business he had here and take his tight ass the hell back to Atlanta. And leave Jack the fuck alone.

* * *

Edward ladled the soup into a bowl, placed it on the tray, and put some crackers next to it. Then he added a glass of iced tea, sweet, of course, and quickly folded a napkin into a swan. A bud vase with a yellow rose from Olivia's garden was the final touch.

Satisfied with the effort, he carried it to her room, knocked, and then entered.

"Lunch, Meemaw."

Olivia sat up in bed, looking much better. Color had returned to her cheeks, and her skin had lost that papery look. Her eyes seemed brighter as she smiled at him.

He placed the tray across her lap.

"Lord, child, you didn't have to go to all this trouble for me."

"Of course I did. Besides, presentation is never any trouble." He shook out the napkin with a snap and laid it across her lap.

She leaned over, inhaled, and sighed. "Chicken soup. It smells perfect."

"I use the wide noodles." He pointed at them. "It's just the quick version. My real chicken soup takes a day."

She took a spoonful, swallowed, and nodded. "Well, you've done a fine job."

"Thanks, Meemaw. One day, I hope to make some lucky man a wonderful wife."

She laughed, slapped his hand, and dipped a cracker into the broth. "This is just what I needed."

"I'm glad." He sat on the chair and crossed his legs. "Now. I want to know what this is all about." He gave her a stern stare. "And I want the truth. I'm not a child to be coddled."

She looked at him over her soupspoon, then took another sip. "It's not something you can do anything about, so what's the point, Edward? I've made my decision about how I want to spend the little time I have left on this earth, and it's not plugged into machines, drugged out of my mind, lying in a hospital bed, praying for the end."

"But what if there were something you could do. Something that would give you more time, more years, even?"

She looked off into some distant place; then her gaze came back to meet his. "I'm not sure, child. I've lived a long time, and it's been good for the most part. I have regrets, true, but who doesn't? However, I've lived my life just the way I wanted to, and I'm happy. More time?" She shrugged. "What would I do with more time?"

Edward picked at the faded spot on the knee of his jeans. "Spend it with me?" he said softly.

"Oh, child." She placed her hand over his. "You're one of my regrets. I should have contacted you and ignored your father's demands to stay out of your life."

Edward's head snapped up. "He said you didn't want to see me."

She shook her head and squeezed his hand. "Never. I never said that." She sat back and pushed her half-eaten soup away. "Even after he died, I should have written you. Or called. But by then you were a young man, and I thought the last thing you'd want was some old lady hanging around."

Once again, his father had interfered with his life. Even from the grave, the man's reach was long. His father had been opinionated, hateful, and could hold a grudge longer than anyone on God's green earth.

"Maybe. I'm not sure. I was going through a lot of stuff when Father died." It was Edward's turn to shrug. "But I sure could have used you in my corner."

"I'm sorry."

"Hey, it's not all your fault. I could have made contact. Not waited almost fifteen years."

She smiled, patted his hand, and cocked her head at him. "And just what was the *real* reason you came? And don't repeat that story about your love life."

"It wasn't a story. Derek, that was...that is his name... I found out he'd arranged to meet me before we'd even met. He'd set the whole thing up just to get to me. Well, to my money." God, it sounded so lame when he said it with his outside voice. He'd never admitted it before, except to Winston. "He swept me off right off my feet. Dancing. Candlelight dinners. Getaway weekends. All on my dime, of course, but at the time, I didn't care. It was très romantic. A gorgeous man swearing undying love to me." Edward rolled his eyes. "Before two months were out, I'd moved him into my condo."

"My, that was fast. Then he dumped you?"

"I wish." He stared out the window, took a deep breath, and told her the rest. "No. Like a fool, I trusted him and gave him the password to my bank debit card." Edward fought the burning behind his eyes, blinking away the tears. "At the ball, the one I told you about, I confronted him about the money. Told him to pack his things and get out." He stared down at his feet. "I was such a little fool to believe all his promises."

She sighed. "Seems to me you didn't do anything wrong but fall in love, and in my book, there's nothing wrong with opening your heart to someone."

"But I so stupid, so naive. I believed him. All the lies he told me. All the promises he made." He closed his eyes, and he was right back to the night of the ball, standing at the ATM in the lobby of the hotel, when he'd discovered there was no money in his account. He'd never forget the horrible, sick feeling that he'd been played by the one person he'd trusted.

"Oh, Edward."

"That wasn't all. I had to borrow money from Mother just to pay my mortgage and take an advance on my quarterly payment from the trust. She wouldn't give me the money until I told her what had happened. I was so mortified."

"I'm so sorry." Olivia shook her head. "Couldn't you get the money back?"

"Not really. The lawyers said I gave him access, and since he was living with me, it could be construed that we were partners. Mother didn't want to drag the Beauregard name and"—he made quote marks in air—"'my lifestyle' through the news in a messy court case, so we dropped it."

"You didn't deserve to be treated like that. No one does."

"Maybe I do." Edward stood, took the tray, and went to the door. "How about I let you rest now? If you're feeling better by dinner, I'll prepare something more substantial."

"That would be lovely." Olivia smiled at him.

Edward turned to leave when she called to him. "Edward?"

"Yes, Meemaw?"

"I love you." She met his gaze.

"I know. I love you too." He left the room and took the tray back to the kitchen.

Chapter Twelve

After cleaning the backseat of the cruiser of all remnants of dog, Jack spent the rest of the afternoon working on training Winston, adding to the repertoire of commands the dog obeyed. Now the dog had Stay and Heel down pat. Winston had made great progress. The dog was eager to please and had real heart.

After the session, Jack found a stick, and they killed some time playing fetch. Each time Jack would throw the stick, the little dog would race after it, snatch it up, and in that rolling gait of his, waddle back to Jack. Then Winston would refuse to give it back. Jack, no longer fearful of him, pried it from those massive jaws, wiped the drool off on his jeans, and then tossed it again.

Jack sat on the grass as Winston came up to him, stick in mouth.

"I'm beat, buddy." He lay back, hands behind his head, and looked up into the sky. Clouds floated past. He couldn't remember the last time he'd just stretched out in the grass and relaxed. Or been on a picnic. Or spent time with someone he cared about.

Winston dropped the stick on Jack's chest and gave him a big, wet kiss.

"Cut that out!" Jack wiped his cheek with his T-shirt. "Edward might like that, but not me." He chuckled as the dog lay down next to him and fell asleep.

Looked like a good idea.

Jack closed his eyes. He could feel a slight breeze and the warmth of the sun beating down on him. The soft breathing of the dog, the buzz of some insect hovering nearby, all lulled him into sleep.

Woof.

Jack woke and looked around. Winston was at the front door waiting to go in.

The sky, once blue, was streaked with orange and crimson. He'd been asleep for at least a couple of hours. Christ, he'd needed that nap. Sitting up, he stretched his arms over his head.

It was great being pain free.

As he stood, he realized he'd never told Edward thank you.

Of course, he'd been damn distracted at the time, but on Monday, when Edward came to get Winston, he'd make a point of telling Edward thanks. It was the decent thing to do.

Once back inside, Jack sat on the couch and flipped the remote, scanning the channels. It was Saturday night; Texas Tech was playing. He settled in and twisted the top off his beer.

Winston curled up next to him. It seemed the little dog craved the human touch. He snuggled his butt up to Jack's thigh, pushing against Jack's leg with his back legs, as if trying to burrow underneath Jack. Then he fell asleep, head on his paws, tongue caught between his front teeth.

Jack's hand strayed to the dog as he watched the game. He scratched behind Winston's ears and gave the bulldog long pets, stroking his short fur. Winston grunted, rolled over, belly up, as if begging to be scratched there now, and Jack laughed.

The bulldog was as demanding as his owner.

Jack took a swig of his beer. Nope. Not going there.

Instead, he threw himself back into the game. His stomach rumbled. At least, he thought it was him, but it could have been the dog.

Jack phoned in an order for a pepperoni pizza and went to pick it up, because he lived too far out of town for the delivery service. And since the Italian restaurant was fairly close to Olivia's house, he drove past again, the pizza sitting on the passenger seat.

The lights were on, and Edward's car was still there. What had Jack expected? Edward didn't know anyone but Olivia in town, and it wasn't as if he'd go trolling the local bars to pick someone up.

And if he had been gone, what then? Drive around with his food getting cold until he found the red Miata? Then what?

Jack drove past, turned at the next corner, and went home. He needed to get back in case the dog had an accident. So far, Winston had been great. Edward had house-trained him, at least.

At home, Winston met him at the door, barking and dancing around him in excitement. His little nub tail shook his entire rump, and his long pink tongue hung out the side of his mouth, dripping dog drool.

"Hey, buddy! Did you miss me?" Jack held the pizza up so the dog couldn't knock it out of his hands. "Ready for some pizza?"

Woof.

Jack went to the kitchen, got down two plates, and put a large slice on each one.

"Dog food or pepperoni pizza?"

Woof.

"I thought so." He put the plate on the floor, and Winston dug in.

Jack took his plate to the living room, got into the recliner, and scanned the channels. "Hundreds of channels and nothing to watch," he told Winston.

Winston finished his pizza and now demanded another slice. The plate clattered on the tile floor as Winston knocked it with his paw until he got Jack's attention.

"More?" Jack got up and put another piece on the dog's plate. "After this one, that's it. Edward will kill me if I let you get fat." Jack chuckled, then sobered.

If Jack wasn't careful, Edward might be the end of Jack's life and everything he'd built here in Spring Lake.

Chapter Thirteen

"Dinner was lovely, Edward." Olivia dabbed at the corner of her mouth with her napkin. "You're an excellent cook."

"That's chef, Meemaw." Edward grinned, then took their plates to the sink. "I'll just get these soaking and wash them later."

"I can get them."

"Absolutely not." He shook his head, then offered her his arm. "You're not to raise a finger until you're feeling better."

She took his arm, and they went to the living room and sat on the couch.

"I do believe you're enjoying this." She winked at him. "It's been a long time since anyone's made such a fuss over me."

He shrugged. "It's my nature. I'm a nurturer. It's a curse, really. Sometimes, I don't know when to quit, so tell me when I get annoying. I guess I just need someone to care for, you know."

"I understand. Everyone wants that."

Jack probably longed for a woman to care for. And he'd be wonderful, Edward knew it. Jack was strong, brave, trustworthy, the perfect mate for some lucky woman. Really, Edward needed to stop beating himself up about Jack. Forget him and move on.

He sat back and pulled one leg under the other. "Now. There is something I'm dying to know. If you were such a sucker for a bad boy, what about Grandpa Frank? Was he a bad boy that you tamed?"

"Your Grandpa Frank? A bad boy?" She laughed. "Oh, dear me, no. He was as straight, as honest, and as kind as the day was long."

"Then how in the world did you wind up with him?"

"I almost didn't." She sighed. "I'd been punished, I guess you'd call it 'grounded' these days. That didn't stop me. I snuck out of the house and hightailed it down to the local hangout. I ordered a hamburger, fries, and a cola, with the intention of not paying for it. I was going to sneak out, make a run for it." Her eyes sparkled.

"Meemaw! I'm shocked! I had no idea you were such a little hoodlum," he teased.

"I was bored. And I suppose all those bad boys had rubbed off on me. I wanted to be rebellious, be wild and wicked." She laughed.

"And Grandpa?"

"Well, your grandfather was there with some friends. I'd eaten and made my way to the jukebox next to the door, pretending to look for a record to play. My plan was just to stroll right out the door when the next person walked in.

Next thing I know, Frank was standing next to me. 'Try fifteen B,' he said."

"Fifteen B?" Edward whispered, his eyes locked on her face.

"Yeah. Ella Fitzgerald's 'Hard Hearted Hannah.' I looked up at him and could see in his eyes he knew my plan."

"What happened next?" Edward sat forward. It was delicious hearing these tales from her. Did his mother have any stories like this? If so, he'd never heard them. Maybe, when he got back to Atlanta, he'd ask her.

"He took my hand and slipped me three dollars. A fortune back then, and more than enough to pay for the food. For a second, I thought about taking it and running anyway."

"Did you?" He'd no idea she had been so wild, so reckless. So Audrey Hepburn in *Roman Holiday*.

She smiled at her memory before she answered. "He whispered to me, 'Don't do it.'" She shook her head. "He knew me. I didn't even know his name, and he knew me. I don't know how he did it, but he saw right through me." Her eyes welled.

"But did you leave?" Edward pressed. He had to know what happened. Yes, he knew they'd married, had his mother, but it was what had happened in between that he wanted to know.

"He offered me his arm, just like you did tonight, and escorted me back to my table, then went back to his friends. I paid the bill with his money." She touched Edward's cheek with her fingers. "You know, you reminded me of Frank when you offered me your arm just now. You're a gentleman, just like he was." She patted his leg. "He wasn't my type. He was like no one else I'd ever fallen for, and I fell for him in that one moment, right there at the jukebox, harder than I'd ever fallen for any of those other men. We dated for a year, he asked me to marry him, and the rest is Rawlings history."

Edward sighed. "That's so romantic."

Olivia smiled. "You'll find the right man. If I did, you will too."

He forced a smile. He'd found the right man, but how could the right man be so wrong? "I hope so, Meemaw."

"Now, I have a favor to ask you."

"Anything. Just name it."

"Tomorrow is Sunday, and I'd like to go to church."

"Do you need me to drive you?" Edward asked.

"Well, yes. But I'd like for you to come with me." She looked into his eyes.

Edward blinked. "To church? Oh, Meemaw, I haven't been to church since…"

"The funeral?" She reached out and took his hand.

Edward nodded and swallowed. "I can't go to church. I wouldn't be welcome."

"Why on earth not?"

He rolled his eyes. "I'm gay, remember? The sin of Sodom? And I'm an unrepentant sinner at that. I can't change who I am, and I won't hide it either." He spread his arms in a flourish. "I'm gay and I'm proud."

Olivia's mouth twisted, and her brows knitted. "Edward, wherever did you get the crazy idea that you couldn't go to church?"

He shrugged. "You know how most religious people feel about queers, Meemaw."

"God loves sinners. No matter what the sin. Jesus taught acceptance, forgiveness, and love, not hatred and condemnation. Anyone who is truly a Christian knows this. All sinners are the same in God's eyes and He welcomes all of them to partake of His grace."

Edward could see that she believed it. And it gave him such a warm feeling inside to believe it too. But just because she believed in God's love and acceptance of him didn't mean the other people in town believed it.

"It would mean so much to me, Edward," she said quietly.

If his mother had asked him to go to church, he'd have flat-out refused. But this was his grandmother asking. How could he deny her? One hour sitting on a wooden pew listening to some boring sermon wouldn't kill him, would it?

"What should I wear? I didn't bring a suit."

"Just a nice shirt and a pair of pants would be fine. Most of the young people don't wear suits either."

"Okay, Meemaw. I'll do it for you."

She stood, leaned down, and bussed him on the cheek. "Do it for yourself, child." Then she left.

Good Lord, what had he gotten himself into?

Church in Hooterville?

* * *

Edward cleaned the kitchen, mopped the floors, and then went to his room. He'd unpacked, hung up his clothes, and put away his shoes in the closet that afternoon while Olivia had napped. Now he searched for something appropriate to wear on Sunday.

He pulled out a pair of navy slacks and a light blue button-down shirt. That should do nicely. Nothing too over-the-top. Definitely nothing with fringe.

Satisfied that he wouldn't embarrass Olivia, he went to the bathroom to get ready for bed, then returned to his room, wearing a pair of dark blue paisley cotton pajamas and carrying his travel kit and a towel. He placed it on the bedside table, within reach, and draped the towel over a chair.

He turned on the fan, turned out the lights, and crawled into bed. For a while, he ran his hand over the light cotton fabric, letting the motion soothe him. His hand moved lower on his body, and he closed his eyes and thought of Jack.

His body's instant response to the man came as no surprise. He'd been fighting off erections ever since he'd met Jack, except when he'd been so exhausted he could barely stand up, much less get it up.

Reaching for the kit, he felt for the lube. His hand touched the box of condoms. What had he been thinking to bring those? As if there would be scads of Brokeback cowboys littering the place? That was a nice image. Dozens of cowboys, striking poses, leaning against their pickup trucks, giving him their come-hither looks.

He'd only found one man here that he'd wanted those looks from, and it was Jack.

He found the lube, popped the top, and squeezed some out.

His cock had pushed through the opening in his pajama bottoms, eager to be touched. Edward's dick wasn't thick; it was slender, long, and he'd been told it was pretty. Right now, it was a velvet-covered steel rod, standing straight up.

His balls ached, and his ass puckered as he began stroking himself. Jerking off was good, but he wanted to be fucked. Really fucked. By Jack. His pace quickened, his hand sliding up and down, squeezing the tip, catching the pearl that oozed from his slit.

Jack could throw him against any wall, fuck him anywhere, anytime. Edward didn't care. All he wanted was one night with Jack.

Edward would suck Jack off. Take Jack's cock deep in his throat, tease and torment the man with his tongue, until he couldn't stand it any longer and begged for mercy. Begged to fuck Edward.

He rolled onto his side and applied more lube to his hand. While he worked his dick, he pressed his slicked-up fingers into his ass, pushing past the outer ring. Hell and damnation, he should have brought his butt plug, but for now, tonight, his fingers would have to do.

Pressing his fingers deeper, he twisted his shoulders to allow more leeway. With a groan, he found his bump and worked it as he increased the friction on his cock, imagining Jack's fingers in his ass, Jack's hand wrapped around his cock.

Jack would lean over, nuzzle his neck, croon into his ear, *That's it, baby, come for me.* And Edward would.

His balls unloaded, his ass spasmed around his fingers, and he came. Milking his cock of its load, Edward shuddered, then fell back, limp and spent. And still craving Jack.

Hell and damnation.

This was stupid. Fantasizing about a man you could never have wasn't very healthy or smart. It was a waste of time. He rose, cleaned up, and then returned to bed.

When had Edward ever been smart?

Well, not anymore. Those days were over. That was the old Edward.

From tonight on, there would be a new and improved Edward.

He'd be smarter, more cynical, less gullible. His heart would be under lock and key, and no one would get near it or his body again. Not without jumping through some freaking big hoops to prove himself.

If Edward meant to survive, meant to find the right man, meant never to be hurt again, he'd have to change *his* ways.

And the first thing he'd have to change was this obsession with Chief of Police Jack Whittaker.

Chapter Fourteen

Edward held the car door open and offered a hand to Olivia as she got out of the Miata. He'd put the top up in deference to her hairdo and her suit. She carried a worn black Bible with faded gold gilt on the edges of the pages and had a perfect pillbox hat perched on her head.

"Jackie O's got nothing on you, Meemaw," he whispered to her. She giggled and swatted his shoulder. Then he offered his arm to her, and she took it. She walked steadier today, another sign, along with eating the hearty breakfast that Edward had cooked, that she was feeling much better.

Edward took a calming breath, gave her a nervous smile, and led her through the parking lot to the front steps of the Spring Lake United Methodist Church. There were people everywhere, all heading for the same destination.

"So many people," he muttered. His eyes darted around to see if he spotted anyone he knew. Not that he knew that many people here. With his luck, he'd run into Phil and Jimmy. He had a vision of Jimmy, like one of the body snatchers, standing up in church, pointing a grease-covered finger and announcing that Edward was one of those "San Francisco queers." The entire congregation would chase

Edward down the street to capture him so he could be reborn as a straight man. He shuddered.

"Good morning, Olivia," sang out an older woman wearing a red hat with white feathers that fanned out from the sides. "Who is this good-looking young man?"

"This is my grandson, Edward. He's paying me a visit. Edward, this is Mrs. Burthe, an old friend of mine."

"So glad to meet you, Mrs. Burthe." Edward nodded and gave her a warm smile.

The woman nodded back. "See you inside, Olivia." Then she went up the stairs and through the doors into the church.

So far, Edward was safe. He only knew a handful of people, and none of them seemed to be here. Maybe they went to another church or just didn't go to church.

Either way, he was thankful. Maybe this wouldn't be so bad.

"Oh look, Edward. Here's Chief Whittaker." Olivia pulled on his arm and turned him around just in time to come face-to-face with Jack.

Everything Edward had sworn escaped him, and all he knew was that Jack was here. And oh my God, the man was so handsome in a dark gray suit, white shirt, and a blue tie that matched his eyes. The flush that ran over Edward's entire body heated him so badly his blush could probably be seen from space.

"Good morning, Miss Olivia. Mr. Beauregard." Jack nodded at him but didn't look Edward in the eyes. Jack's gaze hit him and then danced away. Ignoring Edward.

Despite the pain of that rejection, Edward resolved to do his best to embrace his new attitude. "Good morning, Chief Whittaker. How's my dog?"

"Winston? He's fine."

"That's good." Edward narrowed his eyes. "I trust nothing will happen to him before I get him back on Monday."

Jack's gaze snapped back to Edward, and Jack's lips thinned. "Don't worry. He's safe. You just worry about getting the proof he's had those shots."

"I'm not worried. I know Winston is innocent. You'll have the paper in the morning as soon as they can fax it to your office." Edward's lips felt so tight they might crack. "Then you'll be free of him. And me." He jerked his chin up.

"Good. The sooner the better," Jack growled.

"Too right," Edward snapped.

Good Lord, he wanted Jack Whittaker. All the verbal sparring, their intense gazes, and the heat of the man's body drove Edward crazy. If he didn't get away from Jack soon, he was a dead man. His meager control only went so far and lasted only so long.

"Chief. Care to join us?" Olivia held out her arm to Jack. He blinked, looked at her, then at Edward. Edward could hear the man gulp, see Jack's mind spinning, looking for any way out of it, any excuse to avoid being with Edward.

If Jack's leg had been in a trap, he'd have gnawed it off to get away from Edward.

No no no, this wasn't happening. It was bad enough seeing Edward again, but to sit with him? The one place Jack figured he wouldn't see Edward was at church, and here he was. Jack was damned, all right. So where was the hole to hell, because he'd gladly jump right in.

Why did Edward have to look so damn sexy in those dark slacks and blue shirt? It made his dark hair and eyes stand out. He hadn't worn a tie but left the first two buttons of the shirt undone, giving Jack a glimpse of smooth skin, leaving Jack to wonder about the rest of the younger man's chest. And those were not the kind of thoughts to have standing on the steps of a church.

Olivia waited for Jack's answer, her eyebrows raised. He swallowed. "It would be my pleasure, Miss Olivia." He gave her a nod and offered her his arm.

With Olivia between them, he and Edward climbed the steps to the sanctuary. Edward gave him a slight nod, deferring to Jack to lead the way, and Jack took them down the left side aisle until Olivia said, "This is fine."

Jack motioned for Edward to go in first and waited as Olivia followed. At least she'd sit between them. Hopefully the church wouldn't be packed and he could sit close to the end of the pew for a quick getaway as soon as the service was over.

They settled in their seats. Olivia picked up the hymnal and handed it to Edward. She leaned over and whispered, "The numbers up there are the pages of the songs we'll sing. Here's the program so you can follow where we are."

"Thanks," he whispered back, catching Jack's glance and raised eyebrow.

"It's been a long time since I've been to church," he explained. Why he felt he had to explain anything to Jack was beyond him.

"Uh-huh." Jack sat back and pulled a hymnal from the rack on the back of the pew in front of theirs. Clearly, he doubted that Edward had ever been in a church and probably doubted whether Edward should be sitting in his.

Edward glanced around the sanctuary. Quiet organ music filled the vaulted chamber. At the front, the raised dais had a large podium with what had to be the largest Bible he'd ever seen lying open on it. There were two large flower arrangements on each side, and hanging on the back wall above the choir, a large, lighted cross.

The choir filed in, and the pastor entered. Everyone rose. Edward stood. The organ music swelled, and everyone began singing. Edward fumbled with the hymnal, searching for the page marked on the board. By the time he found it, the song was almost over. He didn't know the tune, so he just read the words. It didn't matter. Edward couldn't carry a tune in a bucket.

Next to him, Olivia's strong voice rose and fell with the melody. Edward glanced at Jack, who faced forward, singing in a wonderful tenor without even looking at the book. Show-off.

Then the pastor said some kind of prayer, everyone said, "Amen" and sat. Edward fell onto the bench, but not fast enough. He was the last person to sit. What more could say,

Hey, I've never been to church? I'm a big sinner, and I don't belong here?

Edward stared at his clasped hands and white knuckles. If he turned around, would everyone be staring and pointing at him, or whispering behind their hands?

Just like always, the urge to get up, excuse himself, and run came over him. His legs trembled as his body and his mind warred over which one would rule him. There was no reason to leave. Everything was fine. He was just self-conscious, that's all.

Olivia's hand reached out, covered his, and gave him a squeeze. He looked up, met her warm gaze, and smiled. His body relaxed, his hands unclenched.

He could do this. It would be all right.

Edward settled back and focused on the pastor. As Edward scanned the program, he followed along and flipped to the pages in the hymnal before they stood to sing. He listened to the sermon, expecting to hear about brimstone, fire, and burning in everlasting hell, but instead he heard a message about love, absolution, repentance, and God's mercy.

He could sure use some of that mercy now.

The service drew to a close with a final benediction. The pastor asked everyone to bow his or her head in silent prayer. Edward dropped his chin to his chest but cast a sidelong glance at Jack.

Jack's eyes were closed, his hands clasped in prayer.

What did Jack pray for?

What should he pray for?

Edward could only think of one thing he needed guidance on, so he closed his eyes and did the best he could to talk to God.

What should I do about Meemaw?

Jack prayed for the courage to make wise and right choices in his professional life, but most of all, he asked God to give him strength against temptation.

If Edward didn't leave Spring Lake soon, Jack didn't know how much longer he could hold out.

As soon as the final chord sounded, Jack turned to Olivia and begged his leave. He moved quickly down the aisle as Edward watched his broad back recede into the crowd. Stopping now and then, Jack shook hands, clapped a fellow or two on the shoulder, and then greeted the pastor at the door. They shook hands, and without a glance back at Edward, Jack disappeared.

"That was a lovely sermon, wasn't it?" Olivia asked as they walked down the aisle.

"Yes. It was. Not at all what I expected." Edward let his grandmother set the pace as they made it to the door and the minister.

"Reverend Mills, I'd like you to meet my grandson, Edward Beauregard."

Edward stuck out his hand, and the white-haired minister took it. "So glad to meet you, Edward. Are you staying long?"

"For a little while, yes. But then I must be getting back to Atlanta."

"Of course. Olivia, I'll see you next week at the board meeting." He gave her hand a small squeeze, and she and Edward moved out the door and down the steps.

His eyes searched the parking lot for the police cruiser, but it wasn't there. Maybe Jack had come in the pickup truck he'd seen parked in Jack's driveway. He wouldn't know it well enough to recognize it, anyway, so there was no use in looking.

Edward took Olivia back to his car, got her seated, and then went around to the driver's side. He nosed the car out of the crowded lot and headed home.

"You and Chief Whittaker didn't sound happy with each other." Olivia looked at him, her eyebrow arched.

"Well. He's just doing his job. I'm just doing what I have to do to get my dog back. That's all." He shrugged.

"That's all?" She scoffed. "Why the tension was so thick between you two, I wasn't sure if y'all were going to kiss or kill each other."

Edward's face ignited. "Meemaw!"

She slapped her thigh and cackled. "I knew it."

"I don't know what you think you know, but I promise you, *I* wanted to kill him. And I'm sure he felt the same about me." The last thing Edward wanted was for anyone, even Olivia, to know about his unrequited feelings for Jack. More grist for the rumor mill.

And if Jack wanted to kill him now, if any sort of rumor about him and Edward got loose, Edward had no doubt Jack would come looking for him and use that gun he carried.

"That was more than just hate, Edward. That was pure grade-A lust between you two. And I should know. I've seen it plenty."

Edward pulled into her drive and parked. This had to be nipped in the bud before it got away from him. Rumors like this could destroy the man's career. Especially here in Hooterville. And the very last thing Edward wanted to do was to hurt Jack. Ever.

He turned to Olivia. "Meemaw. Please. I have to ask you to never, never make those comments again. Not about me and Jack." He took her hands in his. "Don't you see? No matter what I feel, Jack has a position here that could be damaged by such foolish talk."

"Is it foolish?" She stared into his eyes, and he met her gaze with what he prayed would look like determination.

"Yes. It's foolish. Jack isn't gay, Meemaw. Trust me, I know."

"How?" she pressed.

"Haven't you ever heard of gaydar? It takes one to know one? It's like that; we can spot each other a mile away. Jack's not gay. Please."

She sighed. "Too bad. Because I think he'd be perfect for you, and you for him."

So did Edward.

Chapter Fifteen

Jack held Winston's leash coiled in his hand as he shut and locked his front door. Winston sat on the sidewalk waiting for him.

"Heel."

The little dog fell into step alongside Jack. There was no need to attach the leash. He trotted to the cruiser and waited by Jack's door to get in. Jack opened the door, and the dog jumped up, went to the passenger seat, and sat. Ready to roll.

Jack chuckled. He turned the ignition and hit the window remote for Winston. The dog waited until the window had slid down before hooking his paws over the edge and sticking his bulky head out.

Woof.

"I hear you, buddy." Jack backed out and headed to town. Mondays usually sucked, but for some reason, his mood was good. Better than it should be.

Edward would come to the station today, prove that Winston had his shots, and take the animal away. And hopefully, that would be that.

Then Jack could get back to his life. Back to normal.

He shook off the small twinge of tightness in his chest and rolled his own window down, sucking in the cool morning air as he drove to work. If anything had brought home the fact that Edward was dangerous to him, it was yesterday at church.

It just wasn't proper to be thinking about making love to a man while the minister was preaching. But Jack had registered only the first few words of the sermon before his mind had danced into dangerous territory. He'd had to put the hymnal on his lap to hide the fact that he was half-hard.

Edward was sin on two legs, for damn sure.

And Jack had wanted to sin.

That's when he'd made up his mind. Edward had to go, the sooner the better.

Once in town, Jack stopped at the bakery, picked up two dozen assorted doughnuts for the guys, and went to the station.

"Morning!" he called as he entered the main office, Winston trotting at his side.

Kristen looked up from her desk, her eyebrows raised. "You're in a good mood."

"Brought doughnuts." He plopped them down on her desk.

"I'll put them in the kitchen." She stood, picked up the boxes, and went down the hall. "You've got nothing on the schedule today."

"No meetings?" It was too good to be true. A Monday with no meetings? This day was off to a great start. "Hear that, buddy? Nothing but air." His hand made a wave motion.

Woof.

Winston wagged his rump, wide mouth open and tongue hanging.

Jack went to his office with the dog at his heels and sat behind the desk. He flicked on his computer as Winston settled next to the desk.

Kristen appeared in the doorway. "Well, Chief. How was your weekend?"

"Great. I spent most of it training Winston."

"Training him?" She leaned in the doorway, arms crossed.

"Yeah. Watch." Jack stood and came around the desk, eager to show off the dog's new tricks. He moved next to Kristen by the door. "Winston. Come."

The dog stood and trotted over to him and then sat.

"Nice." Kristen nodded.

"Down," Jack commanded.

The dog slid his front legs to the floor.

"He does Stay, Heel, and Off."

"Did you teach him the one where you pretend to shoot him and he falls over?" Her eyes danced at Jack.

"I thought about it, but there wasn't time. If I'd had a few more days…" Jack shrugged and went back to his desk. Winston remained in Down. "Come, boy."

The bulldog rose and padded across the floor to Jack's side.

"Stay." The dog sat. "He'll sit there until I give him another command or say *A-T E-A-S-E.*" Jack spelled the word so Winston wouldn't respond to it.

"*O-K-A-Y.*" Kristen giggled. "You and that dog have gotten sort of close, huh?"

Jack shrugged. "It killed the time. He's so smart; he took to training right off. He should have been trained, anyway. I just saved Edward the trouble, is all."

"Uh-huh." She nodded and rolled her eyes. "What are you going to do once he's gone?"

"Celebrate?" Jack smirked. Sure, he'd gotten used to having Winston around, talking to him, playing fetch, and he'd be sad to see the little bulldog gone, but if it meant getting rid of Edward, Jack was all for it.

All he wanted was to get back to the way it was before Edward Paul Beauregard the Third came into his life.

Kristen chuckled and pulled the door shut as Jack went to work on the force's schedule for the next month.

* * *

Edward waited until nine to make the call to his veterinarian. After explaining the situation to the receptionist, he sat on hold, then explained it again to Dr. Andrews.

The doctor promised to fax over both the record of the shot and a certificate of health to the police station as soon as Edward gave him the fax number.

Edward didn't have the number, but he'd just go to the station, get the number, and call the doctor back. Simple as pie. Once he had the fax, he and Winston would be out of there.

Edward sat at the kitchen table and took a sip of his coffee. "Meemaw, I'm going to the station to pick up Winston. Then we're going up to the hotel and check in. I'll come back to see you once I'm done there." He'd loaded his bags into the small trunk of the Miata earlier.

Olivia smiled at him. "Don't worry about me, I'm feeling just fine. Go get that little dog of yours. I know you miss him something awful."

"I do. He's my best friend. I know that sounds funny. I know I'm a grown man, but"—he shrugged—"he's the only one who's ever been faithful, who's been by my side, thick and thin."

"I understand." She patted his hand. "And I truly wish I didn't have this damn allergy so I could have you both here."

"It's okay." Edward stood, pecked her cheek. "I'll be back around noon. What do you say about a date for lunch?"

She laughed. "Why, I haven't had a date with a handsome young man in over fifty years. I hope we scandalize Spring Lake." She winked at him.

"Well, we'll give them something to talk about." He winked back. "After all, I've had my share of scandals."

"Get out of here, child. Go get that dog. I'll see you later." She waved him away.

Edward left, got in the Miata, unlocked the convertible roof locks, and hit the button. The ragtop opened, then folded neatly down.

All he could think about was getting Winston back as he headed to the station to spring his best friend in the world from jail. He refused to give Jack Whittaker a second's thought. Because a second would lead to a minute and a minute to an hour, and he'd be right back where he was before, pining for a straight man. And that wasn't going to happen.

Not today. Not ever.

He parked in the lot, got out, and practically skipped around to the front doors. Pushing through them, he sang out, "What's the story, morning glory?"

Kristen looked up and laughed. "What's the tale, nightingale?"

Grinning, Edward sat on the edge of her desk. "I talked to my vet. He's all ready to fax the papers over. I just need the number."

She pushed him off and gave him the number on a slip of paper. Then he sat in a chair to talk to the vet's receptionist. After relaying the information, he snapped the phone closed and grinned at her. "It's coming your way."

"Great. I know you'll be glad to get him back."

Edward nodded. "I miss him so much." It was an honest admission, but one he couldn't help but make to her.

"I think the chief's going to miss him too," she said quietly.

He frowned, then brightened. "Not as much as he'll miss me, I bet."

She snorted and rolled her eyes. "Never mind, *I'll* miss you."

"Thank you, darling." He stood. "I can't wait any longer. I want Winston." He walked to Jack's office door. "Is he busy?"

"No. Go on in."

Edward knocked softly on the wood door.

"Enter." Jack's deep, muffled voice still managed to send a tremor down Edward's spine, lodging in his balls.

He took a deep breath, opened the door, and went in. Closing the door behind him, he watched Jack, head bent over the keyboard, eyes shifting back and forth between some papers and the screen.

For a moment, Edward just stared. Good Lord, the man was incredibly handsome.

Edward cleared his throat. "Hi, Jack." His voice came out raspy anyway.

Jack looked up, their eyes met. In that second, Edward knew it was all a lie. Every vow he'd made, every oath he'd sworn to forget Jack, to leave him behind like last year's shoes on the bargain rack at Saks and never to let this man crawl under his skin and touch his heart.

Edward broke the gaze and looked at Winston. "Winston!"

The little dog sat next to the desk and didn't move. Panting, his mouth opened and his tongue lolled, but he didn't rush to Edward.

"Come on, boy!" Edward knelt, waiting for the little dog to race across the room and fling himself into Edward's arms. Winston whined but didn't budge.

Edward's throat tightened until he couldn't breathe. Even swallowing didn't work. "Winston?" It came out like a croak.

The dog just sat there.

His best friend in the world wouldn't come to him.

Edward looked at Jack. "What the *hell* did you do to my dog?" he rasped. His voice still wasn't right. Nothing was right. Hell and damnation, he still couldn't breathe.

Jack stood. "Oh, he's just in Stay."

"In Stay?" Edward stared at the dog, then flicked his gaze back to Jack. "What the hell is that?"

"Stay. It's a command. I trained him." Jack smiled at him as he stood beside Winston.

Edward finally sucked in air. "You *trained* him not to come to me?" He'd known Jack was upset with him, but he'd never thought, not for one second, that Jack *hated* him. That he'd go so far as to hurt Edward like this. That Jack would take the one thing in Edward's life that meant everything to him.

That Jack would steal his best friend.

Edward's hands tightened into fists. He'd never felt so angry, so betrayed, so ready to do physical harm in his life. "You. Had. No. Right."

"What?" Jack took a step back.

"You had no *right* to do that to my dog." Now Edward fought his body to keep from trembling, especially his bottom lip. "You had no right!" he shouted.

"I..." Jack sputtered.

"He's *my* dog. Mine! Not yours." Unable to stop it, a tear rolled down Edward's cheek, and his body shook with fury and hurt.

"Edward, listen." Jack took another step toward him.

"No, *you* listen. You *just* couldn't leave him alone, could you? He wasn't *good enough* for you, was he? You had to *fix* him. *Had* to make him better. He was perfect just the way he was." Edward's vision blurred, unable to stop the flood that poured from his eyes like water over a dam.

"No, it wasn't like that." Jack shook his head. He swallowed and grimaced as if in pain.

"Do you hate me so much?" Edward's voice was small, soft, but he didn't care how hurt he sounded. He was hurt. Mortally. Dagger in the heart hurt.

Jack didn't answer. Instead, he stepped up to Edward. Jack's hand, warm and rough, cupped Edward's cheek, and Jack brushed away the trail of tears on Edward's face with the pad of his thumb. Edward's heart staggered at the tenderness in the caress.

"No, baby. No. I don't hate you." Jack leaned forward, resting his forehead against Edward's. "I'm sorry. I didn't realize... I didn't mean to hurt you." Jack's lips brushed over Edward's forehead, his temple, his cheekbone, each touch a feather, each sweet kiss sending shocks right to Edward's heart. "Baby, I'm so sorry."

Jack's lips found Edward's mouth in a soft, slow, lingering kiss.

Edward's brain short-circuited, and his knees threatened to give way as he buried his hands in Jack's shirt and clung to him. Melted into Jack's body as the man's hand cupped Edward's ass and pulled him closer. Edward's desperate need overcame his hurt.

Jack slipped his tongue along the seam of Edward's mouth, begging entry. Edward moaned, opened to Jack, and accepted the soft, searching tongue, reveling in the connection, the taste of him. Delicious and addictive as Godiva chocolate.

Straight men didn't kiss the way Jack was kissing him.

They don't kiss men at all.

Edward had a moment of clarity, and the truth rocked him. Anger rose like a tidal wave and drowned the desire he'd felt for Jack.

He pushed Jack away and glared up into those unfocused blue eyes. "You lied to me."

"What?" Jack's lips reddened from their kiss.

"You *are* gay. You *lied* to me," he whispered. "You made me feel like I was some sort of pervert because I came on to a straight man. That I was wrong about what I felt between us and that I couldn't trust my own feelings." He'd never felt so manipulated, so foolish. So stupid.

Jack swallowed. "Edward. Let me explain."

"Explain?" He shoved Jack. "You lying bastard. You're just like all the rest of them. You'd do anything to get what you want, no matter who it hurts."

"You're not being fair, Edward. I have a career here…"

"Yes. I know. You're the *fucking* chief of police, and you can do whatever the *fuck* you want." Edward threw Jack's words back at him, then pushed past Jack. "I'm taking my dog and getting out of here."

Jack rubbed his lips with the back of his hand as if erasing the evidence of their kiss. "You can't. I didn't get the papers."

"The vet is faxing them now." Edward picked up the leash from Jack's desk, clipped it to Winston's collar. "Winston. Come." Then he jerked the lead, and the little dog followed him.

"You can't leave yet," Jack sputtered.

"I am leaving. With. My. Dog. If you have a problem with that, you can shoot me." With a final glare at Jack, Edward marched to the door, opened it, and stormed out.

He passed Kristen, her eyes wide, mouth open in a small circle, head rotating as she tracked him. He barreled through the outer doors with Winston at his heels, fully expecting to feel a bullet between his shoulder blades at any moment. That would be just fine. It could match the one he had in his heart.

Edward reached the car, opened the door, and Winston got in. "I'm sorry, Winston. I didn't know he'd do that to you. You were perfect just the way you were."

Keeping it together, Edward pulled out of the lot and drove toward the motel. He needed to check in. He needed to crawl under the covers and never come out.

Nothing had changed. He hadn't changed.

Jack had made a fool of him.

No. He'd allowed Jack to make a fool of him, and that was worse.

He pulled over to the side of the road as a great, shuddering sob exploded from his chest. Winston whimpered, nudged Edward's arm, and Edward gathered him in and held him close, clinging to the bulldog as if he were the last life preserver on the *Titanic.*

Burying his face in Winston's soft fur, Edward wept.

Chapter Sixteen

Jack staggered against the door. What the hell just happened?

He'd looked up and Edward was there and Jack's stomach had jumped and his heart had thudded in his chest and all the blood in his brain went straight to his dick. *Shit.*

Pushing away from the door, he went to his desk and fell into his chair, leaned back and closed his eyes.

Edward was right. He'd been so selfish, so arrogant, to assume that he had the right to train Winston. He hadn't even thought about Edward's reaction, asked his permission, only acted on his need for control over the little dog.

Like he had needed to control Edward.

Uh-uh. Don't go there. Too dangerous.

Dangerous? He snorted and ran his hands over his face. He'd kissed Edward. *Fucking* kissed him. How was that for *fucking* dangerous? In his *fucking* office too. Anyone could have walked in and seen them, and that would have been the end of his career.

Christ, he'd needed that kiss. And more. But what he needed and what he should do were two very different things. Jack had understood that from the first moment he'd met Edward on the side of the road, watched his ass in those tight jeans, and looked into his deep brown eyes.

Fuck. The look of utter devastation on Edward's face. The betrayal in Edward's deep brown eyes. It had ripped Jack's chest apart, exposing his insides. And when that first tear spilled, Christ, he would have done anything to take all that pain away from Edward, like Edward had unselfishly taken away Jack's pain.

Unable to resist the younger man, Jack had reached out to soothe with his hand, and his lips had followed. Jack should have seen it coming. It was inevitable. Like the slow slide of ice breaking off a glacier and sinking into the sea. Like the next wave breaking on a beach.

And there had been nothing Jack could do to stop it. All his self-control fled under the onslaught of Edward's power over him. A power he couldn't ever give into again, knew he shouldn't give in to, and yet Jack knew that he'd gladly step forward again, if Edward ever gave him another chance, and take what he wanted from the younger man.

The only way to resist Edward was never to see him again. Never.

Jack bent over his spreadsheet and looked at the numbers he'd been working on when Edward came in, searching for his place on the sheet with his fingertip.

As he typed in the next number, he put Edward aside.

It was done. Over with. Winston was gone. Edward was gone.

That was the way it had to be.

Jack glanced at the place where the little dog had sat next to his desk.

He was going to miss that dog.

* * *

Edward ran his card key through the lock, the light turned green, and he pushed the door open. He tossed his bag on the dresser, kicked off his shoes, and flopped back on the bed. Winston jumped up, circled, then lay down next to Edward.

Edward had to pull himself together. The clerk at the front desk had stared at him, and Edward knew the guy could tell that Edward had been crying. Didn't anyone cry in Texas? Probably not. At least, not the men.

Edward *so* did not belong in Texas.

He pushed up, went to the bathroom, leaned over the sink, and stared at his reflection in the mirror.

Oh yeah. Puffy, red eyes. They screamed, *Look at me. I'm a big, emotional fag.*

He held a washcloth under the cold water, wrung it out, then went back to the bed.

Draping the folded cloth over his eyes, he hoped it would be enough to take the swelling down. He couldn't face Olivia like this. She'd know. She'd ask what had happened and he'd have to lie.

Because he couldn't tell anyone what had happened.

There was an unwritten code between gay men, and Edward knew he would never out Jack. He'd protect Jack's secret, despite what Jack had done. Despite Edward's hurt.

Oh, he'd wanted to lash out at Jack with words, even his fists, but not destroy the man.

Edward rolled onto his side, lifted the cloth, and peeked at Winston as he slept. The little dog's pink tongue was caught between his front teeth. It was so goofy.

Edward smiled.

It wasn't perfect, but it was Winston. No, Winston had never been perfect, and because of that, Edward had bought him.

He could remember that day six years ago. Could play it in his head like a home movie. He'd been wandering around this huge flea market in a little town north of Atlanta and come across several dog breeders. There had been dozens of crates filled with puppies, all registered pure breeds.

Edward passed a small crate with a single puppy curled up in the corner, whimpering and shaking. He walked on, but something brought him back.

Peering into the crate, he could see that it was a little white bulldog. He'd stuck his fingers between the bars and made kissing noises at the puppy. The little dog's head popped up, and Edward could see the light brown patch of color over one eye.

"How much is this one?" Edward had never owned so much as a goldfish, had never had the desire for a pet, or the responsibility that went with it.

The woman came over, shook her head, and said, "You don't want him. He's not show quality."

"What does that mean?" Edward stared at the little dog. He'd never seen anything cuter, more adorable than that puppy.

"Well, he's registered. But he'll never be able to show." She opened the cage, scooped the puppy up, and held him out. "See. His nose is brown. It disqualifies him." Edward couldn't believe something as insignificant as the color of his nose made this little puppy less than worthy. His nose looked just fine to Edward.

"Oh." Edward reached out a hand, and the dog licked him. "I don't care about that. I want a pet, not a show dog."

"Well, you won't be able to breed him; he'll just pass that nose on to his offspring." She practically tossed the puppy back in the crate.

"Why is he in the crate all alone?" The other puppies were in groups, lying on top of each other, being comforted by the warm bodies of their brothers and sisters. To Edward, it seemed so unfair, so cruel, to be pulled from what little comfort there was in the world for a puppy.

The bulldog moved to the corner of the crate, shaking and whimpering again.

Edward's heart broke at the pitiful sounds.

"I told you. He's just not good enough to be with the others." She shrugged. "If you're interested, you can have him for four hundred and fifty dollars."

"That's a lot. What's a show-quality bulldog sell for?" Edward pushed his fingers through the bars again, and the little dog came to him, gave his fingers a lick, and then chewed them. He smiled.

"My dogs sell for a thousand five hundred."

"Well. I can't resist a bargain. I'll take him."

And from the moment she'd opened the cage, pulled out the puppy, and placed him in Edward's arms, Edward knew this was the dog for him.

Holding the wiggling puppy up to his face, he let the dog kiss him, inhaling that unmistakable puppy breath. "I'm going to call you Winston." The dog gave a happy *yip*, his dark eyes looking so intelligent, so smart, reaching right into Edward's heart.

She rolled her eyes and laughed. "That's original."

Edward shrugged. "He's definitely a Winston." He handed her his credit card, signed the slip, and walked away with the puppy in his arms.

And the rest, as they say, is history.

"We imperfect creatures have to stick together, right?" Edward whispered as he petted the sleeping dog. He put the cloth back over his eyes.

All he needed was thirty minutes to rest; then he'd go back to Olivia's and take her to lunch like he promised.

* * *

"I wouldn't go in there, if I were you," Kristen called as she came down the back hall. Brian, about to knock on Jack's door, raised an eyebrow and lowered his hand.

"What's up?" He went to her desk.

"Jack and Edward had a terrible fight." She said it like JackandEdward, all one word. Brian's eyebrows rose.

Obviously, she wasn't going to tell him unless he begged her. Brian sighed. He interrogated people all day; he didn't want to do it here. "About what?"

"That dog."

Brian frowned. "Didn't his papers come through? Was there a problem with them?"

"No, they're fine. I have them right here." She tapped a folder, then leaned forward. "That wasn't it."

Okay, she was really taking this being mysterious too far. "Look, Kristen, spill it. What's going on?"

"Well, this weekend while Jack had the dog, he trained him. Without Edward's permission." She rolled her eyes. "Now, I couldn't hear everything, but when Edward went in to get Winston, from the shouting I *could* hear, the dog wouldn't come to him. Jack had him in Stay." Tears welled up in her eyes. "Oh, Brian. You should have heard Edward. He was so *hurt.*"

"Hurt?"

"He thought Jack had done it on purpose. So the dog wouldn't come to Edward." She plucked a tissue from the box on her desk and wiped her eyes. "You and I know Jack hasn't got a malicious bone in his body, but Edward didn't know that. Jack just didn't think about Edward's reaction, that's all." Who were all the tears for—Jack, Edward, or both? Had Kristen picked up on something between Jack and Edward?

What the hell *was* going on between those two? Edward had admitted interest in Jack from the start and had sworn he'd gotten signals from Jack. Edward could even be falling for Jack, and that was a shame, because Brian had never gotten a single blip on his gaydar screen about Jack. The man was as straight as they came. Wasn't he?

"I'm sure that's right. Jack's not that kind of man," he consoled her. Glancing at Jack's office door, he made a decision. "I need to see him."

"Enter at your own risk," she warned.

He rapped on the door with one hand, the folder in the other, and waited. About to knock again, he heard, "Come in."

Brian stepped into the office and closed the door behind him. "Chief."

Jack looked up from his work and smiled. No hint of the alleged fight. "Brian. What's up?"

"I wanted to give you that report on Jimmy Wyatt's stolen truck. I found it over by the county line. It'd been dumped in the woods, and it looks like someone took a baseball bat to it." Brian slid the folder onto the desk.

Jack sat back and chuckled. "Question his wife. Or his girlfriend. Or both of them. Or anyone else he might have pissed off in the last week. Your pick."

"That's what I figured." Brian grinned as an idea flashed in his head, and without thinking it through, he said, "Listen, I know it's short notice, but Rush and I are having a few friends over Wednesday evening for barbecue, drinks, and poker. Think you might make it?"

"Wednesday?" Jack clicked his mouse. "Calendar looks clear. I'll put it in." He typed in the date. "Should I bring anything? Beer?"

"No. We play Texas Hold 'Em, so bring some spare change. In the form of ones and fives." Brian smirked. "And I have to warn you. Rush is a shark."

"Well, I don't play a half-bad game myself." Jack leaned back in his chair. "Look, I'll bring the cigars and make it an official poker game."

"That sounds great." Brian nodded. If Jack was upset, he was doing a damn fine job of hiding it. He wasn't acting ruffled at all, not a hair out of place, nothing. "Well, that's all. I'm going back on patrol, maybe drive past Wyatt's place and talk to his wife."

"Good man. Thanks for the report." Jack tapped the folder with his finger.

Brian nodded and left the office.

Kristen looked up at him, eyebrows raised.

"Seems fine to me." Brian shrugged and left.

He wasn't worried about Jack. Jack was one of the strongest men he'd ever met, and Brian had never seen Jack's emotional keel rock even a little.

Edward, on the other hand... Well, Brian worried about Edward. There was just something about the man that brought out the protector in Brian, and he wondered if maybe, just maybe, Edward had stirred something in Jack as well. Something Jack didn't want to acknowledge or make known.

Brian had been down that road with Rush and knew how well Rush had kept his homosexuality hidden. Having known Jack for only six months, Brian had seen enough to know a man as strong as Jack could easily suppress any hint of being gay.

Either way, he'd know for sure on Wednesday.

For now, Brian made a note to keep his eyes peeled for the little red Miata while on patrol.

Flipping open his cell phone, he searched for a number, found it, and hit Send.

"Hello," his best friend answered.

"Mitchell? Did I catch you at a bad time?" Brian asked.

"No, I'm stuck in Houston rush-hour traffic. What's up?"

Brian laughed, not missing the Houston grind one bit and glad he'd decided to leave it behind him and make a new life with Rush here in Spring Lake.

"Rush and I are going to have a barbecue on Wednesday for some friends here in Spring Lake. Wondered if you and Sammi wanted to come out and spend a few days at the ranch. I know it's the middle of the week, and if you guys can't get away, I understand." Rush had started this dinner thing for Edward, and Brian figured what the hell, might as well make it a real party. He couldn't think of two better people to have over than his best friend Mitchell and his life partner, Sammi.

"Hey, that sounds great. We could use some time away. Sammi's been hitting the books hard for the GED test, and he's strung so tight he might snap." Mitchell chuckled. "It's driving me nuts. He just won't relax."

"Well, he can relax out here. He could even bring his books and study, if he wants."

"No way. A chance to have Sammi without those books? I'd kill to get him to think about me for a change."

"He's focused on his goals, and that's good, man. I can't believe you're so jealous."

"I'm not jealous."

Brian snorted.

"Okay, a little. He wants it so bad, and if he's going to get into college, he has to pass this test. I know it's important. It's just that he's so tired between working at the grill and studying that we haven't really, you know…" Mitchell knew he could talk to Brian about anything, even his sex life. In the past, they'd dissected every date either of them ever had, given each other advice, and been there through the death of Mitchell's previous partner, a man Brian had secretly loved.

"Haven't been having sex?"

"Yeah." Mitchell exhaled.

"That sucks."

"I wish it did. Or he did." Mitchell groaned. "I'm dying here, buddy."

"Sounds like you need some time away too. You know, you're both welcome here anytime you need to get away. Rush might put you to work on the ranch, but it's a chance you'll have to take."

"Listen, some good hard physical labor might be what I need to take the edge off. You can count on us for sure."

"Great. Come out in the early afternoon; we need to talk."

"Something wrong?"

"No, I just need your advice. I think Rush and I might be interfering with someone's life." That was an understatement. Bringing Jack and Edward together after such a huge blowup might not be the best idea, but some things needed to be forced.

"Trying to help someone find their way?"

"Yeah, something like that."

"You think Sammi's powers might help?" Sammi could read the thoughts of others, a handy power if you're going to have one. It was Sammi's power that had brought Mitchell and Sammi together, forging a soul bond between them that even Sammi's past as a sex slave couldn't destroy.

"They might. He might be able get a read on these guys. Clear things up, at least. If that's okay with him?"

"I'll ask, but I'm sure he won't mind. You can count on me."

"I always have. See you." Brian hung up.

He'd reached his patrol car, his hand on the handle, when the feeling hit him. He hadn't had a premonition in a long time, but this one was strong, just like all the others he'd ever had in his life. And just like all the others, Brian knew it would come true.

Edward would need him soon. Before the end of the week. Something bad was going to happen. A chill raced down Brian's spine. He shook it off, got in his vehicle, and pulled out of the parking lot to finish his patrol.

Chapter Seventeen

After Edward walked Winston in the grass verge on the other side of the hotel parking lot, he put a bowl of dog food down, and filled another bowl with water. Then he turned on the TV and found the home renovation network, his and Winston's favorite.

With the sounds of the television and the cool air running, Winston would be fine until Edward got back. As he left the room, he placed the DO NOT DISTURB sign on the door handle so the maid wouldn't bother Winston.

Then he hopped in the Miata, pulled out of his spot, and headed to Olivia's. Glancing in the rearview mirror, he was satisfied with his appearance. He'd needed forty-five minutes, not thirty, to take the swelling down around his eyes, but now there was no evidence that he'd cried his eyes out like a heartbroken teenager over Jack.

* * *

Jack stared at the door for a long time after Brian left. Thank God, the man had knocked and given Jack a moment to pull himself together. Only sheer willpower had kept his hands from shaking.

Now they shook like a junkie needing a fix.

Jack willed them still. He willed his heart to stop its yearning. He willed his brain to turn the fuck off and leave him alone.

Because there was no way it could ever work. Not in Jack's life. Not here in Hooterville. Not if Jack wanted to stay chief of police.

But Rush and Brian were together, and no one thought any less of them. Rush was still a respected member of the community. Brian, a respected officer of the law.

But Rush and Brian weren't like Edward. They were big men. Manly. Men who could kick your ass if you got out of line or had the balls to shoot off your mouth about them to their face. No one would look at them and think "fag."

Edward, on the other hand, screamed "fag" from the rooftops while waving a big rainbow flag. No one could doubt his sexual orientation. His body was lithe, his facial features delicate, more beautiful than some women Jack had seen, and... Shit. Why did Edward have to be *so* gay?

Yet those were the very things that attracted Jack.

If Jack had any type of relationship... Shit, had he just used the *R* word? Jack's mind rewound and began again. If he hung out with Edward around here, tongues would wag, and Jack would be labeled "fag" right along with him. The good folk of Spring Lake might not say it to his face, but they'd snicker behind their hands and behind Jack's back. He'd lose their respect and become an object of derision.

Guilt by association.

Only in Jack's case it'd be truth by association.

Either way, it spelled the end of his career and the life he'd worked so hard to build here. So far from that run-down trailer, the hard fists of his drunkard daddy and the abusive put-downs of his mother.

This was just like all those years ago when he had to make a choice about his own survival. Stay with his family, or save himself and cut them out of his life. He'd chosen himself and saved the only person he had the power to save at the time.

Now, it was Edward or him.

Jack chose himself.

Really, there wasn't any other choice.

* * *

Holding his breath, afraid of what he might find on the other side of the door, Edward put his key in the lock and went inside.

"Meemaw, I'm back."

"In the kitchen, honey." Her voice sounded good and strong. He exhaled and let go of the fear he'd find her ill again. His heart just couldn't take that, not today.

"Are you ready to go to lunch?" He stepped into the kitchen and froze.

Olivia was putting a thermos into a large picnic basket.

"What's all this?" he asked.

"I thought we'd do something special. I want to take you to the old ranch. We're going to have a picnic." She smiled up at him.

"That's wonderful! I haven't been on a picnic in ages." He beamed at her. He just barely remembered going once or twice to the ranch as a young child. The horses had seemed so huge to him, all thick lips and big teeth. The cows so small, dotting the wide fields they'd clustered on. "Is it still a working ranch?"

"Yes, if you count the pumping jacks and gas compressors."

"Pumping jacks?" Jacks? Jackrabbits? Jumping jacks? He had no idea what she was talking about, and it must have shown, because she laughed.

"Oil and gas wells. But the old homestead is still there and in good condition. I keep it maintained. The power's been shut off out there for almost fifteen years. Nowadays, I go there sometimes for some peace and quiet. It has a working well, though, so there's fresh water, if you wanted to work the pump." She chuckled and pointed to the thermos. "But I thought we'd enjoy some fresh-squeezed lemonade."

Edward came over to the table and inspected the basket. "What else have you got in there?"

"Just some sandwiches, some fruit, and a slice or two of cake I made this morning." She winked at him.

"Cake?" Dear Lord, please let it be chocolate, because he could sure use some right now.

"Chocolate." She winked.

"Thank God." He sighed.

She laughed. "I figured chocolate can cure what ails a body." She gave him a piercing look.

"Chocolate can never be a wrong choice, in my opinion." He nodded, avoiding her gaze.

"Then let's go!" She slapped the lid closed, and Edward carried the basket to the door. "Wait." She opened a closet door, pulled out a folded quilt, and then motioned for him to go on.

At the car, she put the quilt in the backseat, and he put the basket on top of it to hold it down.

"I hope you don't mind that the top's down?" he asked as he settled her into the car.

"I was counting on it." She grinned. "And I hope you plan on driving fast."

"Meemaw!" He chuckled. "You're a bad influence, you know that?"

"I like that, Edward. I want that on my headstone. *She was a bad influence.* Then she laughed and he laughed, and they pulled away from the house.

* * *

Jack glanced at his watch. Two o'clock and he hadn't had lunch. He couldn't have eaten before anyway. He walked to the door, opened it, and leaned out. "Kristen?"

"Yes, Chief?" She looked up at him.

"Can you order me a lunch from the diner? Whatever the daily special is will be fine."

"Sure. Working through?" She had that look in her eyes, the one that mothers reserved for wayward children.

"I want to get out of here early today. I'm going fishing." He ducked back in his office before she could launch into a round of questions.

Fishing sounded good. He hadn't been thinking about it, but when she asked, it was the first thing that came to his mind. Sure. He'd get his pole and go down to the creek, toss a line in, and just sit. Maybe kill a beer or two. Watch the sun go down.

Not think about Edward.

He ground his teeth and went back to work. If he got this done by four, he could be at the creek by five.

* * *

Edward turned off the road onto a gravel and dirt...well, it was nothing more than two ruts...and came to a gate.

"I'll hop out and get it," she said, her hand on the door.

"No way. I'll get it." He got out and approached the gate. It was almost shoulder high on him, four thick metal posts crisscrossed, with some kind of latch.

"Just push down, it'll lift and unlock," she called to him.

He did, and it swung open without any help from him. He trotted back to the car, got in, and pulled through. "Should I shut it?"

"Better. I let John Macon graze his herd here, so best keep it shut so they don't get out."

He got out and shut the gate. "Now where?" he said as he got behind the steering wheel.

"Just up the road, over that rise." She pointed, and he took off.

The car bumped and jolted over the rut. As the undercarriage of the little car occasionally scraped the ground, he could understand why everyone around here drove those god-awful pickup trucks.

They made the crest of the rolling hill, and Edward stopped the car. It was like a picture postcard. Across a small green valley between the hills sat a white cottage. Well, ranch house, he supposed was the proper term. It had a porch that wrapped all the way around it from what he could see.

Surrounding it were a half a dozen majestic oak trees, as fine as any he'd seen anywhere in the South. All they were missing was the Spanish moss blowing in the breeze. Set to the side and behind the house was an old barn, its white paint worn and faded.

"It's perfect, Meemaw," he whispered. "Just the way I remember it."

She smiled and touched his leg. "I'm glad you remember, child."

He started the car down the hill and followed the road up the front yard.

The house was bordered by a variety of bushes, oleander, camellia, roses. Some bloomed, others had spent flowers, but all looked healthy and vigorous.

"Where do you want to spread the blanket?" he asked as they parked and got out.

"Over there. Under that tree." She headed for it, and Edward followed with the basket.

As she spread the blanket, he looked around. "I can see why you come here." It was lovely, and quiet and...home. He'd never been anywhere that felt so much like home, certainly not his parent's house, and not even his high-rise condominium.

Edward's heart eased.

He put down the basket on a corner of the quilt and sat. Olivia was already pulling off her socks, her shoes already tossed to the side. "Come on, Edward. Get comfy."

He toed off his running shoes, slipped off his socks, and put them next to hers; then he just lay back, his arms behind his head, and looked up through the long, thick branches of the tree.

"I'll bet I can climb it." He smiled.

"You used to when you were nothing but a tiny thing. One time your dad had to go up there after you. You'd gotten up so high, and it wasn't until you looked down that you got scared." She chuckled. "He was so mad at you."

"His perpetual state." Edward snorted.

"But I'd never seen him prouder, child." She lay back next to him, gazing through the branches. "He just kept shaking his head and muttering, 'Why, I never. Look how high he got. Why, I never.'"

Edward's heart caught, and he swallowed. "My father was proud of me?" Even if it was only for climbing a tree, it was better than nothing.

Olivia rolled onto her side and smiled at him. "I know he wasn't much for telling you, but he was."

"Father went out of his way to tell me what a disappointment I was to him. Maybe... I don't know, maybe he did love me. Once." Edward shrugged.

She let out a breath. "If your father were alive right now, I'd tan his hide for how he treated you." She shook her head. "Eddie had his own set of problems, and he let them spill over onto you, that's all." She patted his hand.

"Thanks, Meemaw. But I knew how he felt about me even before he found out that I was gay. Once that happened, the gloves were off, not that he ever held much back. But at least he never hit me." Instead, he'd never touched Edward again. Never hugged him or put his arm on Edward's shoulder in comfort or reassurance.

"Your father was...an idiot." She pished and rolled onto her back again. He had the feeling she wanted to say something else, but had thought better of it.

They were quiet for a while, watching the clouds float by through the limbs and leaves of the big oak. Edward listened to the sounds of the world around him. No cars, no horns, none of the sounds of city life, only the birds, the bugs, and the occasional faraway moo of a cow.

Maybe he was a *Country Living* kind of guy, after all.

Olivia sat up. "I'm hungry, how about you?"

"Now you're talking." He sat up and crossed his legs Indian-style.

She dug out the food, spread it around for them to help themselves, and they feasted.

When the last crumbs of chocolate cake had been licked from their forks, they lay back, patting their tummies.

"Oh God. I'm going to have to run twice a day for a week to work off that wedge of cake. That was the biggest slice I've ever seen." Edward moaned.

"Nonsense. You need to gain some weight."

"And lose my girlish figure?" He chuckled.

She stood and held out her hand to him. "Come on. We need a walk to help us digest, and I want to show you something."

Edward stood, offered her his arm, and they walked around the house. The porch did wrap all the way around, and several doors opened onto it. At the rear of the house, they took a worn path that led over the next gentle hill. They climbed it and stood at the top.

Just below was a hollow. More oaks stood in a circle and beneath them were a dozen-or-so stone markers surrounded by blue wildflowers. A cemetery.

"I want to be buried here, Edward. Next to your grandfather." Her voice was so soft and gentle. No fear, no trepidation. Just calm. Peace. Contentment. "Promise me. You won't let Lillian put me in the ground anywhere else."

"I promise." With his mother that would take a battle, but it was a battle he would win. For Olivia. He owed her that much.

Olivia wrapped her arm around his waist, leaned her head on his shoulder, and they stood there for long minutes. Then he felt her sigh and pull away.

"I want to show you the house before it gets dark."

They went back down the hill and climbed the steps to the porch. She took out a key ring, opened the door, and they stepped inside.

The house was cool. In the sunlight that streamed through the windows and the sheer lace curtains, dust motes floated. He could smell cedar and lavender, and the faded scent of dead flowers.

Olivia had moved into the kitchen, bright and cheery with its empty open-faced cabinets and white linoleum floors. Clean but unused.

On the counter was a cut-glass vase with a bouquet of withered flowers. She removed them, opened a door under the sink, and put them in a garbage pail. "I'll throw this out later."

She opened a drawer, took out garden clippers and a pair of gloves, and went to the back door. "I'll just be a few minutes. Look around."

Edward nodded and went back into the empty living room. A stone fireplace with a simple thick wooden beam for a mantle stood against one wall. He went down the hall and opened door after door, finding four empty bedrooms, each with a door that opened onto the porch. There were two bathrooms. The bath fixtures were from the thirties, at least, and both had old claw-foot tubs and small black-and-white tiles on the floors and walls.

He fell in love with the house as he walked through it, imagining what he'd do if it were his.

Circling back to the kitchen, he found Olivia arranging the flowers she'd cut in the vase. "Your grandfather always liked fresh flowers in the house."

He smiled. "It's a nice touch. Homey."

"Yes. This was our home. When he died, I stayed for a while, but it was too hard. Everything reminded me of him. It hurt too much, so I moved to town."

"But you keep coming back."

"I didn't at first. But it called me home, Edward. He called me home. These days I come quite often just to be with him here." She looked up at him, and tears welled in her eyes.

"Why didn't you move back?"

She shrugged. "It was too far from town, and I didn't want to be so isolated. Besides, when I come here now, it's special."

Edward gathered her into his arms, and they held each other tight.

"You must have loved him so much, Meemaw."

"I did. One day, I hope you'll find that kind of love."

"Me too." Sure. Somewhere over the rainbow where bluebirds and pigs fly.

He stared out the window at the hill that hid the graves of relatives he'd never known but felt closer to than his own family. This place grounded him, made him feel close to his roots, as if he were a part of something bigger than just him and his mother.

She sighed. "I suppose we should get back. That dog of yours probably needs to go for a walk."

"Winston? Oh, he's very good about being inside for long periods. He never has an accident."

They went outside. She folded the blanket, and he put it and the basket in the backseat. Then he held open the door for her.

Once he got behind the wheel, he leaned over and kissed her on the cheek. "Thanks for sharing this with me, Meemaw. It was a wonderful day."

They bumped back over the road, opened and closed the fence, and drove back to town.

Chapter Eighteen

Jack untangled his line for the fourth time as he swore.

Fishing was overrated. "Peace and quiet, my ass," he grumbled.

The line came free, and he reeled it in. The hook, bait missing once more, swung around as he jerked the pole in anger and caught himself on the thigh.

"Son of a bitch!" The barbed end dug into his flesh, and he froze, knowing any more movement would embed it deeper.

It was karma. Cosmic justice. And only a small fraction of the shit he deserved for hurting Edward.

Carefully, he put down the pole, sat on the ground, and, gritting his teeth, worked the hook free of his skin. Blood welled. He grabbed the bottle of water leaning next to his tackle box, and poured it over the small wound to rinse it clean.

Staring at the hook in his hand, he couldn't tell if it was bloody or rusty. To be on the safe side, he probably needed to get a tetanus shot. Actually, he should have had one when Winston bit him, but Jack hadn't wanted anyone to know about that. Now he had a valid excuse, one he didn't mind being known.

His luck was going downhill fast. He'd better leave before he fell in the damned creek. The fish had eluded him ever since he'd arrived, only to swim up to the bank to make their presence and his ineptitude known.

After he gathered up his fishing equipment, broke down his pole, and tossed his empty beer bottles and trash in a plastic bag, he headed back to his truck.

Not a single fish. So much for catching dinner.

Oh well, there was a frozen pizza at home calling his name.

Pizza, a cold beer, and pay-per-view.

What a life.

* * *

Wednesday morning, Jack woke up on the couch in his living room. He sat up, groaned, back muscles aching, and ran his hands through his hair as he got his bearings. The TV was still on, the sound turned down low. On the coffee table was a plate with the half-eaten sandwich he'd made last night. Next to it stood a warm bottle of beer he'd only had a sip of.

He wore jeans and nothing else.

In his bedroom at the back of his house, his alarm clock was ringing. It must have been what had awakened him. He thought he'd fallen asleep around three a.m., same as the night before. He pushed to his feet and shuffled down the hall.

He slapped at the alarm, knocking the clock off the side table. It fell between the bed and the wall, still ringing.

"Fuck," he mumbled as he got on his hands and knees to retrieve it. He reached for it, snagged it by the cord, and reeled it in. After shutting off the alarm, he placed it back on the table. He wasn't sure what was worse, the ringing or the silence.

He stood, slowly, carefully, then went to the bathroom. He needed to piss.

Standing at the toilet, he emptied his too-full bladder, flushed, and turned on the water in the shower. He slipped out of his jeans and tossed them, not caring if they landed in the proper hamper or not. His shirt from last night lay on the floor next to it.

Avoiding his own gaze in the mirror, because reality would come only too soon, he tested the temperature of the water, then stepped in. Warm water fell over his shoulders and down his back as he picked up a washcloth and soaped it up.

Like a robot, he bathed. Rinsed. Toweled off. Got out of the shower.

Showtime.

Jack looked at the mirror.

Oh yeah. He was looking rough. *Shit.* Were the bags under his eyes from only two nights of bad sleep or had they been there before? And he could have sworn the hair at his temples hadn't been that gray last week. The light in this room sucked. Maybe he should switch to those new compact fluorescent lightbulbs.

He ran the water in the sink, splashed it on his face, and then shaved. No matter how slow he went or how careful he tried to be, he cut himself. Three times.

Glanced at his reflection. It should have looked better. It didn't.

He looked ridiculous with three small pieces of toilet tissue stuck to the cuts, dots of blood holding them in place on his chin, jaw, and throat.

Running his hand over his stomach, Jack straightened and sucked in his gut. Turned to the side and exhaled. Still tight, thank God for that. There wasn't a six-pack, but there weren't any love handles, either.

He leaned closer to his reflection as he evaluated his body.

"No no no." A gray hair nestled, like a traitor, among the light covering of dark hairs on his chest. With a frown, he plucked it out and held it up. Squinted.

It was gray all right. He didn't need new lights to see the difference between dark brown and gray.

It was the beginning of the end. The slow slide into middle age. Forty-five loomed closer, mocking him.

He wasn't ready for this.

Jack jerked away from the mirror, dropped the lone hair into the wastebasket, and brushed his teeth without further scrutiny of his forty-three-year-old body.

He had thirty minutes to get dressed, have breakfast, and get to work. He'd skip breakfast; he wasn't very hungry. Hadn't been since last weekend when Winston and Edward had flitted in and out of his life.

This was all Edward's fault.

* * *

"Morning, Chief," Kristen said, then sipped her coffee.

"Morning." Jack flashed Kristen a quick smile and ducked into his office, clutching the coffee he'd picked up at the drive-through, so he didn't have to stand in the kitchen and make small talk with her or anyone else.

He tossed his hat on his desk, put his coffee down, sat, and stared at the door. The last time he'd seen Edward was when he'd stormed out of Jack's office, furious and hurt. Jack replayed the scene in his head, right up to the moment he'd kissed Edward.

It had been the best kiss of Jack's life.

Edward had literally melted into him. Jack could feel the man's body give way, the tug of Edward's hands on his shirt, the complete surrender as Edward opened his mouth and let Jack inside to taste him.

Jack groaned.

He had to stop thinking about it, but all Jack wanted was to feel Edward's body beneath him, feel Edward's entire body melt against his just as it had before. Jack wanted to taste Edward again: Edward's mouth, his skin, his cock. Every inch of him.

That would be insanity.

Fuck. What Jack was going through right now was insanity. Not sleeping. Not eating. And this funk, this depression was sheer weakness. And he'd never given in to his weaknesses.

At this point in his life, it wasn't the time to start. He was right where he'd planned on being. Settled in a nice town, living in a nice house, with a nice job.

Everything nice. Simple. Easy.

No complications.

Edward was the mother of all complications.

* * *

Between taking Olivia all over town and even to San Antonio on Tuesday, Edward had hardly thought about Jack at all. He'd just been too distracted while running around with his grandmother and having lunch at her favorite Mexican restaurant in San Antonio on the Riverwalk. They'd each had two frozen margaritas, and both of them had flirted shamelessly with their young waiter. Edward hadn't talked and laughed so much in months.

Then they'd spent the rest of the afternoon walking along the river, looking at all sorts of shops. Edward even bought Winston a new leather collar that had silver Lone Star studs all the way around it.

Olivia slept on the drive home. She'd been tired but didn't look exhausted. He couldn't wait to see Winston and try on the new collar. He'd dropped Olivia off, settled her in the house, then went back to the hotel. After showing Winston the new collar, Edward had fallen into bed. He hadn't even remembered falling asleep.

Now, it was Wednesday morning, and he had the barbecue at Brian and Rush's ranch in the evening. Dressed only in a pair of black briefs, he stood staring at the small closet where he'd hung most of his clothes.

"What do you think, Winston? Blue jeans or black?"

Winston lay on the bed watching the home decorating channel.

"No opinion?" Edward held each pair up against his body. "It's sort of a casual affair. The blue ones. They're sort of scruffed up." He put the black jeans back in the closet and draped the blue ones over a chair. "Now the shirt."

That would be easy. Definitely *not* the one with the fringe.

After pulling out shirt after shirt, he settled on a plain white button-down shirt and his brown belt and brown boots, then put them to the side to change into later that afternoon.

That settled, he slipped into a pair of sweats and a T-shirt and took Winston for a walk, putting off the call he needed to make to his mother to let her know his progress. More than anything, he didn't want to talk to her. She'd just go on about his inability to do even this one little thing for her.

Back in his room, he sat on the bed and made the dreaded call.

His mother answered on the third ring. "Hello."

"It's Edward." He braced himself.

"Edward, dear. How is it going? Mission accomplished?" she cooed at him. That would change soon enough.

"No, Mother."

"Why not?" And here it was, the voice he knew so well. Hard. Cold. Demanding.

"Well, we've been getting to know each other. I didn't want to rush into it."

"Look, I know you're enjoying yourself, but it's time to stop thinking about you and think about doing what I asked you to do." She gave a long-suffering sigh. "Just do whatever it is you do and make her better." He could just see her flipping her hand and rolling her eyes.

"Gee, Mother, I had no idea you cared so much for Meemaw."

"Don't be snide, Edward. She's my mother. Of course I care."

"Then why haven't you come to see her?"

"Did *she* ask you to ask me that?"

"No. *I'm* asking you that. Why?" he pressed.

There was a moment of silence. "It's between her and me. She knows why."

"But I don't know."

"It's none of your business, Edward." Her tone said he shouldn't ask more, but he ignored it.

"You kept me from seeing her when I was younger, and when Father died you never did anything to encourage me to see her then. I think it's my business. She's *my* grandmother." His voice had spiraled higher, and taking a deep breath, he brought it under control. It would only be more ammunition for her to hurl back at him.

"She's *my* mother." That tone said end of discussion. "Now, don't dilly-dally there; get it done."

Edward gritted his teeth to keep from saying his automatic ingrained response of "yes, ma'am." Instead, he hung up.

He sighed.

Woof.

"You said it." He rolled his eyes and then dressed to visit with Olivia.

As he drove to her house, he thought about his power. He'd never done much with it, never tried to control it, or test it. What if he could slowly bleed the sickness out of her, a little at a time? Make it safe for him and for her.

If he could just take a little of whatever it was or take some of the pain away, that might help. Might even extend the time she had to live. He'd have more time with her.

Which was so odd, because before he'd come here, he'd never really thought about her much at all. He'd lived almost half his life without her in it, so why did that prospect scare him shitless now?

Because if she died he'd be alone, and no one would love him just for him.

If he thought about it, he'd been alone most of his life. It was selfish. But was it any more selfish than his mother's motives in sending him? They both wanted Olivia alive.

What did Olivia want?

Chapter Nineteen

Edward sat across from Olivia as they ate the light lunch he'd prepared, a tuna salad, tomato bisque soup, and fresh fruit. He'd been trying to get around to explaining his power to her for the last half hour but hadn't been able to work up the nerve.

The last thing he wanted was for her to think he was crazy. If she rejected him, he didn't know what he'd do. And that scared him almost as much as taking the risk to heal her.

He cleared his throat. "Meemaw. I want to talk to you about something important."

"You can talk to me about anything, child. I hope you know that." She gave him an encouraging smile.

"This is hard for me. I don't want you to think I'm some kind of a nut."

"I don't think I'd ever think that."

"Just wait until I tell you, then say that." He chuckled.

She sat back in the kitchen chair. "Go ahead. I'm all ears."

He inhaled, held it, then let it out. "I have the power to heal, Meemaw."

She just stared at him as if she were waiting for the weird part.

"Did you hear me? I said I have powers."

"I heard you." She nodded. "What about it?"

Edward's mouth fell open. "What about it? I just told you I can heal people, and that's all you say? Not 'you're crazy.' Not 'I don't believe it.' Not even 'prove it to me'?"

"Edward. I've been alive for almost eighty years, and I've seen a hell of a lot of stuff I can't explain. Lots of people claim they can heal. I've even seen it once or twice." She grinned. "Not saying I believed what I saw, but that don't mean it didn't happen."

"Do you believe me?" He reached out and touched her hand. It was so important to him that she believed. She twined her fingers with his.

"I do. I believe that you believe it. Sometimes, that's all that's needed."

"I want to try to heal you."

She sat back, her smile slipped, and she stared at him. "Heal me?"

"Yes. Whatever you have, I want to help take it away. I can do it; I'm not just pretending." More than anything Edward wanted to do this for her. He wanted to save her.

She smiled at him. Indulgent, as if talking to a child, she said, "That's sweet of you, but…"

"But nothing. I can do it. Give me your hand again." He held his out, waiting for her. They looked into each other's eyes, judging, begging, wondering, and at last, relenting.

She slipped her hand on top of his, palm to palm, and nodded once.

Edward closed his eyes. He had no idea what he had to do; he only knew he had to do something. Just enough.

And it was strange, but he wasn't afraid.

Concentrating, he focused on the skin of her hand, soft and warm against his. Beneath it, he could feel the beat of her heart. He opened his mind to the power, his pulse matched hers, and he breathed in time with her.

Edward opened the thin door between them and searched for the pain. It was buried deep, nowhere near the surface. Unlike Jack's, it didn't come screaming at him. Instead, it hid, lurking in her body, as if it knew he searched for it and meant to take it away.

There was something there. Jack's pain had been red and white and scorching hot, but this was quiet. Dark. Menacing. Waiting for him like a predator lurking in the woods.

More dangerous than anything he'd ever faced before.

If he didn't do this right, it would kill him. For a second, he wavered, instincts for self-preservation almost overtaking him, but he dug into his resolve and held it up like a shield.

And slowly pulled at the darkness. Wicking bits of it away. Absorbing strings, strands of the menace, into himself.

They passed through him, each one searching for an anchor in his body, a place to burrow into him.

He let them continue their journey, offering no anchor, no home, only a conduit.

More dark pieces came at him. The slow bleeding, once a trickle, now seeped. The dam that held them back threatened to burst.

It was time. Edward pulled away, separating himself from Olivia, until they were each their own beings.

Olivia shuddered, and Edward opened his eyes.

"What did you do?" she whispered. Her hand clutched at her stomach, her eyes wide with wonder, not fear.

Edward swallowed. "I took some of it away. Are you all right? Are you hurting?"

"I'm...fine. No, not fine." She blinked and looked down at herself. "I'm not hurting." Then she glanced up at him and grinned. "Good Lord, child. You really did it."

Grinning, he nodded. He'd never felt prouder.

"I never thought you'd do it. That maybe it was some kind of mind trick, like a placebo. But I know the pain I live with each and every moment, and it's gone. Vanished." She sat back and put her hand to her mouth. "Edward. Did you cure me?"

Edward bit his lip. He had to be honest. "No. But I took some of it away. Pain mostly."

"Will it hurt you?" She looked into his eyes. He could see her worry and guilt if anything happened to him because of her.

"No, Meemaw. I'm fine. It sort of flows out of you and through me, and then out into...wherever. I'm not sure where it goes, but it's not in me." He shrugged. "I really don't know why or how, I just know it is."

"How long have you had this power?"

"Maybe all my life, but I've only consciously used it…about the time Father died." He gave her a weak smile.

"Edward. Did you try to heal him?" Olivia whispered as her eyes widened.

The memory of that day flooded Edward. His father lying in the bed, his heart struggling to work. His mother dialing 911, keeping her panic at bay, but Edward could smell it on her. Just as he could smell death clinging to his father.

He'd reached out to take his father's trembling hand.

And his father had jerked away, refusing to let Edward touch him. Even as he lay dying, he couldn't bear Edward's touch. It had been the final rejection in a long string of rejections.

Edward's eyes filled. He hadn't planned on telling her. He'd never told anyone about his attempt to save his father. After all, it was easy to say, "I could have saved him, but he refused."

The hard part was to admit that he hadn't tried hard enough.

"Edward?" She took his hand. He glanced up at her.

"No. It was after that," he lied.

She sighed and her shoulders relaxed. "I'm sure you wish you'd been able to help him."

"Yeah." He gave her a quick smile. "I'm glad I could help you."

"Me too."

Edward paused. "If I could cure you, would you want me to?"

Olivia stared at him for a long time.

Just when he thought she wasn't going to answer the question, she said, "Offering hope to a dying person isn't the worst thing someone could do. The worst thing would be to do it at the expense of your own life."

"I'm not sure what that means."

"It means, I wouldn't save myself and damn you to this hell. I couldn't live with that on my head." She gave his hand a quick squeeze. "Playing God is a slippery slope, child. Easy to slide down and almost impossible to climb up."

* * *

Jack threw himself into his work; he even sat in on the shift change and gave a quick briefing on safety. Then he went back to his paperwork, looking over the warrants for the week. Picking one up, he read it over and grinned.

He picked up the phone and called Brian. "Hey, it's Jack. I see you applied for a search warrant for Jimmy's house to look for the baseball bat his wife used to wreck his truck?"

Brian chuckled. "Yeah. I went to see her the other day, and she was shaking so bad she practically confessed. I'm sure she's still got whatever she used hanging around the trailer."

Jack frowned. "It's a shame. He deserves worse than just getting his truck beat up." The man was a low-life. Trailer-park trash of the worst sort.

"I know that, Chief. I could see bruises all over her. I know he beats her, but unless she calls it in, there's nothing I can do. I gave her that card you had made up about the women's shelter in San Antonio."

"She take it?" Jack had heard about the shelter from a cop he knew in San Antonio and had them made up just in case. She wasn't the only woman around here getting the crap beat out of her on a regular basis. It was something that shamed him about Spring Lake, though he supposed it happened everywhere. He couldn't understand hitting someone you were supposed to love, despite the beatings he'd had at the hands of his father, someone who was supposed to love him.

"Yeah. But I don't think she'll ever use it." Jack could hear the resignation in Brian's voice. "Jimmy's not much, but at least he's paying the bills. And she's got two kids with him."

"The sad thing is most of these women are too poor and too frightened to get out. Until it's too late and someone winds up dead." He'd seen it many times in his job. Too damn often.

"If the judge signs it, I'll pick it up later this morning and do the search before I go off-duty. You're still coming out to the ranch tonight, right?"

Jack had forgotten about the poker game. "Yeah. Be there around six?"

"That's great. Do you remember Mitchell and Sammi, my friends from Houston?"

"Yeah, sure do." Brian's best friend Mitchell had helped him move to Spring Lake. Jack had met him once, when Brian and Rush's relationship was at a rocky point. Mitchell had seemed like a nice guy and a good friend, and Sammi had been with Mitchell. Younger. Sexy. Sammi reminded Jack of Edward. "It'll be good to see them again."

"It will. I haven't seen them in months. Well, I'll see you later."

"If I'm not around, just pick up the warrant from Kristen."

"Will do." Brian hung up.

Jack sat back, an uncomfortable feeling climbed up his back. So far, it looked like everyone at the poker game tonight was gay.

How the hell did *he* figure into this?

His stomach did a flip, and he ran his hand through his hair.

Had Brian figured out he was gay? Jack had never given any hint, had never let it even be suspected. He'd been so careful.

Oh fuck. Jack's body started to tremble as panic rose like bile in his throat. He took a deep breath to calm himself. There was no way Brian knew. No fucking way. It was just Jack's worn-out nerves. He'd been feeling so out of sorts. Lack of sleep, that's all.

Brian didn't know shit.

Unless Edward had told him.

Chapter Twenty

Jack leaned on the bar in the ranch's den as Rush poured him a whiskey.

"Glad you could make it, Jack." Rush smiled at him, then lifted his beer to his lips for a swallow.

"Glad to be here. I haven't played poker in a while. Brian tells me you're the man to beat tonight." Jack took a sip and felt the familiar fire burn its way down his throat.

Rush laughed. "That's 'cause he's such a bad player, I look good compared to him."

"Is that what it is?" Jack didn't believe that for a second.

"Yep."

"Don't let Rush fool you," Mitchell chimed in as he walked in from outside. "He's damned good. The steaks are on the grill," he told everyone. "Another beer, bartender."

Rush chuckled, opened another longneck, and handed it to Mitchell. "Don't tell Jack that or he won't play. Everyone's playing, aren't they?" Rush's eyebrow rose.

"Just more money for you, right?" Mitchell laughed. "Sammi's not going to play. He doesn't know how."

Jack looked over at the couch where Sammi sat, his legs curled under him. He had a glass of cola in his hand. Sammi didn't drink at all, he'd explained earlier. Again, Jack was struck by how much Sammi reminded him of Edward.

They were delicate, lithe, and damned sexy.

Sammi watched them from behind a long dark swath of bangs that covered one-half of his face, making him look mysterious. Mitchell was a brave man, not afraid of what others might think about his choice in a lover.

But Mitchell lived in Houston. Being gay in Houston was a far cry from being gay in Spring Lake. Let Mitchell try running around this town with Sammi on his arm. It'd be another story, for sure.

"We could teach him," Jack offered. "Hey, Sammi. Would you like to learn how to play poker?" Damn, he hadn't meant to say that, but Sammi had looked so alone sitting there on the couch.

Sammi looked up and smiled. "You're sweet, Jack." He shook his head and the bangs shifted, giving Jack a glimpse of his dark eyes. "No, I'm fine. I'll let Mitchell lose all of his money." He laughed and stood, unwinding himself from the couch.

Every man's eyes were on the younger man as he sauntered up to Mitchell. Sammi's jeans-clad hips shifted in a subtle rock and roll, his pierced navel peeking from under the short hem of his T-shirt. He leaned against Mitchell as Mitchell's arms wrapped around him, pulling him even closer. The room stopped breathing as something thick and tangible arced between the two men. Jack could feel their arousal building, and somehow it had spilled over to stiffen his cock.

Brian came in the back door, stopped and stared, then barked out, "Get a room, you two! We have guests."

Mitchell gave Sammi a quick kiss on the lips, and Sammi stepped away. "Sorry." He blushed.

The electricity in the air popped, dispersed, and Jack's prick deflated as fast as it had filled. And from the look on Rush's face, he'd felt the same thing.

Fuck. What had just happened? It was as if they'd been mesmerized by the motion of Sammi's hips.

Jack needed some air or another whiskey. Going for air seemed too obvious, so he turned away and took another sip of his whiskey.

Rush caught his gaze, smiled, and raised his bottle again. "I know what you mean." Knowledge passed between them, and Jack nearly choked.

Shit. Did everyone know? Was he wearing a fucking sign on his back?

* * *

Edward followed the directions to the ranch Rush had given him when Rush had called. It was out in the country, like his grandmother's place, only in the opposite direction. Despite running late, he drove the little Miata slower than usual, looking for the turnoff Rush had said to take.

Just where he'd said it would be was a large gate with the name of the ranch, the Double T, worked in iron on it. It was open, so Edward turned in, jolted over the wide cattle guard, and down a smooth, gravel-packed road lined with oak trees. They weren't as big as the ones at Olivia's ranch, but of a good size. It would be a spectacular alley of trees in about twenty years.

Ahead he saw a cluster of buildings. A two-story house and two barns. In front of the house, there were two pickup trucks, a Jetta, and a Tahoe. Edward eased the shiny red Miata between the trucks, parked, and got out. Was there a law in Texas that pickup trucks could only be white, silver, or black, because those were the only colors he'd seen around here.

The trucks dwarfed his car, their side steps at almost the same height as the top of his door. His car could fit in the long back bed of the black one on the left.

It was as if the trucks had overdosed on testosterone.

Edward looked at the convertible. Looked back at the mud-splattered trucks.

The Miata screamed "sissy." He groaned. These were real men, even if they were gay. What was he doing here? He didn't even know how to play poker.

Now, if they needed him to make a kick-ass potato salad, bake a killer crème brûlée, or redecorate the house, he was the gay man for the job. He didn't know a damn thing about ranches, pickup trucks, or cows. Hell and damnation, he couldn't even spit without gagging.

He should get back in the car and go home. He had his hand on the door handle when his nostrils caught a whiff of heaven.

The undeniable aroma of steaks on a grill.

His stomach rumbled and overruled his doubt-filled mind.

Edward headed toward the front steps.

* * *

Jack turned away from Rush and leaned against the bar. This wasn't going well at all. He had to do damage control before the night spiraled out of control. Before anyone here talked to anyone in town.

The doorbell rang, and Brian went down the hall to the front door. Voices floated back to them, but Jack couldn't hear the conversation.

"Is someone else coming?" He turned back to ask Rush.

"Yep." Rush nodded and took a long swig of his beer, finishing it off.

Another gay guy? Who the hell was left? Jack couldn't take any more shocks.

"Everyone, this is Edward," Brian introduced the new arrival.

Jack's knees turned to Jell-O, and he leaned on the bar for support. "Pour me another whiskey. Make it a double," he rasped at Rush. No fucking way could he turn around and face Edward, but he couldn't stand here all night. He was so fucked.

"Hello, everyone." Edward's soft voice washed over Jack, making him hard.

Jack listened as Mitchell, Sammi, and Rush welcomed Edward. Jack could face it like a man or make a run for it, right past Edward, out the door, hood slide across his pickup truck, and sling gravel getting the hell out of there.

Jack turned around. In one heart-stopping moment, he took Edward in. White button-down shirt, undone to expose throat and a hint of smooth chest, dark hair tousled by the wind, and the sexiest pair of faded, torn blue jeans he'd ever seen wrap a body.

Shit. Jack was a goner.

"Evening, Mr. Beauregard," he drawled as if he didn't care.

Edward's lips parted as he feasted on Jack. For a moment, he forgot where he was, and the urge to throw himself into Jack's arms and let Jack kiss him like he'd done in his office almost overpowered him. Edward's eyes darted around the room at four pairs of eyes staring at him. Staring at Jack. Hell and damnation.

"Hello, Chief Whittaker." Edward's voice cracked as if he were going through puberty again.

Jack gave him a curt nod, then turned back to take a drink. It looked like whiskey, amber, rich, and heady. Fortifying. Edward could use some liquid strength.

"Edward, what would you like to drink?" Rush asked. "We have beer, soda—"

"I'll have what the chief is drinking. A double." Edward swallowed hard and gave Rush a quick smile.

"Whiskey it is." Rush poured a tumbler. "Neat?"

"Yes." Now Edward had to go and get the drink. Right where Jack stood.

Jack snatched up his drink and stalked to the back door. "Gonna see what's happening with the steaks." Then he was gone, and the screen door slammed behind him.

Edward exhaled. Rush pointed to the drink, and Edward darted forward, picked it up, and tossed it down. He coughed as the warm liquor ate its way down his throat, hit his empty stomach, and warmed his toes.

This was bad.

Edward glanced at Brian. One raised eyebrow met his gaze. Edward walked over and whispered, "Why didn't you tell me Jack was going to be here?"

Brian shrugged. "Didn't think it was important."

"Why didn't you tell Jack I was going to be here?" It was obvious by Jack's reaction that he hadn't known Edward would be there. And he hadn't liked it. At all.

"Didn't think it was—"

"Important," Edward finished. "I get it. Well, you're wasting your time, Cupid. Jack's not gay. He's not even interested in me. In fact, he hates me."

"Uh-huh." Rush snorted.

"Can we just forget it?" Edward begged. "Really, let's act like this isn't happening."

"What isn't happening?" Mitchell joined them.

Sammi piped up from the chair he'd curled up in. "That the chief of police and Edward are..." He paused, gave a ghost of a smile, and let the unspoken words linger in the air.

"Nothing. We're nothing. Please." Edward didn't care if he was begging. "I admit to being attracted to him, but Jack's *not* gay. End of discussion."

"Okay. Whatever you say," Rush replied and winked at Brian as the big cop slipped out the back door after Jack.

Edward knew they didn't believe him. Oh, he was so fucked. If Jack had hated him before, he'd probably find some reason to arrest Edward, then have him killed while in custody. It would look like an accident. He'd be shot escaping or for assaulting an officer.

Who would take care of Winston if he were dead?

Jack paced back and forth across the flagstone patio, sucking down air as if he were a fish out of water.

No no no. This could not be happening to him. What had he done to deserve this? Did everyone in the room think he was gay now? Jack's stomach knotted up so bad he thought he'd busted something.

And what the hell was Edward doing here? And why did Jack's body have to respond to Edward's voice, the sight of him. And oh goddamn, those ripped jeans he wore.

Brian cleared his throat.

"What the fuck is going on?" was all Jack could get out as he spun to face Brian.

"What's the problem, Jack?" Brian looked up as he checked the steaks.

"Edward. What's he doing here?" Jack took another sip of his whiskey.

"Rush invited him. I didn't think it would be a problem. Are you okay?" Brian stared at him.

Jack pulled himself together and got control of his voice. "It's not a problem. I was just surprised, that's all." He took a deep breath and then exhaled. "Look. I don't have a problem with you or your friends. Being gay and all that." He ran his hand through his hair. "I just didn't want you thinking...that I was..." His voice faded out.

"That you were gay?" Brian's eyes widened. "Hell, Jack. In all the time I've know you, I've never thought that."

"It's just that it felt like a setup, you know." Jack chuckled, trying to act casual. "Because there were couples. You and Rush. Mitchell and Sammi. Except me. And then Edward showed up, and I thought..."

"Oh. Like a blind date sort of thing." Brian's eyes twinkled. "I understand."

"Yeah, right. A blind date." Jack laughed again. It sounded strained even to him.

"Nope. Just a bunch of friends getting together for dinner, drinks, and poker." Brian slapped him on the shoulder, then leaned in. "And for the record, Jack, I wouldn't think any less of you if you were gay." He winked. "Some of my best friends are gay."

Jack stared at him. Absolutely nothing came to mind for him to reply to that statement. He was better off keeping his mouth shut, for damn sure.

Brian looked at the steaks. "These look ready. Help me carry them inside. Have dinner; then if you want to leave, go ahead." Brian had given Jack an out. If he was smart, he'd take it.

Instead, Jack finished his drink, put down the glass, and helped Brian take the steaks off the grill and put them on two huge platters. Each steak was at least an inch thick, and from what Jack could tell, they were cooked to perfection.

"I think I'll hang around. Eat my steak. Give Rush a run for his money."

Try not to stare at Edward.

Chapter Twenty-one

Jack and Brian brought the steaks to the table. It had been set for six, and Sammi was pouring iced tea into tall glasses. Through the kitchen door, Jack could see Edward bustling about in the kitchen.

Sammi said, "Edward has worked some magic on the baked potatoes. He showed me his recipe for restuffed potatoes." Sammi licked his lips. "Delicious."

Mitchell came to the table. "Sounds like it. Jack, did Sammi mention he's entering culinary school next fall?"

"That's great. I can't boil water." Jack smiled at the younger man.

"Well, I have to pass my GED first. Then take the SAT." He looked nervous. "I'll bet you all have been to college." Jack could see Sammi's vulnerability as he bit his lip.

"A and M," Brian said.

"Me too." Mitchell raised his hand. "That's where Brian and I first met."

"Texas Tech," Jack added.

"University of Texas, Austin." Rush chuckled.

Edward entered, carrying six fluffy potatoes on a plate. "Don't mind them, Sammi. I went to Georgia State for one year and dropped out." He gave Sammi a grin. "College isn't for everyone."

Sammi blasted him back with a wide grin of thanks. "What do you do, Edward?"

Everyone started to sit down. As hosts, Rush and Brian took the chairs at the head and foot of the table, Mitchell sat across the table and Sammi slipped into the chair next to him.

That left Edward and Jack sitting side by side.

Jack pulled back the chair and sat.

"I've done lots of things." Edward shrugged as he sat. "Waited tables. Worked in a bank. I even sold aluminum siding over the phone one summer."

"Wow! That's a lot of different experiences," Sammi said.

"Yes. But now I'm a licensed masseur." Edward looked up.

"Massages?" Rush quipped, chewing around a piece of his steak. "If I'd have known that, I'd have had you out here sooner." He rubbed his shoulder. "I could use a *good* back rub." Jack saw Rush's eyes sparkle and the slight wink he gave Brian.

"Good back rub? I thought I gave good back rubs." Brian looked offended.

"They are, until you forget what you're doing." Rush gave him a sexy grin. "He's got roamin' hands."

Brian rolled his eyes. "Can't help it."

Edward laughed. "Sometimes it's a problem, even for me, if I don't concentrate on what I'm doing like what my patient needs or what I find wrong."

"Like what?" Sammi asked.

"Well, lots of times, a patient says, 'My shoulder hurts.' But when I'm exploring his muscles, I find that the problem isn't in his shoulder, it's farther down his back, maybe in the muscles along his spine. Your body is so interconnected that if you throw something out in one place, it can affect somewhere else. It's called referred pain." Edward spoke with such confidence that it impressed Jack, and he felt a small flicker of pride. Edward might not be the most conventional person, but he was serious about what he did. Jack had personal proof of Edward's talent. Of course, Jack couldn't tell anyone about that. Ever.

"Really? That's interesting." Rush nodded. "I wouldn't know. Brian never seems to make it past my shoulders." He snorted.

Brian glared at his lover. "Like you're any better."

Rush threw his hands up in surrender. "I admit it. I can't get past your neck."

Everyone laughed, even Jack. The warm humor and the gentle teasing between the men drew him in, and his shoulders relaxed. He could do this. He could get through this evening.

"So, Edward. How do you know Jack?" Sammi smiled.

Oh shit. Jack's stomach knotted, and he fought the urge to bolt.

"He arrested my dog."

"Your dog? Jack, how could you?" Sammi cried.

Jack cringed. "It wasn't like that."

"What was it like?" Sammi demanded.

"Yeah, Jack. Tell us what really happened." Brian leaned forward, his chin in his hand.

Jack stared around the table. Everyone waited. There was no getting out of this.

"Okay." He sighed. "I was parked on the side of the road." He left out the part about the headache and his blurry vision. "And this little red Miata goes flying past me, doing about sixty."

"Sixty-five," Edward quipped.

Jack shot him a glare. "So, I pursued."

"Lights and sirens and everything." Edward rolled his eyes. "It was so news-at-eleven." Sammi rolled his eyes, and the others smirked.

"As *I* was saying"—Jack gave Edward another glare—"he pulls over, and before I can run his plates, he gets out of the car and proceeds to walk this bulldog down the side of the road."

"Oh shit." Brian laughed. "That must have really pissed you off."

"You bet." Jack nodded.

"Winston had to go. What was so wrong with that?" Edward took a sip of his tea and tried to look innocent.

"When you get stopped by the law, you're supposed to listen to what they say, obey orders, not go for a fucking stroll," Jack growled.

"So you say," Edward shot back.

Jack's hand strangled his fork. God, the man made him crazy.

"Go on," Sammi encouraged. "Then what happened?"

"I was going through his insurance and registration papers when the dog comes up to me and bites me on the ankle."

"Oh no! What did you do to the poor dog?" Sammi gasped.

"Poor dog! I didn't do anything, did I?" Jack turned to Edward.

"He didn't. I have to admit it. Winston just walked right up to him and bit him."

"Then?" Rush asked.

"I pulled my gun."

"You weren't going to shoot him?" Sammi's hand flew to his mouth.

"He couldn't. I grabbed his arm."

"Hey, I'm telling this story." Jack grinned at Edward. "So Edward grabs my arm, the one with the gun, and we're struggling, and the dog is shaking my leg like it's a dead rat, and I lose my balance."

"I let go." Edward shrugged. "He said to let go and he wouldn't shoot either of us. I was obeying orders." He smirked at Jack.

"I fell on my ass in the middle of the road, the gun went off..."

"He shot my tire."

"You screamed."

"I did not!"

"The dog let go, and I did what any self-respecting cop would do. I arrested the dog." Jack paused. The entire table exploded in laughter, and he joined them. It really was a great story, and now, days later when his ankle no longer hurt, he could see the humor in it.

Laughing, Edward reached out and put his hand over Jack's hand, and for a moment, it felt like the most natural thing in the world.

The moment passed, and Jack slid his hand from under Edward's.

The laughter died, and an uncomfortable silence took over.

Edward stared down at his plate. Pulled his hand back and placed it in his lap. Jack stared at his food, not wanting to see the hurt on Edward's face. Or whatever he'd find on the faces of the other men.

Rush cleared his throat. "Well, if you guys give me a few minutes, I'll get the poker table set up." He stood and left the dining room.

"I'll man the bar and get everyone's drinks." Brian followed Rush.

Sammi stood. "Since I'm not playing, I'll get the dishes and clean up."

Edward stood. "I'll help you."

"That's great. We can talk more." Sammi's tone suggested they'd more than talk, and he gave Edward a sexy wink. A surge of jealousy rushed over Jack.

Oh no. Not good.

Jack stood. "I need another drink." He followed Brian without a single glance at Edward.

Edward sighed and picked up his plate and Jack's.

Mitchell stood, gave Sammi a kiss, and said, "Don't be long. You're my lucky charm."

Sammi snorted. "There's no such thing as luck." He leaned in and whispered, "And I'm not going to help you cheat to win." Sammi gave his lover a knowing look, and Mitchell grinned and shrugged his shoulders.

"That's okay. My superior talent and skill will win out." Then he left, leaving Sammi and Edward alone.

"I get the feeling we're the 'designated women' for tonight," Edward said. "I should have worn heels."

"I don't mind." Sammi laughed. "I really did want some time alone with you."

"Me?" Edward squeaked. "Why? I thought you're with Mitchell. Life partners and all that."

Sammi came around the table, close to Edward. "I am." He slid his hand over Edward's arm. "But I want to know all about you and that dishy chief of police."

"Jack? There's nothing to tell." Edward picked up another plate and headed for the kitchen, trying not to let Sammi see the truth in his eyes.

Chapter Twenty-two

Jack placed the box of cigars he'd brought on the table. "Can we smoke inside?"

Rush nodded. "I smoke all the time. It's *one* of my vices."

From Rush's quick glance at Brian, Jack had the notion that Brian was one of his other vices.

Brian shrugged. "I don't mind. I've gotten used to it." He shot Rush an equally hot stare. Jack knew he didn't mean the smell. Probably meant the taste of it in Rush's mouth, on his tongue. Shit. He had to stop thinking like this. It had to be from being around so much blatant sexual energy. Between Mitchell and Sammi, Rush and Brian, Jack had a hard time not getting hard. *And Edward, don't forget Edward.*

Rush laid out the table with chips and cards as the others sat.

"I'll deal. Texas Hold 'Em. Five-dollar limit. You know the rules." He dealt the cards like a pro. Each of the men tossed a five on the table, and Rush pushed them their chips.

Jack's eyebrows rose at Rush's skill as a dealer. "Hope I brought enough cash."

"I'll take a marker, Chief." Rush grinned as he lit up a cigar. He passed the box and clipper to Brian, who took one.

"Might as well." He shrugged.

Jack took the box from him, chose a cigar, clipped the end, and lit it up. He passed the box to Mitchell, who followed his lead.

"I've never smoked cigars," Mitchell confessed. He inhaled, choked, and laughed.

"Cigar virgin," Rush proclaimed and Mitchell blushed.

"You'll get used to it." Jack motioned with his cigar. "Just don't inhale too deeply the first time."

"Okay." Mitchell tried again, this time without choking. "Nice."

"Good smokes," Rush said. "Now that we've got our cards, our cigars, and our drinks, let's play."

The game started, and for a while, lost in the game and the camaraderie, Jack forgot about Edward.

* * *

Edward sat at the kitchen table with Sammi and picked at a place mat. They'd rinsed the dishes, put them in the dishwasher, and put away the leftovers. He didn't want to go in the den where the others were. Where Jack was.

He should think about something else. Like healing his grandmother.

Sammi stared at him; then his eyebrows rose. "You've got a power."

"What?" Edward straightened. Where did that come from?

"The power." Sammi paused, his head tilted as if he were listening to something. "To heal. You can heal people." He smiled.

"How did you know that?" Edward stood, knocking his chair over.

Sammi stood, came to him, and took his hand. "Don't be scared. I have a power too. I can hear people's thoughts."

Edward's mouth dropped open, and he stared at Sammi. "You can hear my thoughts?"

"Yes, if I concentrate."

"Can you hear Jack's thoughts?" Edward had no idea why his mind flew to that. Well, he did, he just didn't want to admit it.

"Yes." Sammi leaned close, his lips brushing Edward's ear as he whispered, "You make him crazy."

"Crazy good or crazy bad?" Edward whispered.

Sammi's tongue flicked Edward's earlobe, sending a shot of arousal through Edward. "Crazy good. As in, you make his dick very, very hard." Sammi's hand slid over Edward's arm, and Edward shivered at the caress. If he didn't step away, he'd be in big trouble, but hell and damnation, it was as if he was rooted to the spot. Hypnotized.

"Do you think Mitchell would like what you're doing?"

"I'm not worried about Mitchell." Sammi nuzzled his neck.

"Oh?" Edward's brain was shorting out, his eyes closing as he fell under Sammi's spell. He couldn't take much more of this before he gave in.

"I'm worried about you."

Sammi licked his ear and turned Edward's face to him. Edward closed his eyes as soft lips cushioned his, and he leaned into the kiss.

"What the fuck?"

Edward jerked away. Jack stood in the doorway, glaring at him. Fire ignited in Edward's cheeks and flamed up to the roots of his hair. His heart hammered in his chest as a rush of adrenaline swept over him.

Sammi slung his arm around Edward's waist, pulled him back, and nuzzled Edward's cheek.

Jack's eyes widened, then narrowed. Edward could feel the fury pouring off Jack. Confused, Edward didn't know what to do, or why he felt as if he'd just betrayed Jack. With Sammi. And there was Mitchell. And…hell, he didn't understand anything, except he'd never seen Jack so mad.

"Sorry for interrupting," Jack spit out, spun, and disappeared.

Edward pulled out a chair and slumped into it. "What just happened?"

Sammi sat next to him. "Well, from what I can tell, you just made Jack insane with jealousy." He crossed his arms and smiled.

"You did that on purpose." Edward ran his hand through his hair. Jack insane? He could believe that. Insane with jealousy? No way.

"I'm sorry. But Jack needed a wake-up call." Sammi looked unrepentant.

Brian, Rush, and Mitchell appeared in the doorway.

"What happened? Jack just lit out of here like his boots were on fire." Rush stepped into the kitchen.

Edward jerked his head at Sammi. "Ask him."

"I kissed Edward. Jack saw it."

Mitchell shook his head. "Perfectly timed, no doubt." Edward stared at him. Why wasn't he upset? His lover had just kissed someone else. A stranger. If it had been Edward, he'd have thrown a fit.

Sammi gave Mitchell a soft smile, went to him, and wrapped his arms around Mitchell's neck. Mitchell bit Sammi's jaw, then devoured his mouth with a kiss. Edward's toes curled just watching it, so he was sure it had wiped away any memory Sammi had of kissing him.

"Why is it I feel like I'm coming in at the middle of a play and I don't have the script?" Edward looked at each of the men.

Brian cleared his throat. "We thought that maybe Jack needed a little push."

"Oh fuck." Edward put his head in his hands. Could this be any worse?

"I know, we meddled." Mitchell sighed. "And we're so sorry if we messed things up between you and Jack."

Edward looked up. "I keep trying to tell you. There *is* no me and Jack. Look, I know you were trying to help. But honestly, this was the worst possible thing you could have done." He stood and shrugged. "I think I'd better go now. I'm sorry if my drama screwed up the evening."

"Don't go." Sammi reached for him, but Edward stepped away.

"I have to, really. And please, for God's sake, don't spread any rumors about Jack. For the official record, Jack's not gay." Fuck, he was getting so tired of repeating himself. "I need to be alone." Edward needed to curl into a ball, hug Winston to him, and forget the look on Jack's face. All the denying Edward had done, all his adamant cries of "Jack's not gay," everything he'd done to protect Jack, had blown up in his face.

Brian went with Edward to the front door to see him out.

"Edward. I'm so sorry." Brian looked miserable.

"I know. And thanks for caring enough to try something so stupid." Edward stretched up and kissed Brian on the cheek. "Jack's lucky to have you guys for friends. I wish I had such good friends back in Atlanta." Maybe if he had, they would have warned him about Derek instead of just watching and waiting for Edward to crash and burn.

Edward went down the steps to his car and got in.

It was going to be a long drive back to the motel.

Chapter Twenty-three

Jack let up on the gas pedal. The truck was flying down the blacktop. Going this fast might get him killed, but right now, that sounded damn fine with him. His life was over anyway.

They all knew. What a fool he'd been. All his hard work, all his control, shot to hell. Years of repression and denial wasted.

It was all Edward's fault. All of it. If he hadn't come to Spring Lake, if he hadn't been speeding, Jack would never have met him, never have felt the attraction, the hunger, oh fuck, the longing for Edward.

Jack didn't know what to do. He'd have to call Brian and talk to him. Do some damage control. Even if it meant admitting he was gay. Shit. If he had to, he'd beg Brian not to out him.

He slowed and drove through town to his house. Pulling into his drive, he parked and turned off the lights. Closed his eyes and sat. Thinking.

No, thinking was bad. If he thought, he'd just think about how furious, how hurt, how fucking jealous he'd been seeing Sammi kiss Edward. And he didn't want to think about how strong his feelings about Edward had become in such a short time.

He'd never been so at a loss and so on the verge of losing control.

He pushed the palms of his hands into his eyes, trying to block out the scene in the kitchen, but it was burned into his brain or on the back of his eyelids, wherever graphic scenes of destruction were stored.

He'd wanted to jerk Edward away from Sammi, rip him from Sammi's arms, and claim Edward as his own. Thank God, he'd had some control left. Not much, but enough.

Edward had come into his life only six days ago, threatening everything Jack had worked so hard for.

Yet why could Jack recall every moment that he'd spent with Edward, even the bad ones? Like the one in his office, when he'd made Edward cry or when Edward had wrestled him to the ground over the dog. And the good ones like tonight as he told the story of how they'd met, and Edward kept interrupting. Or when Edward had taken Jack's pain away, nearly died, and saved Jack's life.

And all Jack had ever done to Edward had been to hurt him.

Oh shit. He'd fucked up royally.

Jack turned the key, fired up the truck, and backed out of the drive.

* * *

Edward shut the door to his room and slumped against it. Winston hopped off the bed and danced around his feet.

Edward glanced at the bed, wishing he could crawl into it and bury himself under the covers, but duty called.

Woof. Woof.

"Okay, boy. I know you need to go out. Just hold on." Edward got Winston's lead and snapped it on. "Come, Winston." He opened the door, made sure he had the key, and then left his room. The door shut, and he crossed the parking lot with Winston in the lead.

Fifteen minutes later, after he'd walked Winston, he unlocked his door and went inside, unsnapped the leash, and let Winston loose. Then he sat on the bed and yanked off his boots and socks.

Barefoot, he went to the bath to get ready for bed. He'd pulled his shirt out of his jeans and unbuttoned it when there was a knock on the door.

"Who could that be?" he asked his reflection.

His reflection shrugged.

"Winston, come in here." He called the bulldog and then closed him in the bathroom so he wouldn't be a pest or run out of the room.

Edward went to the door and looked out of the security peephole.

Jack.

Hell and damnation. What was Jack doing here, and why did Edward's heart pound as if he were an excited schoolboy with a crush on his teacher? Edward leaned against the door, his mind racing. If he let Jack in, Jack would probably kill him for what happened tonight. If he didn't let him in, he would probably kick the door down, kill him, and then who would pay for that?

If he let Jack in, at least he wouldn't have to pay for a broken door. He'd be dead, but debt free. Not quite win-win, but it had its advantages.

The door jumped with another round of knocking, each thud rocking Edward's body.

"Go away." Edward prayed Jack would listen; then he prayed Jack wouldn't.

"Edward. Let me in. We need to talk."

Edward sighed. It was inevitable. Whether it was here or later, they'd have to have this out, whatever "this" was. He stepped away from the door, swung back the security latch, and opened the door.

Jack's face struggled to remain composed; Edward could see a small twitch in the corner of the man's mouth, and a vein throbbed in his temple.

"I want to apologize," Jack said. His voice was all raspy and gruff and sexy as hell.

Edward stared up into his face, waiting. Jack scuffed his boot against the cement but didn't say anything else. He shoulders hunched, as if he'd curled up inside himself but still walked upright. Something ate at Jack. Served him right. As far as Edward was concerned, there'd been too many "somethings."

"So which one are you apologizing for? Lying to me about being gay? Trying to steal my best friend away from me? Making me think I was nuts? Or manipulating me?"

Jack winced with each item Edward ticked off. "All of it, I guess."

"Apology accepted. Good night." Edward shut the door, but Jack's arm shot out and stopped it.

"Wait." He licked his lips.

"There's more?" Edward arched a brow.

Jack stood there, looking at his feet. Maybe be was trying to figure out which one to shove in his mouth first.

Edward sighed. "Why are you here, Jack?"

Jack looked up, and Edward could see some internal battle being waged as demons danced in the depths of Jack's blue eyes.

Hell and damnation. Why did the man have to be so damned sexy? So in need of healing?

"Come in." Edward reached out, grabbed Jack's arm, and pulled him inside. Jack stumbled on the threshold and caught himself on the door frame.

"Shit." He stepped past Edward. Edward shut the door, catching a whiff of whiskey in the air.

"Are you drunk?"

"Not drunk enough," Jack muttered.

"Why did you come to me?" Edward wanted answers, not excuses.

"You know why." Jack's voice deepened; his eyes flicked up, smoldering as he gazed at Edward. No one had ever looked at Edward that way.

Oh fuck. Edward felt like dessert, and Jack was starving.

Jack stood an arm's length away, his hungry gaze boring straight through Edward's body with laser-beam accuracy.

Direct hit to the heart.

Edward would deal with regrets tomorrow morning. Tonight, he would be bananas Foster. With a cherry on top. God, he hoped Jack liked whipped cream.

Edward stepped close, wrapped his hand around the back of Jack's neck, and rose up on his toes. "You're here because you want me." He brushed his lips across Jack's, teasing him. "You need me." Another brush. "You crave me." He licked Jack's bottom lip.

Jack moaned and slipped one hand under Edward's open shirt; the warmth of Jack's palm singed Edward's skin. Jack slid his other hand around Edward's shoulders and pulled him against Jack's hard body. Edward's legs threatened to give way as he melted into Jack.

"Christ, I need you," Jack whispered; then he crushed his mouth down on Edward's. The taste of whiskey and Jack went straight to Edward's head.

Edward's heart soared. Jack wanted him. He'd risked being seen coming to Edward's motel room. It was foolish and reckless and so fucking romantic, Edward thought he'd die.

Jack could do whatever he wanted to Edward; Edward just wanted Jack. Wanted his tongue, his touch, his cock. Edward's knees buckled under a wave of complete surrender.

Jack grabbed him, hands tightening on Edward's arms, lifting him, pushing him, forcing him backward. Edward's legs hit the bed, and with a hard shove from Jack, Edward fell backward.

Jack straddled Edward at the hips and flung wide the sides of Edward's shirt, exposing Edward's smooth chest and taut stomach. Edward had never seen such passion, desire, and lust, but it was all over Jack's face, in his eyes and in the heat of his demanding hands.

"I crave you, Edward." Lowering his head, Jack nuzzled Edward's neck, taking deep breaths, sucking air in as he drank in Edward's scent. "You smell so fucking good, baby."

Edward cradled Jack's head and buried his fingers in Jack's hair. Jack licked his neck and sent shivers down Edward's spine. His cock, trapped in his jeans, begged for Jack's touch.

Edward's hips surged up, but Jack's weight held him down, pinning him to the bed. Jack's cock, a thick lump in his jeans, rubbed against Edward's belly. The rough fabric abraded and heated his skin, yet the metal buttons were cold. His body didn't know whether to shiver or shudder.

For a starving man, Jack moved slow, taking his time, relishing his dessert. Edward had expected fast and furious, but so like Jack, even in his passion there was control.

"I tried. God knows I tried to resist you, Edward. But tonight, I couldn't stand it another moment." The anger in Jack's raspy voice told Edward more than just his words had that he'd fought the attraction, struggled with whatever demons raged inside him, and lost.

Jack licked Edward's neck, below his ear, traced down his throat, nipped his skin. Tasting. Stroking, Using his tongue like a finger, teasing and prodding. Moving lower,

Jack baby-kissed his way to Edward's chest, to encircle an already hard nipple.

Edward moaned, his fingers digging into Jack's scalp, guiding him to where the ache lay. "Oh yes." Jack's warm tongue flicked against his nub, and as if there were a direct line from Edward's nipple to his cock, he felt the zap. It was such sweet torture, and Edward wanted it to last as long as they both could stand it.

Jack captured Edward's hands and held him down, fingers entwined, pressing him into the bed. Overpowering Edward as he feasted on Edward's body. Nipples, chest, belly, ribs, even under his arms, all were tasted, nipped, licked, and sucked in excruciating slowness as Jack, draped over Edward's body, fed on him like some incubus.

Edward would give Jack anything he wanted, whatever he needed. Tonight, Edward would hold nothing back.

Jack looked up as his tongue zigzagged down Edward's stomach. "You're so beautiful. Christ, you taste so delicious." Their gazes met. Edward smiled at the desire he saw in Jack's darkened eyes. Had anyone ever lusted after him like this? Had he ever been so desired or felt so sexy?

Edward had had his share of lovers, anonymous and known, but none of their eyes had held the depth, the intensity, the sheer need, that Jack's eyes did right now. Edward ached with the realization that this was everything he'd been searching for and all that had been missing from his life.

And he'd only have it for this one night.

Jack slipped lower on the bed, between Edward's legs and flicked open the button on Edward's jeans.

"Did you pick these jeans out knowing they'd drive me crazy?" He nipped Edward's hip bone above his jeans.

"I didn't know you would be there."

"Then who did you wear them for?" He laid a kiss beneath Edward's navel.

"For me." Edward held back.

"Bullshit. You're aware of how fucking hot you look in them. You're a tease, aren't you?" He fingered the rip on one thigh, just above the knee. The soft, frayed edges tickled Edward as Jack's nail scraped his skin. "Was it Sammi?" His inquisitor was subtle, insistent, and ruthless.

Edward gasped. "I didn't know he'd be there."

"Rush or Brian then? Tell me." Again, the scratch of hard nail against soft skin. Edward shuddered, his resolve crumbling under his lust.

"Rush. I wore them for Rush." Edward gave up his secret.

"Why? He's with Brian." Jack nudged Edward's zipper down, each *click click click* like the report of a gun, loud and shocking.

"When I met him, he flirted with me. He said my butt was cute."

"Your ass isn't cute." Jack smirked. "It's fucking gorgeous. I couldn't keep my eyes off it at the traffic stop." He rubbed his face over the bulge in Edward's pants and took Edward's zipper between his teeth.

Edward watched as Jack unzipped his pants. Jack's hands slid down Edward's arms to trap Edward's hands. So dominant. So alpha male. So in control. Edward wanted to be dominated, wanted Jack to manhandle him. To feel Jack's superior strength and be helpless against it. Helpless against the force that was Jack.

To be taken by such an incredible man as Jack.

Edward had never felt so turned on, so on the edge of coming, so in need of a fucking.

And his dick let Jack know all about it. It strained at Edward's precum-soaked black briefs, giving Jack all the proof he'd need.

Jack splayed Edward's pants, exposing the length of his cock hidden under the soft cotton fabric. Jack mouthed Edward's dick as he sucked it through the cloth.

Edward groaned and arched his hips, but Jack held him down as he nibbled along the length, reached the tip, and then with his teeth, lowered the waistband to expose the angry, red head of Edward's dick.

"Oh please, Jack," Edward begged. Just one touch and he knew he'd be gone.

"What do you want, baby?" Jack's piercing gaze skewered Edward.

"Lick me. Suck me. I don't care, just touch me." Edward didn't bother to hide the need in his voice; Jack could see it in his eyes, feel it in the trembling of Edward's body, and in the leaking of his cock.

God, if his balls were any tighter they'd be inside him. Edward hovered on the edge of coming, the slow fire tickling his spine, building, ready to explode.

Jack tenderly rubbed his face against the tip, his lips brushed over it in a caress, then parted as his tongue darted out to taste the fluid that dripped like pearls on a string from Edward's slit to his belly.

Jack took the head of Edward's cock in his mouth and sucked.

Oh sweet, merciful God. Warm, wet, Jack was a haven, a home, a place where Edward felt safe and secure and, Edward's heart stuttered, loved.

Great shudders ran through Edward, and he bucked, cried out, and came, spilling down Jack's throat.

Jack leaned his cheek against Edward's belly as his moist mouth captured Edward's cum. Jack's strong hands had captured Edward's body. And his tenderness had captured Edward's heart.

Chapter Twenty-four

Jack released him, gave a few quick licks to Edward's balls, then climbed back up to lie next to Edward. Cupping Edward's face, Jack kissed him, and Edward opened for him. Lazy tongues stroked each other, and hands relaxed but remained joined.

It was perfect. They cuddled. Actually cuddled. He'd never figured Jack for a cuddler, but he wasn't complaining. Edward floated in the afterglow that came with sex, but he wasn't tired. He was oddly energized. Ready to go, to do more. So much more.

So was his cock. Just the idea of Jack fucking him got him hard, and they hadn't even gotten all their clothes off yet.

Jack's kisses deepened as he roamed over Edward's neck and down to his chest again. Lapped his nipples. Edward arched like a cat, purring.

"Baby, I want you." Jack's breath warmed Edward's skin.

"You've got me. From the moment you shot my car."

Jack laughed just like he had at the dinner tonight, let Edward go, sat up, and pulled off Edward's jeans and briefs as Edward got out of his shirt. Naked, he stretched out on the bed, stroking his cock in a wanton display for Jack.

"God, you're so beautiful. You're the most beautiful man I've ever seen." Jack sat back on his legs as he ran his fingertips over Edward's body, sending tremors traveling like tiny aftershocks after them.

Edward cupped his balls and never let his gaze stray from Jack's. There was no need to speak; their eyes told their intentions. Jack ran his tongue over his lips. His eyes darkened, his pupils large and liquid. Hungry again.

Reveling in Jack's desire for him, Edward pumped his dick, feeling the sweet ache of building arousal. Jack watched, eyes shifting between Edward's hand and his face, as if Jack couldn't decide which one he wanted to focus on.

"I seem to be the only one naked." Edward raised an eyebrow.

Jack stood and stripped for him. Each motion was slow and deliberate, designed to tease and titillate Edward. And it did. It made Edward crazy, impatient, more than ready for Jack to fuck him. Edward didn't know how Jack could have such control.

It took forever for Jack to unbutton his damned shirt and give Edward a glimpse of chest, but when Jack's shirt fell away at last, Edward was not disappointed.

Brown hair covered the space between Jack's pecs, trailing down over his belly to disappear in his jeans. He had the sexiest dark brown nipples, hard as bullets, that Edward had ever seen. His skin wasn't pale, but a nice, light tan as if his summer tan had faded. Strong, muscular arms, broad shoulders, everything about him turned Edward on.

And when Jack flicked open the buttons to his jeans, pushed them down, and Edward realized Jack had been going commando, Edward shivered.

Jack's long, thick cock stood straight out from dark, thick curls. Blood-engorged, brown, its skin looked velvet soft. Jack's balls were full and heavy and made Edward's mouth water.

"Talk about beautiful. *You* take my breath away." Edward held out his hand, inviting, beckoning. "I want you inside me."

Jack climbed onto the bed and covered Edward with his body. Their cocks slid and scraped against each other, as Jack wrapped Edward in his arms.

"Oh God, baby. It's been so long since I've done this," Jack whispered, as if Edward couldn't hear the longing, the desperation, in Jack's voice. Jack's hips' slow grind and the feel of Jack's prick pressed into his belly drove Edward nuts.

Edward pointed to the nightstand. "Condoms. Lube."

Jack slid off him and retrieved the needed items. He tossed them on the other side of Edward, then went back to stroking Edward's body as if he couldn't get enough of the feel of Edward's skin, as if memorizing it because he feared it would be a long time before he did this again.

Edward lay there and experienced every stroke, every glide of Jack's hands. His fingers were gentle, but with a strength that hid just below their surface. Slightly rough, but not hard and callused, it was Edward's turn to commit their touch to memory.

When Jack reached Edward's belly, he stopped, grabbed the lube, and slicked up his fingers. "Spread 'em."

"Yes, sir." Edward moved his legs apart. "I hope this is the body cavity search."

Jack chuckled. "An officer has to be thorough."

"Of course." Edward bent one leg up and to the side and lifted his balls out of the way to give Jack a clear view.

"Christ." Jack hissed and ran his finger from the tip of Edward's weeping cock, dragging down the midline of his scrotum, to the soft skin underneath and straight to his hole. Edward shuddered as the touch ended with a gentle pressure against his opening.

Edward's hands gathered in the bedspread, clutching at it in his readiness to be penetrated. He loved that first breaching, the straining of his muscles, their fight not to let the intruder in, and then the pleasure in their ultimate defeat.

Jack's slick fingers pressed once, twice, then as Edward pushed out, Jack slipped in.

"Oh God, you're so hot, baby. So tight." Jack watched as he finger-fucked Edward. "I haven't touched a man like this in so long."

"How long?"

After a long pause, Jack whispered, "Years."

Edward couldn't think of a thing to say to that admission.

To Edward, it was unthinkable to go years without being touched or touching. Without physical contact or a relationship with a man. What would such denial do to a man's soul? What had it done to Jack? Perhaps Edward's need to be cared for, his longing to be loved, were the reasons for all his failed relationships.

But he'd rather die than never be touched, caressed, fucked.

Jack seemed to have controlled that need, or eliminated it.

Until now. Edward didn't know whether to be flattered or sad. Flattered that Jack couldn't resist him, or sad that Jack had been alone and untouched for so long.

"It's so good, Jack." Edward purred as he rode Jack's finger, his hips begging Jack to take it deeper. "More," he whimpered.

Jack smiled. "More? Like this?" His finger pushed in farther and brushed across Edward's gland.

"Oh God!" Edward arched off the bed, his cock slapping against his belly. If Jack kept this up, he'd come in no time.

"That's it, baby. I know you want it."

"Yes. I want it. Fuck me, Jack. Before I come." Edward grabbed his balls and pulled on them, cutting off his orgasm. "Now."

But Jack didn't pull out, he kept working Edward's bump. With each pass, Edward groaned. Sweat beaded on his brow, and his hand shook as it clutched his balls.

"Please!" Edward cried out. "Wanna come!"

"Then come. I'm in no hurry to fuck you." Jack leaned down, licked the inside of Edward's thigh, gave him a quick nip, then latched onto the tender flesh and marked Edward.

Edward thought he'd lose his mind. He let go of his balls, and in a single breath was right back at the top of the roller coaster, on the crest of the big drop, and Jack just kept it coming, kept raking over his sweet spot, kept driving him right over. The. Fucking. Edge.

"Jack!"

Edward's cum spurted, hot, ropy jets, splattering against his belly as his body shook, convulsing around Jack's finger.

"That's it, baby. I can feel you. Ride my finger."

Edward collapsed. Jack had wrenched one of the strongest orgasms he'd ever had from him. It had been mind shattering, because clearly Edward had lost his mind and the ability to speak.

He opened his mouth, but only a low, long moan came out.

Jack leaned over and filled Edward's open mouth with his tongue. Limp, Edward couldn't fight Jack. Dominating Edward, Jack's tongue made its presence known as it stroked every inch of Edward's mouth.

"Now, I'm going to fuck you, baby." Evil. Jack was evil and wicked and unbelievably hot. He was unrelenting. Unstoppable.

Thank God.

Edward's arousal soared again. Eager, he reached down and pulled his knees back, spreading himself for Jack. "I'm all yours."

Jack put his hands on the back of Edward's thighs, pushed up, and leaned down to lick Edward's hole. "I've always wondered what this would be like." Jack lapped him a few times and pulled back.

"And?"

"Fucking delicious. Just like every part of you." Then he gave Edward a sexy grin, dived back between Edward's thighs, and licked at Edward's tight rose.

Edward's hands trembled as he held his legs. "I'm ready, baby. Now. Please."

"Please?" Jack looked up, his hair falling carelessly across his forehead. Oh fuck, he looked so hot, so sexy.

"Please. Need you," Edward begged.

Jack sat up, ripped open the condom, rolled it on, and squeezed out some lube. He slicked up all eight inches and climbed back over Edward. Positioning his cockhead at the entrance to Edward's body, he pushed in.

Edward relaxed, let out his breath, and with Jack's next push, opened for him.

"Oh God. Sweet fucking Jesus," Jack groaned. "So tight. Yeah." Another push and his cock slid all the way in.

Filled with Jack's dick, Edward groaned, caught his breath, and let his body adjust to the needed intrusion.

"Gotta move." Edward wasn't sure if Jack warned him or if he begged him.

Edward pulled back and then surged up, taking the first stroke, letting Jack know he could move. "Fuck me."

Jack did. Slow at first, his pumping was rhythmic, intentional, controlled. Each stroke designed to bring Edward pleasure. Above him, Jack's body stretched tighter than a drum, the muscles in his arms and chest corded with the effort it must have taken to go so slow, when all he must have wanted to do was hammer Edward's ass.

Edward wanted to be pounded. Wanted to be handled.

"Harder."

Jack picked up the pace, his breath coming fast and harsh. Edward's cock came to life. Amazing. He couldn't believe it. As if he were sixteen again and so randy that he would get hard just thinking about dicks.

Jack sat back and pulled out of him. The look on his face had changed from concentration to something wild, dangerous, and uncontrolled.

Oh yes.

With a growl unlike anything Edward had ever heard, Jack grabbed Edward and flipped him over onto his stomach. Grabbing him by the hips, fingers digging into Edward's flesh, Jack dragged him up onto his knees. It was rough and harsh and felt just like when Jack had thrown him against his office door.

He was so fucking turned on. His cock stiffened with the handling, the wanting...

"Let go, Jack. Do what you want to do to me."

Jack's intake of breath filled the room. "You're so impetuous, baby. So wild. You need...to be tamed."

"Then tame me."

"You like it, don't you? When I'm rough. When I let you know who's the boss." Jack's eyes glittered, hungry, like a predator.

"Yes," Edward croaked out. So close, so aroused, he lost the ability to speak again. Single syllables only, thank you.

"Who's the boss?" Jack's cock touched his ass, slipped between his cheeks, and found its home.

"You."

Jack shoved in. Pain and pleasure blended as Edward cried out.

"Goddamn." Jack gasped. "Oh...fuck." Jack seemed to have lost speech also. Edward grinned. He'd done that; he'd reduced Jack to one-syllable words.

Jack gripped Edward's hips, holding him in place as Jack pressed down and rammed Edward's ass as he rode him. Jack's head thrashed, his eyes shuttered, and a low, steady moaning rumbled in his chest, bypassing his throat.

Edward rested his head in his folded arms and went along for the ride. And it was a fucking wild ride as Jack's growls turned to grunts, his balls slapped Edward's ass. He shafted Edward deep and fast, taking Edward higher and further than he'd ever gone. To know that Jack felt safe enough with him to let go, to lose himself, to take what he wanted, turned Edward on like nothing else.

Edward reached down and stroked his prick. At this pace, Jack couldn't last long. He'd done so much to Edward, Jack had to be ready to unload, and Edward wanted to come with Jack. Wanted Jack to feel him come around Jack's cock.

"Fuck! God. Yes!" Jack leaned over Edward's back, burying his face in the back of Edward's neck. Edward's back and Jack's chest sealed together, sweat as their glue, Jack's hips pumping, jerking, out of sync, back in rhythm, faltering; then in a final burst of rapid fire thrusts, Jack groaned. Stiffened.

Edward's balls drew up, his hand raced over his cock, and he felt the warm flood of cum as Jack emptied inside him. Edward flew over the edge, joining him.

Jack shuddered, clutching Edward, his head working from side to side against the back of Edward's neck, soft, sweet lips brushing his hair.

Edward slid flat on the bed, carrying Jack on his back. Jack slid to the side but didn't let go.

He didn't let go.

Edward fought to stay steady, not to succumb to the feelings that rocked him, that almost pushed those three damning words from his lips.

Then Jack pulled Edward to his chest, his face still at Edward's neck, his hand making a lazy circle over Edward's chest.

And for a glorious moment, Edward felt treasured. Loved.

He sighed.

In the morning, after the regret set in and the lust wore off, Jack would leave. He knew it because Jack had lost control with him. Had taken chances he'd never in a million years take, like kissing him in his office or storming off because he'd seen Sammi kiss Edward or coming to the motel to see him.

And Edward knew that for Jack, that made Edward dangerous.

Chapter Twenty-five

Unable to sleep, Edward watched Jack sleep. Jack's face and body had lost all the tightness, the wariness, the tense struggle for control that Edward now recognized was the man's state when awake. He'd hoped that for a short time he'd made Jack happy and relaxed, because Edward never expected Jack to fall in love. Want him, sure. Love him, no.

Edward had been in love too many times to count, but none of the men he'd fallen for had ever loved him back. And if a bunch of bad boys and twinks hadn't loved him, what made him think a remarkable man like Jack Whittaker would?

No. Jack would leave and never look back, like everyone else.

Edward had known that going into this, and for his own good, for once in his life, Edward would do the smart thing. There could be no future with Jack. None.

Edward craned his neck at the clock on the nightstand. Four thirty.

"Jack. Wake up. You need to leave." Edward didn't trust himself to touch Jack. One touch wouldn't be enough. It would just lead to others, and they'd lead to fucking, and

Edward just couldn't do more without losing what was left of his heart to Jack.

Jack's eyes fluttered as he focused on Edward. Edward braced for the realization and regret to show in Jack's face.

Jack smiled, reached for him, and pulled him close.

Why did Jack have to do that? Why couldn't he have just let his regret show? Edward closed his eyes and basked in the warmth of Jack's body next to his. It was foolish, and he knew it.

"You have to leave."

Jack groaned and sat up on the edge of the bed, reaching for his jeans.

"Can I see you again?" Jack didn't face him, just stood and pulled his pants up.

"I'm free for dinner tonight," Edward quipped.

Jack froze, then continued working his buttons. "You know I can't do that."

"Because you've got another date, or because you don't want to be seen with me?" Edward had to push, unable to do anything else or be anything else. He wouldn't know how or where to start.

"I'm the chief of police, baby." Jack sighed, as if he were explaining something to a small child. Edward pushed himself up against the headboard, surprised at his sudden anger.

"You can fuck me, but you can't have dinner with me?"

"I want to see you again, but here." Jack slipped on his shirt, buttoned it.

"What for, Jack? What's in it for me?" Besides the phenomenal sex? Oh, sure, there would be the heartbreak, the self-flagellation, the knowledge that Edward hadn't been enough for yet another man.

Jack shrugged, sat, and pulled on his boots. "I have some vacation time coming. I was thinking I could take a trip to Atlanta." Jack turned at last and faced Edward, a flicker of hope in Jack's eyes.

Edward sat with his arms crossed, to keep from reaching for Jack. It was a tempting offer, if sex were all he wanted. He felt like Julia Roberts in *Pretty Woman*. A motel outside of Spring Lake or Atlanta—it was just geography.

He shook his head. "Where would that leave me, Jack? Living for those two weeks a year when you showed up, then spending the other fifty getting over you, only to do it all again the next year. And then what happens when you can't come or eventually don't show up?" Edward sighed.

"What do you want from me?" Jack's hands fisted, his gaze avoiding Edward's.

"I want to be with a man who loves me, who isn't embarrassed to be with me."

"I'm not embar—"

"Don't lie to me or yourself." For the first time in his life, Edward was going to be smart, even if it broke his heart. "I want the fairy tale. I want what Brian and Rush have, what Sammi and Mitchell have. I want forever."

"Edward, I—"

"Can't give that to me. I know. You're the chief of police. Respected by the good people of Spring Lake. You can't go traipsing around town with a fag like me." Edward was so numb he couldn't feel his toes. Bitter and numb, not a pretty combination.

"Edward."

"Shut up, Jack. Don't say anything else." Edward closed his eyes, took a breath to steady himself. "Just go." If Jack didn't leave right now, Edward would give in, and he couldn't do that. For once in his life, Edward wanted someone to beg *him* to stay, to beg Edward to be with him, to beg Edward to love him.

Jack went to the door, turned back as if to say something, then opened the door and left.

Edward stared at the door for a long time.

Woof.

He got out of bed and let Winston out of the bathroom. The little bulldog jumped up on Edward's legs, trying to climb up.

"Sorry, boy. I forgot about you." Kneeling, he pulled the dog into his arms. Winston gave him a lick on the chin.

"Jack's gone," he whispered in Winston's ear.

Woof.

"I know. I'll miss him too." He stood up, went to the dresser, and pulled out his sweats. Going back to bed with the sheets smelling like Jack, male sweat, and their mingled cum would be too much.

"It's for the best, you know. It would never have worked. I'd have just been hurt again." He dressed and grabbed Winston's leash. "A quick walk, and then I'm going for a long run."

Without another look at the bed, Edward snapped the lead on, and they left the room. It was still dark, but the lights from the parking lot illuminated the grassy area.

He'd drive to Meemaw's, then go for a run from there. Then he'd take care of what he'd come here for.

If it went well, he'd be on his way back to Atlanta by Saturday.

* * *

Jack pulled into his drive, parked, got out, and went inside. He stood in the hall, unsure of which way to go, what to do, or what he wanted.

A week ago, he'd known exactly what he'd wanted from life. He'd have told anyone who asked that he was happy. He had it all, was content with his life, had met all his goals, and was living the dream.

He looked around the empty, darkened house. In the kitchen, frozen dinners for one waited to hit the microwave. In the living room, no arguing over the remote or which movie to watch. In the bedroom, he had the bed all to himself.

How did he think it would end with Edward? Did he really think he could fuck him once, or even twice, and not lose his heart? Not realize that Edward was the best thing he'd ever seen?

Edward probably hated him, and he had every right. Jack's need for control, his fear of embarrassment, of being shamed and ridiculed, had ruined the most beautiful thing that had come into his life in a long time.

He started down the hall. He needed a shower to wash away the memory of what he'd done with Edward. Of how free he'd felt, of letting go and taking what he'd so desperately needed. Edward had awakened feelings that Jack had suppressed for years.

It didn't matter now. Nothing mattered. It was over.

He stripped, tossed the clothes at the growing pile around the hamper, and turned on the shower, adjusting the temperature to hot. Then he stepped in and let the scalding water beat down on him, pour over his head, run down his face, into his mouth, over his chest, his back, his flanks, thighs, feet. Rinsing Edward off him.

Edward clung to him like guilt.

With the soap clutched in his hand, Jack scrubbed. And scrubbed. And scrubbed until his skin was red and raw, but Edward, as tenacious as his bulldog, wouldn't leave. Wouldn't go away and leave him in peace. Just leave him the fuck alone.

Edward refused to go.

He could still feel Edward's body, still smell the scent of Edward's hair, the taste of his mouth, his sweet cock, his musky balls, his salty, bitter cum. They inundated Jack's senses, and all he could see, taste, feel, was Edward.

Jack beat his fist against the tiles. Then his other fist hit the tiles. He heard a cry of frustration and hit the wall again to stop it. Another cry, another punch. Over and over until his cries were too hoarse to be heard, his shoulders and arms trembled, too heavy to lift, and his busted knuckles splattered blood on the tiles. The drops swirled on the floor and slipped down the drain.

* * *

Edward jogged up to Olivia's house. His dawn run had been good. This time he'd gone the opposite way to avoid the mechanics at Smith's Garage. He'd pushed himself until the sweat poured down his face, nearly blinding him. His clothes were soaked and clung to his body.

It was too early to bother his grandmother.

He got back in the car and drove to the motel, stopping at the fast-food place to pick up some breakfast. He ordered coffee and one of those meals with everything.

In his room, he tossed the food on the minuscule table, sat in one of the two chairs, and opened the containers. Didn't look at the bed.

"Winston. Here, boy. Breakfast." Edward held out a sausage patty, and Winston took it from him and swallowed it whole. "You need to chew, Winston."

Winston ignored Edward's suggestions.

Edward looked at the food, then dropped the container on the floor. Winston buried his face in the tray and feasted. Edward went to the bathroom. A shower first, then go to see his grandmother and discuss his plan to heal her.

He undressed and ran the shower. After testing the water for warmth, he stepped into the cramped little tub and pulled the shower curtain closed. A tiny bar of soap sat in the holder. He'd forgotten to bring his good soap into the shower.

Too tired to care, he ripped the paper off the motel soap and washed the sweat off. His shampoo and conditioner sat on the edge of the tub. He pumped out a small amount and lathered, rinsed, and repeated.

Finished, he got out, toweled off, and wiped the fog from the mirror.

Stared at his reflection. How could he look so normal? Look just the same as yesterday, when nothing now was the same? He was different now, changed, the new, improved Edward. Smarter. Braver. Able to leap heartbreak in a single bound.

No one could see the cracks in his heart.

Chapter Twenty-six

Somehow, Edward hadn't been able to get around to talking to Olivia about healing her. They'd spent the day chatting, and he'd driven her to the church for a board meeting, waiting in the car until she came out an hour later. They'd had lunch at some ladies' lunch place that served soup, dainty sandwiches, tea, and salads. He'd been the only male in the place. Olivia had introduced him to all the ladies, and they'd been very friendly and welcoming.

They ran errands to the post office and brought a casserole she'd bought at the little café to a sick friend; then he took her to the local Wally World and followed her around as she wandered the store, greeting the workers and the other shoppers by name.

After cooking dinner together, they'd watched some television until she'd announced she was ready for bed. He'd gone back to the motel, took Winston for a walk, and then at last, he faced his own bed.

Thank God, earlier that morning, the maid had come in while he walked Winston and cleaned the room. He'd begged clean sheets along with towels from the young Hispanic woman.

Winston had jumped up on the bed and settled down in his spot. Edward drew back the covers, climbed between the cool, unscented sheets, and only took two hours to decide to get up and take one of his sleeping pills.

Now it was Friday morning, and he'd planned to leave town tomorrow. It was now or never, and never wasn't an option, not as long as his mother was alive and kicking and in control of the purse strings.

Edward dressed, walked Winston, put down food and water, and hung the DO NOT DISTURB sign on the door. He got into the Miata and drove to Olivia's.

He knocked on the door and waited. It was almost nine thirty, so she should have been up by now. He rang the doorbell.

Still no answer.

Edward dug in his pocket and pulled out the key to her house. He opened the door and stuck his head inside. "Meemaw?"

The house was silent. Had he forgotten something? Did she have an appointment and had arranged for someone else to take her?

He entered and shut the door. The front room was lit, the TV on. Some chatty blonde interviewed a second-rate movie star. Edward walked into the kitchen.

It was empty, clean, everything in place.

He trembled as he turned toward the hall and her bedroom.

"Meemaw? Olivia?" His call echoed in the empty house.

He pushed open her bedroom door. The bed had been made. Nothing out of place. It was strange. His gaze darted to the door to her bathroom.

He crossed the room and listened. No shower running.

He knocked. "Grandmother? It's Edward."

He turned the knob and pushed the door open. Olivia lay curled up on the floor, her face so white that he thought she was dead.

"Oh God," he whispered as he knelt next to her. She was so small, her knees drawn up to her chest, her arms wrapped around her belly.

Edward touched her cheek. "Meemaw?" he croaked. He'd been too late. Oh God, he'd blown his chance to heal her, and she'd died. A sob broke from his chest.

"Edward." It was a whisper, and his heart thudded double time in his chest. She didn't move, and for a moment, he thought he'd only imagined her voice, but her eyes shifted behind closed, translucent lids.

"I'm here. I'm calling an ambulance." He sat on the floor next to her, afraid to leave her alone. He pulled out his cell phone, called 911, and gave them the address.

Then he took her chilled hand in his, opened the barrier between them, and searched for the darkness that lurked in her body.

* * *

Brian leaned against the counter of the ER nurses' station and finished his paperwork. He'd followed the ambulance from the car accident he'd been working to get the rest of the information from the kid who'd run his truck into a ditch.

He suspected the teenager was drunk, but without the official alcohol level from the blood test, Brian couldn't arrest him, only write a ticket for losing control of his vehicle. Thank God no one else had been involved and the kid had only broken an arm.

Brian glanced up as the automatic doors to the ER swung open and two EMS guys wheeled a gurney in.

Edward trotted alongside the trolley, holding Olivia Rawlings's hand.

"Edward! What happened?" Brian pushed off and met them halfway down the hall.

"She collapsed. I found her at home in the bathroom," Edward said as they wheeled her into a room. The nurse stopped him from coming in, and he stood in the hall next to Brian looking stricken, pale, and lost.

"Shit." Brian took Edward by the arm. "Let's go over here and get out of their way. You can't help her now."

"I can. I did." Edward stared through the glass wall to the room as a doctor joined the nurse. They hovered, fussed, adjusted, and inserted needles and tubes, doing whatever it was they were supposed to do to the small figure under the white sheet.

"You called 9-1-1 and got her here." Brian nodded as he pulled Edward to the closest waiting room.

"She was on the floor. I sat with her until they arrived. I took—" Edward faded out as he allowed himself to be led down the hall. He was pale, shaking, and looked only an inch away from death himself.

Brian sat him in a chair. "Wait right here. I have to make a call."

Edward grimaced, wrapped his arms around his belly, and doubled over.

"You okay?" Brian hesitated.

"Fine." It was more a groan than speech.

Brian stepped out of the room, pulled out his cell phone, and searched his contact list. Hit Send.

"It's Brian. You need to get down to the hospital."

* * *

Edward had had no choice, and he'd do it again if given the chance, but hell and damnation it hurt so *badly*. He just had to remember to breathe.

He tucked his head between his legs as wave after wave of nausea swept over him, his jaw clamped shut to keep from vomiting. After a while, the pain and nausea dissipated, but it had taken its time, leaving him weak. He prayed the cancer had left with it.

He checked his watch. It had been almost thirty minutes since he'd brought Olivia here, and no one had reported her condition to him yet. Forcing himself to sit upright, he took a few deep gulps of air and searched the room for Brian. He'd been in and out, had brought Edward some water, sat with him, given him a few comforting words.

No Brian.

He needed to call his mother. He pulled out his cell phone, and too tired to care, hit her number.

"Mother, it's Edward. You better come. Meemaw is in the hospital, and it doesn't look good."

There was silence, then his mother's strained voice, "I'll be there as soon as I can." She hung up. Edward snapped the phone closed and leaned his head back against the wall. Took a few breaths until he felt better.

He stood, shook off the last of the dizziness, and went to the door. Leaning against the frame, he looked up and down the wide hall. Doctors and nurses bustled in and out of rooms all along the white corridor.

At the far end, Brian stood near the nurses' station talking to someone. Edward headed that way, hoping Brian knew Olivia's condition.

"Where is he?" Jack asked. He would never admit how hard his heart was pounding or how fast he'd driven, lights and siren on, just to get there. He didn't need to admit it because Brian had called knowing that Jack had feelings for Edward and that he'd drop everything to be there.

Brian knew, and Jack didn't care.

"In the waiting room. He looks bad, Jack." Brian scratched his chin.

"Is he in shock?"

"No, I don't think so. It's like he's in pain."

"Shit," Jack hissed, guessing what had happened. "That little fool." He stepped around Brian, determined to have a word or two or three with Edward. Maybe grab him by the neck and shake him, if he didn't just grab Edward, hold on tight, and never let go.

He couldn't do that. He'd blown his chance with Edward.

Edward came down the hall, looking bone tired. Jack knew the moment Edward recognized him from the rapid flashes of emotion that played across Edward's face. Not all of them were good, but he deserved that.

"What are you doing here?" Edward asked as his eyes darted from Jack to Brian.

"I called him." Brian gave no excuses.

Edward looked up into Jack's face. "Chief Whittaker." He turned away. "Brian, have you heard anything about Olivia?" Edward had dismissed Jack, but Jack wasn't going anywhere. One look at Edward had made that impossible.

"I was just coming to get you when Jack caught me. You can go in to see her now."

"Thanks." Edward went past them to her room.

Unable to leave, Jack followed Edward. Brian trailed him, but Jack was glad the younger cop had decided to stay.

At the door to Olivia's room, Edward paused, then went in. Jack hung in the doorway, uncertain if Edward would need him or not. Unsure what the hell he was doing there, but positive he wasn't leaving until Edward told him to go.

Brian stood on the other side of the glass, watching.

"Meemaw?" Edward sat in the chair by the side of her bed and took her hand. She looked frail, old, and if Jack read the signs right, she was dying.

"Edward." She smiled at her grandson, love lighting her eyes. "I'm so glad you're here. I have so much to tell you."

"Shhh. You don't have to say anything." Edward kissed her hand.

"But I do. I know what you tried to do for me, back at the house." She frowned. "Don't do it again." Her voice was soft but adamant.

"But I have to, Meemaw. It's why I came. I have to heal you." Edward petted her hand.

"I know. And I want you to stop." Her eyes flicked to Jack's, and she gave him a nod. "Come in here, son. Don't linger in the door."

Jack felt Brian push him forward. He stepped in as Edward looked up and frowned.

"Jack. Tell him. He mustn't try to save me. I won't live knowing I passed this cancer on to him."

Edward shook his head as Jack came closer. "Baby, you listen to your grandmother. She's telling you what she wants."

"No." Tears welled in Edward's eyes. "Meemaw, I can save you."

"Edward. I don't need saving. Jesus and Frank are waiting for me, and I'm ready to join them."

Jack came up behind Edward and placed a hand on his shoulder, expecting Edward to shrug it off. Edward accepted his touch, and Jack gave Edward a reassuring squeeze.

"Now you listen to me, Edward. I forbid you to try to heal me." Olivia's tone said she'd stand for nothing less than total obedience. Jack almost asked her if she knew whom she was dealing with, but he kept quiet.

"But if you go, I won't have anyone." Edward sounded like a child, lost and alone, and Jack's heart broke at it. Edward's tears spilled and ran down his cheeks. Jack kept his hand on Edward's shoulder, offering support.

Olivia glanced up at Jack. "Jack, you take care of my grandson." Recognition passed between them, and somehow, it didn't frighten Jack. He'd been asked to tend something precious and fragile, and in that moment, he realized it was a priceless treasure.

"No, Meemaw. Jack can't promise that." Edward shook his head. "Don't ask him what he can't promise."

Olivia looked up at Jack, and he gave her a nod but said nothing. Edward didn't see Jack's promise. Edward didn't have to know, not now. Maybe not ever.

Edward pressed his cheek against her hand. "But I just found you. You can't go now."

"I have to. It's my time." She winced. "And it's your time to live, child. Promise me you won't try to do anything to stop this."

Jack could feel Edward's body shaking under Olivia's demanding stare. "I promise," Edward whispered, and his breath dragged in, the sob caught in his throat. "But you're in so much pain."

"I refused the drugs. Don't want to be all drugged up, in some kind of coma. That's no way to live, and I want to live until I take my last breath." She shook her head. "Besides, I have things I need to tell you. Secrets that should have been told fifteen years ago when your father died."

"Father?" Edward's back stiffened.

Olivia nodded. "I want you to know the truth. About why I never spoke to your father. Why he and Lillian took you away. Why your father treated you the way he did."

"I know that; he hated that I was gay."

Olivia shook her head. "No, that wasn't it. He was afraid of what he was, that he'd passed it on to you. That you were a punishment for what he'd done to Lillian by living a lie."

Edward sniffed again. "What are you talking about?"

"Edward, I was in San Antonio. You know how I love the Riverwalk. I saw him there with his lover. A young Hispanic man. They were going into a hotel."

"I don't understand."

The light dawned for Jack. Holy shit.

"Eddie was gay. I found out and told him if he didn't tell Lillian, that I would. We had a terrible argument over it, and he admitted that he'd had lovers. That's when he left, cut off all communications, and took the family back to his home in Atlanta."

Edward didn't say another word. Jack figured the light had hit him too.

"Gay?" Edward whispered. "I don't understand. How could he be gay and treat me the way he did?" He slumped back against Jack. Jack put a hand on each of Edward's shoulders to support him.

"I never understood it either. I told you that Eddie put his own problems on you."

"Did Mother know?" Edward looked at Olivia.

"I think she did."

"And she let him…" His voice caught, and he shook his head. New tears welled and fell.

Jack wanted to pummel someone, but Edward's father was dead and his mother was a woman. Up until this moment, he'd believed a man should never hit a woman. Her treatment of Edward made him reconsider his beliefs.

Christ, Jack didn't know how much more of this truth Edward could take, and he wasn't sure Olivia was doing Edward any favors.

"Is that all?" Edward sighed. He seemed to accept what she'd said.

"No, there's one more thing." She gasped and clenched her hands, and a small moan escaped her. "Maybe I should rethink those meds." She chuckled gamely, but Jack could see the pain and fear in her eyes.

"Let me help you." Edward leaned forward.

"No. I won't let you risk it."

"Let me just take some of the pain away. So you can bear it," he pleaded.

Olivia looked up at Jack again. "What do you think?"

Edward turned and stared up at him, as if seeing him for the first time.

Jack cupped Edward's face in the palm of his hand. "Baby, can you just take the pain? Can you stop it if it goes too far?" Jack had promised Olivia to look out for Edward, and he meant to, whether Edward wanted him to or not.

"I can. I can control it." Edward nodded, his eyes begging Jack to believe him. Jack knew Edward needed to do this, needed to help his grandmother and ease her passing, for her sake and for his own.

"If I think you're getting in too deep, I'm going to break it off," Jack warned, as if he had any right to care for Edward, as if what he said mattered.

Edward nodded, accepting Jack's help. Jack didn't fool himself that it meant anything more than what it was.

"I believe he can control it. Let him try, Olivia." Jack dropped his hand from Edward's face.

Olivia nodded, closed her eyes, and lay back against the pillow. "Before you do, I have to tell you something else." She took a breath, opened her eyes, and looked straight at Edward. "Everything is yours, child."

"What?" Edward looked at Jack, then back at Olivia.

"Everything I own. The ranch, the house, all the leases. All yours. You're my sole beneficiary and have been since your father took you away."

Edward sat back. Jack gave a soundless whistle.

"If I said you can have it all back, would you let me heal you and stay with me?" Edward choked out through his tears, but Jack knew Edward already knew her answer.

"No. I've got my heart set on seeing Frank." She gave his hand a pat.

Edward leaned forward and kissed her forehead. "I love you, Meemaw."

"I love you, Edward. Unconditionally."

Chapter Twenty-seven

"Jack, you better take your hand off my shoulder. I'm not sure if you could be hurt if you're touching me." Edward knew what he needed to do and knew that he could do it. If anyone was going to be hurt, it would be him.

Jack nodded and dropped his hand, but didn't move away. Edward could feel the warmth of Jack's body behind him, could smell Jack's scent, and it reassured him. Jack would be there for Olivia, and that was enough.

Olivia closed her eyes, and Edward brought her hand to his lips, then lowered it to rest on the bed. He took a deep breath and let it out in a long, slow exhale. Closing his eyes, he placed his hand on top of hers and closed the distance between them.

Nothing rushed at him, but from the two times before, he knew he'd have to seek it out, go back to the place he'd found it before and confront it and his fears.

Edward's way seemed clearer, the path not so strange, and in an instant, he was there.

Dark, pulsing, ominous, it lurked near the center of her being. It had grown bigger, even from this morning. Edward's fear kicked in, and he hesitated. Before, he'd rushed to pull it away from Olivia, only to take more than he'd planned, and his rashness had left him ill and struggling to throw off its effect on him. If he were going to survive this and help Olivia, he'd have to take a lesson from Jack.

Edward reached down deep inside himself, found control, and mastered his fears. He approached it and drew on his power. As he wicked it away, nipping at small bits, his mind eased, his breathing was a slow rise and fall, his heartbeat perfectly timed to Olivia's.

He could do this.

The pain flowed through him in a continuous stream, not stopping to inflict harm, and dissipated into the cosmos, the ether, or wherever it went, but he knew it hadn't nested in him.

More confident than he'd ever been, he knew if things got out of control, Jack would be there. Jack might not love him, but Jack believed in him and his abilities.

The mass grew smaller, more concentrated, and wisps of the smoky tendrils disappeared. As Olivia's pain lessened, Edward felt her body relax, her breathing grow less ragged, her heartbeat stronger.

Was it enough? He could do more, but that would mean attacking the thing itself, drawing the cancer into his own body, and he'd promised her he wouldn't do that.

Edward pulled away, putting distance between them, backing out until he could barely feel her; then, with a final step back, they separated.

He opened his eyes.

Olivia slept, her face a study in peace and contentment.

"You did it, baby."

Jack had to stop calling him that, really. That one word from that one man, more than any other word he'd ever heard from anyone else, stabbed his heart. He would never belong to Jack, and they both knew it.

"Thank you for watching over me." Edward gave Olivia's hand a final pat and stood. "She'll be okay for a while."

"Do you think you'll have to do it again?" Brian asked. Edward had been so absorbed in his work, he'd forgotten about Brian being in the room.

"Maybe. It depends." He left out the rest of the sentence, "on how long she lives." He didn't want to think about that. Not right now, when the knowledge that he'd helped ease her pain was fresh.

"I need some coffee," Edward mumbled. He was tired but not exhausted.

They left Olivia's room and went to the waiting room.

Rush, Mitchell, and Sammi sat in a row on the chairs against the wall. Edward had no idea they'd come to the hospital. Brian must have called them. Sammi spotted Edward, stood, and rushed over to him. Smiling, he pulled Edward into his arms.

"You did good, Edward," he whispered into Edward's ear and gave it a quick kiss. This time it wasn't sexual, just a kiss of congratulations.

Edward pulled away. "I know." He sighed. "I just wish…"

"That you could save her. I know." Sammi nodded. There went that reading people's thoughts thing that Sammi did.

"Thanks for coming, y'all. Olivia would appreciate it. So do I," Edward said as he slumped into a chair. Rush handed him a cup of coffee, with cream and sugar. Edward cradled it in his hands, letting its warmth transfer to himself.

Now he wondered what next? How long?

Jack stared at Sammi, eating the hard taste of jealousy. The same bitter taste had sat in his mouth when he'd discovered Sammi and Edward kissing. He glanced at Mitchell, but he seemed to take it in stride. Maybe he was used to his lover kissing other men, but Jack would never stand for that crap. Maybe they did threesomes. He didn't care what they did, as long as Edward wasn't involved.

Sammi looked up and gave Jack an unsettling, knowing smile.

He gave himself a mental kick. He had no control over Edward. Never had. Never would. Edward was not a dog Jack could train to behave. Edward was Edward.

Jack wasn't sure if he could ever accept all that Edward was, and without that acceptance, Jack could never claim Edward as his. Edward wasn't going to change, not to suit Jack or anyone else.

And he shouldn't have to.

"I need to be going." Jack smiled as everyone turned to him. Sammi's eyebrows rose, Mitchell looked like he'd expected it, and Brian and Rush looked pissed.

Edward never looked up.

Jack left the room and headed down the hall to the exit.

Please don't leave, Jack. Edward's unspoken words were wasted.

Sammi leaned over to Edward. "Go after him."

Edward shook his head.

"Tell him."

"I can't. It wouldn't matter anyway."

"It matters. Tell him you need him." Sammi nudged Edward with his shoulder.

Edward stood. "I'll be right back."

In the hall, Edward jogged toward Jack. He'd almost reached the doors.

"Jack! Wait!"

Jack stopped and turned. For a second, Jack's face lit; then wariness descended.

"Yes?"

Edward stopped in front of Jack. "I wanted to thank you. For believing in me."

Jack, tight-lipped, nodded.

Edward didn't know what else to say. They stared into each other's eyes, searching for something that would let them reconnect.

"I don't know how long I'll be here. Can you take Winston for me?"

Jack stared at him.

"He needs to be walked, not cooped up in a small motel room. You know him and he knows you, and you know what he likes and…" Edward rambled.

"Sure." Thank God, Jack didn't say "baby." Edward couldn't take another endearment from Jack.

Edward dug in his back pocket, pulled out the card key to his room, and handed it to Jack. "Thanks."

Jack shoved it in his pocket, turned away, and left. He got to the door, paused, and turned around.

"For the record, you were right."

Edward tilted his head, unsure what Jack meant.

"About Winston. He was perfect just the way he was. I had no right to try to change him."

Their gazes locked, and Edward's heart thudded like a bass drum in his chest.

"He was a little…undisciplined," Edward offered. "A little control's not so bad."

"Maybe." Jack gave him a nod and stepped through the doors.

Edward watched him disappear into the darkness. It was night. He'd been at the hospital most of the day. With everything that had happened, he'd lost track of the time.

He returned to the waiting room.

Sammi stood. "Well?" Everyone else waited for Edward to speak.

"I asked Jack to take care of Winston. Until." He went to the chair he'd left and sat. Picking up his coffee, he sipped it, not wanting to talk to anyone.

Brian slipped to the door. "I need to make a call."

Rush looked up, gave him a wink, pushed his hat back on his head, and smiled at Edward. "You did a good thing for Olivia, Edward."

Edward smiled. He *had* done a good thing.

He just wished he could have done more.

Brian stalked down the hall, his cell phone pressed to his ear.

"Jack? What the hell?"

"Let's not get into this."

Brian ran his hand over his face. "What's wrong with you? Why did you leave? Edward needs you here."

He could hear Jack breathing. "I'm going to get Winston."

"Now you are, but before you were just leaving him here. Alone."

"Everyone's there. He doesn't need me."

Brian's hand curled into a fist as he fought the urge to deck someone. Preferably Jack. Instead, he shook the phone, then sighed and put it back to his ear. "Of course he does. I don't know what's going on between you two, but…"

"Nothing is going on."

"Try that bullshit on someone else. 'Baby'? I heard you."

Jack swallowed; the gulp came over the phone loud and clear.

"Please, Brian." Jack's voice sounded ragged and tired.

"Jack. I care about you. And about Edward."

"Thanks. But everything is okay."

"Bullshit!" A nurse walked past and put her finger to her lips. Brian leaned against the wall in a corner and lowered his voice. "Jack. I don't know much, but what I do know is this. If you love him, don't let him go."

There was a long silence as Brian waited.

Jack exhaled. "It's too late for that. I blew it."

"It's never too late."

"Let's just call it irreconcilable differences, huh? Night, Brian." Jack hung up.

"Shit." Brian closed his phone and slipped it back on the holster, then returned to the waiting room.

"I'm going home to change and get some sleep. I'm on duty in the morning," Brian told their little crowd.

Edward looked up, his face haggard. "Thank you, Brian. For everything."

Brian nodded. "Guys," he said to Mitchell and Sammi. "You've got a key to the house. Come and go as you please."

"We rode with Rush," Mitchell replied.

Sammi took Edward's hand. "I'll stay with Edward. We'll call you if anything changes."

Rush stood. "Mitchell and I will stay a little longer. Hold on."

Together they walked into the hall. Brian slumped against the wall.

"Darlin', you look beat." Leaning in, Rush ran his finger across Brian's lips.

"I am. It's been a long day. I hate when the shift changes, one day working nights, then switching over to days." He gazed into his lover's eyes and saw the promise there.

"Can I wake you when I get home?" And hunger. With a surge of pride, Brian could see the hunger that still burned in Rush's eyes, even after six months.

"You better." Their eyes spoke of what they longed to do, but they both had the good sense to know making out in the hallway of the emergency room wasn't a good idea and knew that their acceptance in the small town came with the price of control.

"Later." Rush pushed off and strolled, slow and sexy, down the hall to the waiting room as Brian savored the sight of his cowboy's slim hips and perfect ass.

He sighed and left for home.

As he walked to the patrol car, Brian worried about Jack. He might be in denial now, but any fool could see Jack and Edward had deep feelings for each other.

Brian just wished he knew what had happened between them. Not the details, just the events. Maybe Sammi would find out. Sammi and Edward seemed to have made a connection, not sexual, but between fellow similar souls. Both of them appeared fragile, their hurts so transparent, but they both had an inner core of strength far greater than anyone would imagine.

Brian hoped Jack would wake up, before it really was too late.

Chapter Twenty-eight

Jack opened the door to the hotel room. Winston stood up on the bed and barked, his hindquarters doing a happy dance.

"Hey, buddy!" Jack greeted the little dog.

Woof. Woof. Woof.

"Edward's tied up right now. You're coming home with me." Jack gathered the dog's food and water bowls and a few cans of dog food that sat on the dresser, and placed them in a pile on the table next to the leash.

He scanned the room. Walking over to the dresser, he opened it. Edward's clothes lay neatly folded in the drawer. He shut it and went into the bathroom.

Maybe he should bring some of Edward's things to the hospital. Then he thought about how bad Olivia had looked and decided that Edward wouldn't be there that long. He picked up a bottle of aftershave, opened it, and inhaled.

The scent surrounded him. Close but not quite Edward. The light musk of the cologne combined with Edward's own personal scent into something heady that left him aroused and aching. Jack could recall it as clearly as he remembered the smell of turkey on Thanksgiving, freshly baked chocolate chip cookies, or the heavy scent of jasmine on the vine that grew on his fence.

Would it haunt him forever? His regrets would, for damn sure.

Jack closed the bottle and put it back exactly where he'd found it. Then he gathered Winston's things and opened the door.

"Winston. Come."

The little bulldog trotted out the door and straight to Jack's patrol car.

They got in, and Jack headed for his house. He needed a hot shower and his bed.

"I think I'm in love with Edward," Jack mentioned to Winston as they drove.

Winston, hanging out the window, turned his head to look at Jack.

Woof.

"I don't know what I'm going to do."

Edward said good-bye to Rush and Mitchell around seven p.m. when they headed back to the ranch. Sammi, true to his word, stayed. He scooted his chair closer to Edward as he looked up from his second cup of coffee and smiled.

"Are you okay?" Sammi touched Edward's leg.

Edward shrugged. "You don't have to stay, you know."

"Leave you here? Alone? Jack's the asshole, not me." Sammi grinned and nudged Edward.

"Jack's not an—" Edward started, leaping to Jack's defense, but with a glance at Sammi, he stopped. "He's just…" He searched for words that wouldn't sound as bad when said aloud.

Sammi stared at him; then his eyes widened. "Ashamed of you?" He gasped. "Did he say that?" Sammi took Edward's hand and pulled it to his chest. "You must have been furious."

"Furious. Hurt." Edward shrugged. "Jack holds an important position here in Spring Lake. He doesn't want to be ridiculed, be made fun of, because of me."

"Why would that happen?"

"Here in Hooterville? Are you joking? No one would blink at him and me together in Atlanta or Houston, but here?" Edward shook his head. "Some of the people here are practically Neanderthal. I can't blame him."

"Stop it. Stop making excuses for him."

"I'm not." Edward sighed. "Look, I'll just say it. Jack might want me, but he's not *in love* with me. And I want someone who'll love me, all of me, not just my body."

"Did you tell him that?"

Edward nodded. "After the party at Brian and Rush's place. Jack came to my motel room. We had sex," he confessed.

Sammi's eyes twinkled. "And it was wonderful. The best sex of your life. Of his life. Right?"

"For me, yeah, it was. For Jack? I don't know. There were times when I thought… I felt so loved, and then… Sammi, he'd not been with another man in *years*. Can you imagine that? Not touching anyone or being touched." He probably shouldn't tell Jack's secrets, but Edward needed to talk, needed to share with someone, and it felt so right to talk to Sammi like this.

"I used to dream of a time when my body was my own, Edward. That no one would touch me and that I didn't have to touch anyone else." Sammi's eyes filled with a sorrow Edward hadn't seen there before.

"Really? Why?"

Sammi sat back. "I was a whore, Edward. A sex slave. Men paid to have sex with me. I met Mitchell when I ran away from my owner, Donovan. Mitchell and I fell in love. He's my soul mate, and he can hear my thoughts as well as I hear his. He helped me escape from Donovan and risked his life to do it. Brian helped him."

Edward listened as the young man spoke. Would anyone ever love him that much? "I've had sex with a lot of men."

"Did any of them force you? Or pay you? Did you do it just to survive? Were you punished if you refused?"

Edward clamped his lips together and shook his head.

"I can understand wanting control of your life and your body. But I'm not sure that's what's driving Jack." He leaned forward, his elbows on his knees. "From what I can gather, Jack is afraid, overly so, of being laughed at, like you said. But it comes from something that happened a long time ago. When he was younger."

"He never said anything about that to me. But then, we didn't really talk." Edward rolled his eyes.

"You should. Just talk and find out what's going on with him. Jack needs you, Edward, and you need Jack."

Edward laughed. "I think you're an incurable romantic, Sammi."

"I am. I was a damsel in distress, and Mitchell was my knight in shining armor. He rescued me, and I'm going to spend the rest of my life making him glad he did."

"I wish I had what you and he have. What Rush and Brian have."

Sammi nodded. "I know. But there's one thing I've learned. Anything you want, anything that's worth having, is worth fighting for. Fight for him, Edward."

"Doesn't he have to *want* me to fight for him?" Edward asked.

"He does. He just doesn't know it yet."

Edward smiled. He stood. "I'm going back to Olivia's room and sit with her."

"I'm coming with you." Sammi rose and followed Edward.

Edward settled into the chair at Olivia's side, Sammi in the chair near the door. The quiet noises of the equipment attached to his grandmother were the only sounds in the room. Edward stroked Olivia's hand, relishing the touch of her skin. Still warm. Still alive.

His eyes filled with tears every time he thought of her dead.

Sammi sighed. "Don't think like that."

Edward sniffled and wiped his eyes on the back of his sleeve. "Can't help it."

"You know, I just met my grandmother for the first time a few months ago."

"Really?"

"Yes. I never knew my mom and dad. I was raised by a string of foster parents until I couldn't stand it anymore and ran away from home at sixteen. I understand how important Olivia is to you."

Edward leaned over and rested his head against Olivia's hand. "Thanks for understanding."

Just then the nurse came in, checked Olivia's vitals, took her blood pressure, then left. Edward and Sammi returned to their vigil.

Twenty minutes later, a doctor came in.

"I'm Dr. Franklin, Olivia's oncologist."

"Edward Beauregard, her grandson." They shook hands. "Can you tell me what's going on?"

"Well, your grandmother has cancer. I suppose you've already figured that out. It's terminal. In case she didn't tell you, she's signed a living will. It states that she refuses any efforts, any treatments, to prolong her life. She's determined to live her life just as she always has, on her own terms." He chuckled. "She's one of the most strong-minded people I've ever known."

"I know."

"She seems to be resting comfortably for now." He held up the charts he carried. "To put it bluntly, she's dying."

"How long?" Edward's voice managed not to break.

Franklin shrugged. "Hours. Days. Not much more. Her numbers are very bad. Her kidneys are shutting down, and her other organs are beginning to fail."

"I understand."

"All we can do right now is to be here for her."

Edward nodded. Sammi stepped up next to him, wrapped his arm around Edward's shoulders, and hugged him tight.

"We're not going anywhere," Sammi said.

"I'm glad to meet you, Mr. Beauregard. I'm glad she has family to sit with her. I was afraid she'd go through this alone."

"Thank you for following her wishes." Edward shook Dr. Franklin's hand.

The doctor left, and Edward went back to his chair.

"Here, it's getting cold." Sammi found a blanket somewhere and wrapped it around Edward's shoulders. Edward accepted it and pulled it around him.

Sammi sat down, pulled his legs underneath him, and rested his chin on his knee.

Edward resumed stroking Olivia's hand.

Olivia slept.

* * *

Somewhere around three in the morning, Olivia's monitors went off. Edward jerked awake and stared at a multitude of red lines and beeping lights. A nurse bustled into the room, checked the frail woman in the bed, and turned off the alarm.

She turned a sad smile to Edward. "It might not be long now."

Sammi came to Edward. "Give me your phone, honey. Let me make some calls."

Edward nodded and thrust his phone at Sammi, unable to take his eyes off his grandmother. Sammi slipped out of the room to use the phone.

Scooting his chair closer, Edward took Olivia's hand in his. The temptation to do something, to open the portal between them, to leach away the cancer killing her, built in him along with his anger and helplessness, and the slow, sliding certainty of her death.

Panicking, he closed his eyes and focused on the portal, then stopped.

He'd promised her not to do it. Not to play God.

Edward cried out with the frustration of it all. He *had* the power. He *could* do it. She could stay with him a little longer. They could go on more picnics, ride around in his car, top down, the wind in their hair. He would still feel her love and acceptance of him.

Edward rested his forehead on her hand, his sobs choking him.

No one had loved him as she had, and it terrified Edward to think that no one ever would and that the only love and acceptance he'd ever known would die with her.

"I love you, Meemaw." Her hand was wet with his tears, but he dabbed at them with the edge of her sheet. "I'm so sorry I didn't come sooner. So mad at Mother and Father for keeping us apart. I'm going to miss you so much."

She lay silent on the bed, the life fading from her.

"I don't want to be alone, Meemaw," he whispered to her. "Don't leave me."

She didn't answer, but it didn't matter. She'd said all she needed to say to him, and that would have to be enough.

There was nothing left to do but pray.

Chapter Twenty-nine

Brian, Rush, and Mitchell met Sammi in the waiting room. Sammi flew into Mitchell's arms and buried his head in Mitchell's neck. "She's dying. It's so sad."

"It's okay, baby." Mitchell looked over Sammi's head at Brian. "Edward?"

"I'll check Olivia's room." Brian left and went down the hall.

Leaning in the doorway, he watched Edward, head bowed, his hand clasping Olivia's. It was very quiet. No beeps, no machines running.

Brian stepped in and went to Edward. "Edward. When did she pass?"

"I don't know. A little while ago." He straightened and looked up at Brian. "It's okay. She was ready to go. I just wasn't ready to let go." He gave Brian a sad smile and stood, still clinging to Olivia's hand.

Brian wrapped an arm around Edward's shoulder. "The others are waiting outside. You need to get some rest. We can make all the arrangements later."

Edward nodded. He let go of her hand, leaned over, and kissed her forehead, then let Brian lead him away.

It was surreal. As Edward walked down the hall, he couldn't feel his body, which was odd. Numbness radiated outward from his heart. And he was cold, so cold. Even Brian's arm on his shoulder, Brian's hand on his other arm, didn't give warmth.

They entered the waiting room, and three big men rushed him. Each one enfolded him in his arms in turn, each offering support and words of comfort. Edward was stunned. They had come for him, to help him through this, even though they'd only just met and barely knew him.

What had he done to deserve such friends? Had he been any different in Atlanta? He didn't think so. Maybe he'd just been hanging with the wrong people. A fast, wild life loaded with bad boys galore. A *Metropolitan Living* sort of life. All he'd done here was show up in Spring Lake and be Edward.

New, welcome warmth spread through Edward. As tears filled his eyes, he smiled at his new friends. Control came easier, and he blinked the tears away. "I'm okay. Really. Having y'all here right now is just…amazing. It means so much to me. Thank you."

A small voice came from behind him. "Edward. I'm so sorry about Olivia."

Edward turned. Kristen stood a little way from the group. "Oh, Kristen, thank you so much for coming. How did you know?"

"Brian called me. I wanted to be here for you. To let you know I cared." She reached out a hand; he took it. She pulled him in for a quick hug; then, her hands on his shoulders, she pushed him back and looked into his eyes. "Anything you need, just let me know."

"I will." He nodded. His eyes darted to the door. It would be too much to ask where Jack was and hear any answer except "he's on his way." His control could only stand so much.

Kristen squeezed his hand, as if she could read his thoughts, but didn't say anything.

What could she say, really? And what did he expect of Jack?

"I guess we should go." Edward shrugged. He had no idea what anyone did in this situation. Were there papers to sign? Bills to pay? Someone would stop him at the door if they really needed him.

Mitchell tucked Sammi under his arm. "We'll head back to the ranch with Rush, Brian. Don't worry about us."

Brian nodded. "I'll take Edward wherever he wants to go. Then I've got to go to work."

The logistics settled, the small crowd left the waiting room and stepped into the corridor.

Jack came through the automatic doors, and Edward dragged in a deep breath and stumbled. Just the sight of the man shook him to his core. His heart soared. He wanted to sing out, "Jack came!" at the top of his lungs. Struggling not to let anything show on his face or in his eyes, he kept walking.

Jack looked as bad as Edward felt. Demons warred in Jack's blue eyes as he stood there devouring Edward. It must have taken so much out of Jack to be here for Edward right now.

"Thank you for coming. Olivia would have appreciated it, Jack." His voice was almost normal and barely shook at all.

Jack's gaze searched his. "I couldn't stay away. You okay?"

Edward nodded. "Fine. Now."

As he stared at Jack, Edward wondered if the others could see the hunger in his eyes. Unsure of what Jack had told or what he'd kept secret, Edward had no idea what to do or say next.

Jack ended the uncertainty by stepping up to Edward, saying, "Come here, baby," as he folded Edward against him. Jack's smell, his warm, hard body pressed against Edward's, his sweet endearment, spoken aloud, not whispered, was too much for Edward. It broke what little self-control he'd found. He was safe in Jack's arms. Jack would catch him when he fell.

Edward fell. "Oh, Jack! She's gone!" he wailed, buried his head in Jack's neck, wrapped his arms around Jack's neck, and wept. Jack held and rocked him as Edward melted against Jack.

"I know, baby, I know. It's okay. She's happy and in a better place. This is what she wanted, remember?" Jack petted his head, stroking his hair, running his fingers through it.

Edward nodded, his face still hidden in the crook of Jack's neck.

"I've got him," Edward heard Jack say. "I'll take him home to my house. I've got Winston there." Then to Edward, "You want Winston, baby?"

Edward nodded, but this time he choked out, "Yes."

Jack's hands smoothed up and down his back.

"He's all yours, Jack," Brian said.

"Yeah." Jack leaned back, lifted Edward's tearstained face, and kissed him. Right there in the hall of the county hospital emergency room. With a crowd of people watching. With Jack's secretary standing there, for God's sake. Even a passing nurse or two.

Hell and damnation, Chief of Police Jack Whittaker kissed him. In public.

Edward broke their kiss as his eyes darted around the hall. "Jack. People."

Jack kissed him again, stopping any words from Edward. Only a soft moan managed to escape from Edward.

"I told you, honey. Just give it time." Sammi chuckled.

It seemed all Edward could do was cry, nod, or speak in monosyllables. How could his heart hurt so badly and rejoice so completely at the same time?

"Sure?" Edward asked Jack.

"Never been surer in my life. Let's go home." Jack tucked Edward under his arm and they left the hospital, followed by their friends.

Edward had no recollection of his feet touching the ground or of saying good-bye to the others or even getting in Jack's truck. All he knew was that he was with Jack. That Jack had come for him and been there when Edward had needed him. That Jack had claimed him in front of their friends and assorted members of the hospital staff.

"Jack. Everyone in town will know by lunch."

Jack was silent.

"You did think this through, didn't you?"

"Let me handle it."

Edward's stomach tightened as a gaping black sinkhole began crumbling away under his feet. "Tell me you'd made a decision to come out before you got to the hospital. That you didn't just let your emotions get the better of you. That this wasn't a huge mistake you're going to regret later."

More silence.

The sinkhole grew, huge, black, the ground beneath him disappearing.

"Jack?"

"I wanted to be here for you, Edward."

With nothing under Edward except black air, Edward threw out a lifeline. "But you didn't mean to let everyone know you're gay, did you?"

There was a long sigh. "Edward. Since you've come into my life, I don't know anything anymore. Not how to fish, not how to be content in my own house, not even how to sleep at night. All I know is that without you, all those things have become impossible. I tried to fight it, I did." His voice rose, anger seeping into his words. "I lost. If I mean not to go crazy, then I have to admit it."

"Admit what?"

It was now or never. Jack screwed his courage up. If he couldn't say it to Edward, how the hell was he going to say it to anyone else? Like Brian? Or his old friend Bill Lansing, the mayor of Spring Lake?

"I'm gay, and I love you, Edward. All of you. Just like you are. No changes. No training. You're perfect as is, and if I can't deal with that, then I don't deserve you." Jack caught the rope and pulled Edward out of the abyss.

Edward slid across the seat toward Jack as far as his seat belt would let him. He placed his hand on Jack's warm, muscular thigh. "Thank you, Jack. I know that must have been hard for you."

Jack chuckled. "Well, you know how they say, 'You can't teach an old dog new tricks'? I guess it took a little bulldog to teach this big dog that a person can be perfect just the way they are."

Edward leaned over and pecked Jack on the cheek. "I have a confession to make. Without you, I never could have helped Meemaw. Before you, I would have rushed in, done my thing, taken on the cancer, and probably gotten myself killed, or worse, hurt her in some way. Maybe spread it instead of taken it away." Edward shrugged. "But you taught me a little control goes a long way, and I used it, learned how to take just her pain. You saved me, Jack. In more ways than one." He squeezed Jack's leg. "So, maybe an old dog can teach a young dog a few new tricks."

Jack growled. "You saying I'm old?"

"Well, older than any of the men *I've* ever been with. Older than me."

Jack slung his arm over the back of the seat, his fingers playing in Edward's hair. "Age has its privileges, you know."

"Like age before beauty?" Edward quipped.

"Edward." Jack gave another warning growl.

"With age comes experience?"

"That's better."

"How about age will win out over youth and beauty every time?"

"More along those lines; that's what I was thinking."

Edward leaned back, happy but exhausted. "I need some rest, Jack. I just want to curl up in a warm bed and get some sleep. Then I need to tackle the arrangements for Olivia's funeral."

"Did you call your mother?"

"Oh shit!" Edward sat up, dug out his cell phone, and punched in the number.

"Mother?"

"Edward. I'm at the airport in Houston getting a rental car. I should be there in two hours."

"Don't hurry, Mother. Meemaw died early this morning. I'm so sorry."

There was a long silence; then her voice came back. "I see." He could hear her breathing. "Where are you staying?"

"I have a room at a motel off the I-10, but I have the key to Meemaw's house in town. Do you want to stay there?"

"Yes. That would be fine."

"Call me when you get to town, and I'll meet you there and let you in."

"All right." She hung up without another word.

"That doesn't give you much time for some rest. Let me take the key to her, baby," Jack offered.

"I'll see. While the idea of not dealing with my mother is tempting, I wouldn't want to inflict her on you."

"We'll have to meet at some point. After all, I'm her son's lover." Jack grinned and heat shot right through Edward's body.

"I like the way that sounds. However, I think I like 'partner' better. It's much more permanent." Edward raised an eyebrow as he waited for Jack's response.

"Partner it is." He winked. "How's this? Good morning, Mrs. Beauregard. I'm Jack Whittaker, your son's partner."

"That should throw her for a loop." Edward laughed. He closed his eyes, and before he knew it, they were at Jack's place.

They got out. Edward, with Jack's help, made it to the bed. Jack's bed. He crawled under the covers, inhaled Jack's wonderful scent, and promptly passed out.

Chapter Thirty

Jack sat in his truck outside Olivia's house, drumming his fingers on the steering wheel. Edward's mother should arrive at any time. Jack had left Edward sleeping when she'd called, and Jack had told her that he'd meet her and driven right over.

A white Cadillac Escalade pulled into the driveway and parked. Jack gave a whistle.

Why would he expect anything else? The Beauregards had money, he knew that, he just never expected such a display of wealth. The door opened and a woman slid out of the driver's side. She was petite, dressed in stylish pants and jacket, with perfectly styled dark hair.

Jack got out of his pickup truck and walked over to her, his hand extended.

"Mrs. Beauregard? I'm Jack Whittaker. I spoke to you on the phone."

"Hello, Mr. Whittaker." She took his hand in her graceful, well-manicured hand. "Where's my son?" Deep brown eyes took him in. Jack could see where Edward's looks came from, except his nose. Edward's nose wasn't turned up like hers.

"Edward is resting. He's been through a lot."

"Well, yes. I suppose so." It didn't sound as if she believed Jack.

"He was at the hospital all night with Olivia. I'm very sorry for your loss." Jack used his best diplomatic tone of voice, the one he used to soothe the ruffled feathers of important people.

"I got here as soon as I could. Edward didn't give me much warning." She patted her hair, as if a strand of it were out of place.

"He didn't have much warning. He found Olivia collapsed, called the EMS, and they took her to the hospital." Jack shrugged.

"Did you know my mother, Mr. Whittaker?" She eyed him.

"Sure did. Everyone knew Olivia." Jack smiled.

"I was just wondering what connection you have to my son and Olivia."

"Well." Jack took a deep breath, then let it out. Here it was, the first hurdle. "I'm seeing your son, ma'am."

"What?" She blinked and took a small step back. "Seeing Edward? What are you talking about?"

"You do know your son is gay?" Jack chuckled.

"You're gay?" Her eyebrows almost hit her hairline as her sharp gaze raked over him.

He hadn't meant to shock her, but if he intended on telling people, he'd have to get used to it, he supposed. Starting with people like Brian and Edward's mother was like riding a bike with training wheels. He'd have to work damn hard at falling off.

"Yes, I am, ma'am," he drawled, laying the accent on thick.

"My word." She stared at him. "You're older than Edward's usual fling."

"Yes. But I'm not a *fling*." Jack tried to keep the growl out of his voice.

"Nonsense." She waved her hand, dismissing him. "Flings are all Edward does. All he's capable of."

"Not anymore, ma'am." He shook his head, trying to stay civil. He was not going to argue with her about it.

She gave a very unladylike snort. "Edward changes lovers the way I change shoes. Don't say I didn't warn you."

A flicker of fear ran through Jack. Edward had mentioned he'd had lovers. What if his mother was right? What if he'd outed himself over a fling? Jack's stomach did a slow barrel roll, but he pushed the seeds of doubt she'd planted away.

She held out her hand. "The key, please."

Jack put it in her hand. "Edward says it opens the front and back doors."

"Thank you." She turned and went up the steps. "Oh. Tell Edward I want to see him as soon as possible. We have plans to make."

Edward had been summoned, and Jack had been given his orders and dismissed.

Christ, no wonder Edward didn't want him to meet her. She was a dragon, and Jack just bet she could breathe fire when she was riled up. He'd have to wear asbestos underwear to deal with her again.

Shaking his head, Jack got into his truck and watched as she opened the door and went inside. He pulled away from the house, unable to help the smile on his face. Edward waited for him at home. Asleep in Jack's bed.

His house was now a home.

* * *

"If my mother thinks she's going to run the funeral the way *she* wants it and not the way Olivia wanted it, she's mistaken." Edward paced back and forth across Jack's bedroom with Winston at his heels.

The fact that Edward wore only a pair of black boxer briefs completely distracted Jack from the conversation. The way they hugged Edward's thighs, the material cupped Edward's package and showed off his tight ass, just made Jack's mouth water.

And the younger man's bare chest? Christ, Jack wanted to suck on those pink nipples, run his tongue over Edward's abs, delve into his navel. Jack sighed. Now was not the time for such thoughts.

"Baby, you don't know what she's got planned. Why don't you wait and hear what she has to say, then go ballistic?" Jack tried to be the voice of reason, but Edward was not having it.

"I don't have to wait, I know." He stopped and faced Jack, who had sat on the edge of the bed to wake Edward up with a kiss. After telling Edward his mother's message, Edward had leaped out of bed and began pacing and ranting.

Winston sat too.

"Well, you know her better than I do, of course. I just met the woman." Jack shrugged. "But she is Olivia's daughter, and she should have some say in the plans."

Edward couldn't argue with that. He just rolled his eyes.

Woof.

"See?" Jack pointed at the dog. "Even Winston thinks you should cut her some slack. Both of you are upset over this. Her mother and your grandmother just died. Emotions are going to be high."

"Don't you start on me too, Winston." Edward glared at the dog, then sighed. "Thank you for running interference, by the way. Did you really tell her you were my lover?" Edward fell to his knees in front of Jack and sat. Winston trotted over to them and inserted himself between the lovers and stretched out, waiting to be petted.

"I did. She didn't believe I was gay." Jack chuckled.

"You don't look it." Edward grinned. "Face it. You had everyone here fooled."

"Yeah, well." Jack rubbed the back of his neck. "She also didn't believe I wasn't one of your 'flings,' as she put it. She said you weren't capable of sustaining a long-term relationship." He searched Edward's eyes for the truth.

Edward winced. "It's true that I've never been very successful with my relationships. You should know that. In fact, most of them have crashed and burned. However, it wasn't because I didn't want them to work. It's always been my heart that got broken." He stared down at his hands resting on his knees. "I always pick the wrong men."

Jack reached out, cupped Edward's chin, and leaned down to place a soft kiss on Edward's full lips. "Until now."

"Until now," Edward repeated, eyes still closed.

Woof.

"It's okay, buddy. You're going to have to get used to me kissing your daddy." Jack reached out and scratched the little bulldog behind the ears.

"I don't think his daddy will ever get used to it." Edward looked up at Jack from under impossibly long, thick lashes, and Jack's dick went rock hard.

"Now, why'd you have to go and do that, baby?"

Edward laughed. "Me? What did I do?"

Jack rolled his eyes, gave Edward a kiss, and stood. "Tease. Get dressed, and I'll take you to see your mother. I need to speak with the mayor."

"The mayor?" Edward got to his feet and took Jack's hand.

"Yeah. He should hear it from me, instead of at the coffee shop."

"Will it be bad?" Edward nibbled on Jack's knuckles, not helping his erection go down at all.

"Not as bad as your meeting with dear old Mom." Jack pulled his hand away. Any more attention from Edward, and he'd throw Edward on the bed and fuck him, and right now, that sounded like the best thing they could do, or at least the most fun.

With a huge, loud sigh, Edward headed for the closet.

"But after I see Mother, I get to say I told you so."

Edward always wanted the last word.

* * *

Jack sat in a chair and waited for Bill to get off the phone. He looked around the mayor's office and wondered if this was the last time he'd ever see it. He knew Bill couldn't fire him for being gay, but what if he asked for Jack's resignation, what would Jack do then?

Go without a fight? Stay? Jack knew that a good working relationship between the mayor and the chief of police made everyone's life easier and made things move smoother. He couldn't imagine the hell his life would be if they were at odds.

Bill hung up the phone and smiled at Jack. "What's so important, Jack?"

"Thanks for making time for me, Bill."

Bill nodded his encouragement.

Jack took a deep breath. "I wanted you to hear this from me, not passed along like some gossip."

Bill stiffened. "Is something wrong?"

"Not wrong. Well, you might think it's wrong, but for me, it's about as right as it gets."

"Are you resigning, Jack? What the hell?" Bill leaned back, bracing himself on the arms of his big leather chair.

"No. I'm trying to tell you that I'm gay." Jack waited for Bill's reaction.

Bill's body slumped into the chair as if all the air in him had escaped. "Shit, Jack."

"I know it comes as a shock to you, but it's time I admitted it."

"Gay?" Bill rubbed his hand over his face. "Gay." His gaze searched Jack's, and he shook his head. "Well, you certainly fooled me and everybody in this town."

"I know. Fooled myself most of the time. Spring Lake isn't exactly 'gay friendly.'"

Bill sat up. "I'd like to think we're at least fair. You've proved yourself time and again in the last four years as chief of police, and for over ten years before that as one of the finest cops this town has ever seen. Obviously, being gay had little to do with your ability to do your job."

"Thank you, Bill. That means a lot to me." Jack nodded. "I know that's the official stand, that's what you have to say to be legal." He looked up into Bill's eyes. "But what about you and me? We've been friends a long time, and I value your friendship. Are *we* all right?"

"That may be the official stand, Jack, but I hope you know me better than to think I'd just spout some politically correct crap at you and think something else. If I have a problem with it, I'll tell you straight up."

"That's why I came here first."

"Relax. I'm fine with it. Just wish you'd told me sooner." Bill rubbed the back of his neck. "Sorry about the time I tried to hook you up with my cousin."

Jack chuckled. "That was years ago, man. She was a nice lady."

"She married a rancher on the other side of San Antonio." Bill laughed. "So, what brought about this confession?" His eyes narrowed. Bill had always been as sharp as a tack.

"I've got someone in my life that I'm not going to be able to hide." That was an understatement. Edward's light couldn't hide under a bushel basket.

"I'm glad to hear that. It's not my business, but does this mean you're in love?"

"Yeah, I guess it does. Remember the little bulldog?"

"Winston?"

"Yep. Edward is Winston's owner."

"Wow. Olivia's grandson? Didn't you just meet?"

"Last week. I know it's fast, but…"

Bill held up his hand to stop Jack. "Don't explain to me. I remember the first time I saw Caroline. I knew right then and there I was going to ask her to marry me."

"Well, I can't marry him. It's not legal in Texas and probably never will be. Not in my lifetime, at least." Jack shrugged. "If he'll have me, I mean to live with him here in Spring Lake."

"Have you asked him?"

"No." Jack shook his head. "But I thought you'd better know about it so you wouldn't get blindsided. So you could decide what to do. About me." Jack looked into Bill's eyes.

"There's nothing to do."

"But what about the city council? They may not see it the same way."

"Let me handle them, Jack. We'll deal with it, if it comes up. Okay?"

"Okay." Jack stood and held out his hand.

Bill stood and shook it. "I'm glad for you, Jack. Don't really know what to say…congratulations? Best wishes?"

"Don't say anything, man. I'm just grateful for your understanding and support."

"You got it. Now, when do I get to meet him?"

"At Olivia's funeral. He's making the arrangements with his mother right now."

"I'm sure I'll like him."

"He's…" Jack hesitated, on the verge of warning Bill about Edward.

"He's what?"

"Wonderful. Gorgeous. A flirt and a tease, and I'm so fucking in love with him I can't believe it."

Bill laughed, came around the desk, and slapped Jack on the back. "You old dog."

"Funny you should say that." Jack grinned at his good friend, relieved this had gone so well.

With that, Jack left. Now, he just had to face his men at the department.

And everyone in town.

Chapter Thirty-one

Jack stood next to Edward as the minister talked about Olivia's life. Edward had asked Jack to be there as moral support. He'd told Jack that by having Jack stand next to him, it would be like putting them on display, letting the townspeople get used to seeing them together in a safe venue.

Edward's mother stood on the other side of Edward, her face hidden by a black veil. There had been a small argument about burying her under the oaks, but Lillian had given in faster than Edward had thought she would.

Wildflowers bloomed around them, the air thick with their sweet scent. It was incredibly peaceful. Olivia had made a good choice. The grave was next to her late husband, Frank Rawlings. Forever together.

That's how love should be. How Jack wanted it to be for he and Edward.

Half the town stood behind them in the little grove on Olivia's ranch.

Jack glanced around, seeking support of his own.

Mayor Bill Lansing and his wife were there to pay their respects to Olivia. Bill raised an eyebrow and gave Jack a small nod at Edward, then smiled, showing his approval and support. A small flicker of pride in his lover ran through Jack, and he remembered how he'd gushed over Edward in Bill's office. *Shit.* Jack had actually *gushed.*

Brian met his gaze and gave him a small nod. Like Jack, Brian had worn his dress uniform. Jack checked out several other officers who'd shown up. There had only been a few of his men who'd let Jack know they weren't happy with their chief being gay.

He could deal with the ones who were open about their dislike. It was the ones who hid it who were dangerous. Looking down the line of his officers, he ticked off whether they stood with him or against him. Shit. Now was not the time for that.

Behind Brian stood Rush, Mitchell, and Sammi. Jack was glad they had all returned for the funeral in support of Edward. He needed all the friends he could get, especially now that the news was out and things had begun to heat up.

The day before the funeral, Edward had come out of Olivia's house to find his car had been vandalized. Someone had spray painted FAG GO HOME on the side of it. He'd called it in, and a report had been filed. Jack was certain it wouldn't be the only act of intolerance they'd face and doubted they'd ever catch who'd done it, even though Jack had a good idea who the culprit was. Edward had told him about the incidents at Smith's Garage, and Jack would lay odds it had been Jimmy Wyatt.

Jack didn't care, as long as no one got physical. Edward was no match for most of the men around here, and Jack couldn't guard him every minute of the day.

Still, they'd get by. Or they'd leave. Jack had decided he'd resign if the town couldn't accept them or if it got too intense. He'd give up everything he'd worked so hard for to protect the man he loved.

Jack's attention came back to the minister as he closed the ceremony with a prayer. Most of the men slid their hats back on their heads, including Jack.

Next came the hard part.

Edward had arranged for everyone to go back to Olivia's ranch house and have lunch. It's what she would have wanted, he'd said. He'd wanted a picnic, complete with blankets, but Lillian had fussed, so they compromised with tables and chairs under the oaks.

Lillian had been calm, almost eerily so, and Jack had been bracing himself for when she blew. He could see it building and knew that Edward felt it too.

Jack wandered through the crowd, his gaze searching for Edward every now and then. Edward and Lillian stood near the tables of food laid out under the oaks in front of the house and greeted their guests. Kristen and some of the women from church had helped to organize the reception, cooking food, making Igloo coolers full of iced tea, setting up tables, and now they served the food.

Surely no one would disrupt Olivia's funeral. She was probably one of the most beloved people in the town. No, they'd give *her* their respect.

It was tomorrow Jack worried about, and the days after that.

Sammi approached him, linked his arm in Jack's, and pulled him along.

"Don't worry, Jack. I've been listening to everyone."

Jack stared at the young man on his arm. "Listening?"

"Yes. I can hear everyone's thoughts." He shrugged. "It's a gift. Like Edward's ability to heal. Most of the people here are cool with it."

"With what?"

"You're being gay. With Edward. They like him, but they *love* you." Dark eyes flicked up to meet his.

"Love me?" He'd never thought about the people of Spring Lake caring for him.

"Love. Respect. Care about." Another shrug. "Don't worry. This town will accept you and Edward, just like they accepted Rush and Brian."

"Not everyone is here."

"No. Not everyone. But enough." Sammi sounded so sure.

"Thanks for letting me know." Jack stared at Sammi. After all, he'd just told Jack that he could hear people's thoughts. In their heads. Odd thing was, Jack believed him.

"There's no need for you to leave Spring Lake. You're needed here. So is Edward."

"Edward?"

A sly smile parted Sammi's full lips. "He's been thinking about the future. Ask him."

Then Sammi let him go and slipped back to Mitchell's side. Mitchell wrapped his arm around his lover and pulled him close even as he stood speaking to someone. Unashamed of Sammi.

Time for Jack to man up.

He made his way to Edward's side and put his arm around Edward's shoulder. Edward leaned into him, seeking comfort. Lillian looked at them and frowned.

"Sorry if this bothers you, Mother." Edward smiled as Jack pulled him closer.

"I'm just worried about Jack, dear. He seems such a nice man."

"He is." Edward tensed under Jack's arm.

Lillian turned to face her son. "You're going to destroy him, you know."

"What?" Edward's voice rose.

"Lillian." Jack sighed. "Edward isn't going to hurt me, just like I'm not going to hurt him. We're going to be together for a very long time."

Edward looked at Jack as his brows shot upward.

"I want you to live with me here. My place is small, but it's big enough for two."

"Actually, I had other plans."

Jack's heart stuttered. "What?" He let Edward go. Took a step back as everything came crashing down around him in one sharp blow to the gut.

Lillian let out a little noise of triumph.

Edward faced his mother and stepped away from Jack. "Olivia left everything to me, Mother. Both houses, including the ranch and all its income. I won't need my trust fund, at least until I'm forty when it comes to me. You can't control me anymore."

"Everything?" She gasped.

"Yes. All of it. And I want to—"

"You had her change her will?" Lillian hissed as her eyes narrowed. "That's why you were so eager to stay. That's why you didn't heal her. To get the money."

"No! She asked me not to heal her. She had a living will and refused my help, just like she refused the doctor's help. She'd changed her will when you took me away. And she told me the truth about Father."

"Truth? What truth?" Her head snapped back.

"That Father was gay. Like me." Edward's hands curled into tight fists. "And you never told me. And you never stopped him, never came between us. You knew, and you let him treat me as if I were worthless. Less than a man. I'll never forgive you for that." Edward's eyes went liquid.

"She said that? She told you he was *gay*?"

"Mother. She caught him with one of his lovers. Threatened to tell you if he didn't tell you. That's when he packed us up, cut her out of our lives, and left Texas."

Lillian clutched at her chest, her hand searching for something to sit on. Jack rushed to a nearby chair, snagged it, and placed it under her. She hit the chair as if her knees had given way.

"Gay?" She shook her head. "Your father was *not* gay." She said it as if he'd accused his father of being an alien from outer space.

Edward knelt beside her. "As long as I can remember, you and Father had separate bedrooms. Whose room did you have sex in, Mother?"

"Sex?" she whispered.

Edward stood. "Sex. Did you *ever* have sex with Father after I was born? I'm gay, and I'll tell you the truth. I could never have sex with a woman. Just couldn't. Some gay men can and do, in order to live the lie. If Father did have sex with you, it was probably infrequent, every now and then."

She rubbed her hands over her crisp black linen skirt. "Once in a blue moon." The she looked up, tears in her eyes. "I just thought he didn't want me that way and that I didn't please him anymore. I thought he had mistresses."

"No. It wasn't you; it was him," Edward said. "I guess he deceived us both." He took her hand in his and brought it to his lips. "I'm so sorry he hurt you."

She brushed his bangs from his forehead. "I'm sorry I let him hurt you, but he always knew what was best for us. I believed him when he said we shouldn't coddle you or give into your phases."

"Phases? Being gay is a phase?" Jack snapped. "Pretty damn long phase, if you ask me."

"Father was very persuasive." Edward gave his mother's hand a squeeze and let it go. "I'm going to live at the ranch house. I'm going to use Olivia's house in town to open my massage business." Jack marveled at how confident and sure Edward sounded, like a completely new Edward. The Edward who didn't want Jack. Who didn't want to live with Jack.

Christ. He'd been such a fucking old fool.

Jack's heart hurt so bad he thought he'd just die. He needed to get out of there, leave before he made a complete fool of himself. Lillian had been right. Jack had destroyed himself over Edward.

There was no taking this back. No way to make it right. No way to go back to his nice, safe little life.

He lurched away, pushing through the last of the guests, to get to his truck. He had his hand on the handle when a hand on his shoulder jerked him around.

"Jack? Where are you going?" Edward looked up into Jack's face.

"I'm getting out of here. Have some pity for me, Edward. Leave me some dignity," Jack gritted out.

"What are you talking about?"

"I gave up everything for you. My career. The respect of my friends and my men. I was even willing to walk away from this town, the only real home I've ever had, for you. And you tossed it to the side."

"I don't know what you're talking about."

"I'm talking about us, dammit." Jack growled, taking Edward by the arm, his hand convulsing. "I'm talking about being in love with you and you dumping me, like all the others." Jack's heart shattered, and it took the breath from him, leaving him gasping.

Edward's mouth hung open. "Dumping you? Others? Where did you get that idea?" What the fuck was Jack talking about?

"I guess your mother was right. I was just another fling." He gave Edward's arm a shake as he let him go. "Leave me alone, Edward." He got in the truck and slammed the door.

Lillian. Edward should have known. If he didn't act fast, he'd lose Jack, and that was not going to happen. Not this time. This time, he'd fight for his man.

Edward jumped onto the running board and grabbed Jack's arm through the open window. "Jack! Listen to me. She's wrong. She's just trying to break us up. I love you. You have to believe me. Those other men, the ones she's talking about, they dumped me. They. Dumped. Me." Edward hung on, even as Jack tried to shake him off. "I wasn't good enough. Not for them." Edward's voice caught in his throat. "When you said you loved me, as is, well, that was the most wonderful thing anyone has ever said to me. But if you don't believe in me, in my love, then I guess I'm not really good enough for you either." Edward didn't know what else to say, so he let go and stepped down off the truck.

Jack shook. Unable to get the key into the ignition, he gave up. It all came down to this. He loved Edward, but did he believe Edward?

Raising his head, he looked into Edward's eyes. They were large, deep brown pools that pulled him under every time he gazed into them.

"I want you to live with me at the ranch," Edward whispered. "I should have talked to you about it first, not sprung it on you."

"Live with you? At the ranch?" Jack dropped his hands into his lap and laid his head on the steering wheel. "Christ,

Edward." His entire body turned to mush, and he was afraid he'd never be able to lift his head again. He'd stormed off like a petulant lover in the middle of Olivia Rawlings's funeral.

The town would be talking about this for years.

He'd let himself get so out of control with Edward. Over Edward.

Oh fuck, yes, Edward was dangerous. And Jack had developed a taste for danger.

"I'm so sorry, love. I didn't mean to hurt you like this. I love you," Edward said.

Jack pulled himself together, opened the door, and stepped out of the truck.

"Edward." He grabbed Edward by the lapels of his black suit jacket and hauled Edward against his body. "If you *ever* do that to me again, I won't be responsible for what happens."

Then Jack crushed his mouth to Edward's.

Applause and cheering went up around them. Jerking back, Jack looked around. A small crowd, with Brian, Mitchell, and Sammi at the front, had gathered around them. The uniforms of the Spring Lake police force were scattered among the people. Kristen stood there, tears painting her cheeks.

"Oh shit." Jack groaned.

"He loves me!" Edward waved to everyone.

"Edward," Jack growled.

"Shut up and kiss me again." Edward pulled Jack to him, and their lips met in a scorching kiss.

"Get a room!" Mitchell shouted, and laughter erupted.

"Okay, everyone, show's over. Break it up." Brian waved his hands to disperse the crowd.

"Excuse me. I have something to take care of." Edward's eyes narrowed, and he spun away from Jack. He made his way through the crowd, back to the tables, to where his mother sat, as Jack followed, unsure of what Edward was going to do.

"Mother. We need to talk." Edward planted himself in front of the table, leaned down on his fists, and glared at her.

She shrank back and said nothing.

"If you ever try to interfere or come between Jack and me again, that's it."

Jack smirked. The Dragon Lady had just met Son of Dragon Lady, and Jack had a good idea who was going to win this battle.

"What?" Her mouth gaped open, and her eyebrows hit her hairline.

"You heard me. I know what you're up to, and it won't work. You're not going to sabotage Jack and me. If you try it again, you're out."

"Out?"

"Out of my life, Mother. Alone."

"But darling…" she stuttered.

"Your word. I want your promise."

Mouth open, she turned to Jack for support. Jack shrugged. "If I were you, I'd make that promise." Then he wrapped his arm around Edward and tugged him close.

She exhaled. "Are you sure, Edward? Is he the one?" Suddenly, Jack could see the concern for Edward in her eyes. Maybe she accepted him, after all.

"Yes, Mother. Jack's the one and only man for me."

"And I guess you know I love Edward enough to risk everything," Jack added.

She looked from one to the other and then sat back. "You never cease to amaze me, Edward. If you're happy, then I'm happy." She stood. "Take good care of my son, Chief Whittaker."

"I intend to, ma'am." Jack doffed his hat to her.

"And Edward?"

"Yes." Edward grinned up at Jack, then looked at his mother.

"Take good care of Jack."

"I will." Edward gave Jack a peck on his cheek.

"I'm leaving this afternoon, as soon as everything is over here." She stood and brushed off her skirt. "I'll expect the two of you for the holidays."

"Yes, ma'am," they chorused, as she walked toward the house.

Chapter Thirty-two

Jack shut his bedroom door, unbuckled his holster, and placed it on his dresser. He jerked off his tie and shrugged out of his jacket.

"Man, I thought they'd never leave. Good thing the food ran out." It had been a long afternoon, and only the knowledge that he'd have Edward all to himself had made it bearable.

"It was a good service. And a great turnout. Olivia would have been so pleased." Edward flopped back on Jack's bed.

Edward must have been exhausted; he'd been on his feet all day, meeting and greeting the people who'd attended the service, listening to condolences and stories about Olivia.

Jack sat on the bed and ran his hand over Edward's thigh. "Been wanting you all to myself all afternoon, baby."

Edward laughed, reached up, wrapped his hands around Jack's neck, and pulled him down into a soft kiss. Jack went willingly. Christ, Jack loved kissing Edward. He had the softest lips, like tiny pillows to rest his mouth against. And the taste of him? Just one taste and Jack got so hard he ached.

Edward pulled on Jack's shoulders and rolled Jack onto his back. Edward looked down at Jack, mischief glinting in his eyes. Christ, Jack hoped it was more than mischief.

"Me too. I know it's weird, but all I could think about was dragging you inside the ranch house and making love with you with everyone still standing around on the front lawn. It's made me crazy, not getting to be with you for the last three days." Edward's fingers flicked open the buttons on Jack's white dress shirt.

"Well, I think it was best for you to stay at Olivia's house with your mother and get things ironed out." Jack relaxed as Edward undressed him.

"I'm just glad she went back to Atlanta after the funeral." Edward spread Jack's shirt wide open and sighed. "Good Lord, Jack. You've got the most scrumptious body I've ever seen." Edward ran his finger around Jack's nipple. It pebbled and sent a small aching to Jack's loins.

"What? This old thing?" Jack chuckled, pleased that Edward, younger and much more handsome than himself, found him desirable. That pleasure urged Jack's stiff cock to escape its containment.

Edward unzipped Jack's pants, pushed down Jack's briefs, and wrapped his soft hand around Jack's throbbing dick. "No, this old thing." Edward leaned down and took Jack in his mouth. Jack arched off the bed as wet warmth surrounded his flesh.

"Fuck." Jack groaned. Edward sucked him down, taking him to the root, burying his nose in Jack's thick pubes, then pulled back, sucking and working his tongue around Jack's shaft.

Edward deep throated him a few times and took Jack right to the fucking edge.

"Shit. Wanted to last. Longer," Jack gasped. His balls pulled up, the buildup in his groin intensified, and he knew he was going to shoot his load. He fought it, trying to make it last, trying to enjoy Edward's gifted tongue.

Could Edward heal him with a blowjob?

He didn't know. All he knew was that he loved Edward more than anything or anyone in his entire life. He would gladly face the entire town's wrath just to be with his lover.

Edward dug his tongue into Jack's slit. Jack gurgled, thrust deep into Edward's mouth, and spilled down Edward's throat. Edward sucked him until he stopped spurting, then licked Jack's dick clean and left it with a kiss.

"Sorry." Jack gulped air, his body still shuddering.

Edward stretched out next to him, his fingers playing in the hair on Jack's chest. Edward's chest was smooth. It was a wonderful difference that Jack, as a man, appreciated, just as he loved the way Edward's body was smaller, tighter, younger.

"Don't apologize. I love that I can make you lose control." Edward's lips turned up in a sly grin.

Jack took Edward by the arms and pulled him on top of his body. "I know. You have this power over me, baby. I can't help myself. You make me so hot, so turned on, so fucking furious, all at the same damn time."

Edward laughed, kissed him as he ran his hands over Jack's chest. "Get naked."

Jack sat up, kicked off his shoes, pushed off his pants and briefs, and yanked off his socks. When he lay back on the bed, Edward was naked and crawling between his legs.

"I want inside you," Edward whispered. He bit his lip and looked down at Jack from under dark, long lashes.

A shiver of fear ran down Jack's spine. "It's been a long time since anyone's had my ass, baby." It would hurt, no doubt, but he wanted it.

"But you like it?" Edward's hands trailed down Jack's body, over his hips, along his thighs. Every stroke of Edward's soft hands felt like lightning dancing across Jack's skin, raising the fine hairs on his body.

"Not as much as I like fucking, but yeah, I like it. At least I did the few times I tried it." Jack may have been older than Edward was, but he definitely wasn't as experienced, and most of his sexual encounters had been a very long time ago.

Edward ran his hands up, cupped Jack's balls, and then he leaned over and took one in his mouth. Jack's hips surged back as if he tried to bury them in the mattress. His dick came to life, as blood filled it. Edward switched to the other ball and worked it over until Jack quivered.

Jack closed his eyes, his breathing came deeper, and he just let go. He was safe with Edward. He could lose control, and Edward would be there to catch him.

The sound of the top of the lube being flicked open brought the fear back, and he tensed.

"Relax. I'm not as thick as you, lover. I'll go slow."

Jack nodded. Edward eased his hand under Jack's balls, stroking his lube-covered fingers down the sensitive underside all the way to his puckered hole. Jack couldn't tell if the ache was fear or longing, but he wasn't going to let fear stand in the way of pleasing his lover.

Another dab of lube across Edward's fingers and they pressed against his ass. Jack pushed back, and Edward's slender finger slipped inside him.

"Ah." Jack grunted as the feeling of fullness fought with the pain of being stretched. Edward waited a moment, then went deeper. Pulled out, then back in, building a steady rhythm of in and out until Jack was humping Edward's finger.

Edward nailed his gland, and Jack cried out, his back arching off the bed, his fingers twisting in the covers. Edward kissed Jack's belly, his tongue delving into Jack's navel, nibbling flesh as he finger-fucked Jack.

And Jack loved it. He fucking loved it. Wanted more. Wanted Edward's dick in him, wanted to feel Edward lose his load, fill him with his cum, warming him from the inside.

"Do it, baby. Fuck me." Jack humped Edward's finger.

"Sure?" Edward rested his cheek against Jack's belly and looked at him. Jack drank in dark, liquid eyes, dark hair, swollen red lips, and a soft, stubble-covered chin. Everything about Edward turned him on.

"Fuck me."

Edward pulled out, tore open a condom, and rolled it on. Jack wrapped his legs around Edward's waist, angling his ass upward. Edward brought his velvet rod to Jack's entry and pushed. Jack pushed back, needing Edward inside him, all fear gone, nothing left but the ache and the desire and the fucking want.

Another small thrust and Edward was in. Jack's ass screamed; then, as he gulped down air, his channel relaxed.

Full. So full. Edward's long, slender cock wasn't all the way inside. As Jack's prick sprang to life, he knew he could do this.

"Move." Jack slapped Edward's hip and impaled himself on Edward's dick.

Edward didn't hesitate; he pulled out, shafted in. They danced the age-old dance. The push and pull. The in and out. The back and forth.

Each giving control, and each taking it.

Jack fisted his dick. "Gonna come."

Edward nodded, his lip bit between his teeth, unable to say a word, only groan and roll his eyes. He shifted and nailed Jack's bump. Jack thought he'd lose his mind, it was so good. He hadn't remembered it as being this good. Maybe it was because Edward was fucking him. Maybe it was because for once, he'd given someone else control.

"More, baby." Jack begged for it.

"Fuck, Jack." Edward's hips jerked. He opened his eyes and looked down at Jack.

"I love you," Jack gasped as he coated his hand and his belly with spunk.

Inside him, Edward erupted, cried out, and froze, pumping his release, filling Jack's ass with the heat of his cream.

Jack lowered his legs and sank into the bed. Christ, he'd been fucked and it had hurt so damn *good*. Despite his screaming ass, he wondered how long it would take before they could do it again.

With a final shudder, Edward pulled out. He got a damp cloth and cleaned Jack, then climbed back into bed. As he fell to the side, Jack pulled him into his arms, spooning his chest against Edward's back.

"Thank you, love," Edward whispered.

"For what?" If anyone should be giving thanks, it should be Jack. He'd never been happier than at this moment, holding his lover in his arms, nuzzling the soft nape of his lover's neck.

"For loving me." Edward brought Jack's hand to his lips and kissed it.

"Unconditionally," Jack whispered as he tucked Edward's head under his chin.

* * *

Two months later

Edward swung through the double doors of the police station.

"What's the story, morning glory?" He perched on the edge of Kristen's desk.

"What's the tale, nightingale?" she sang back. "How's business at the Spring Lake Day Spa?"

"Growing!" He snagged her hand, peered at her nails, then tsked at them. "I've got you down for the full treatment next week, right?"

"You bet. I can't wait. I'm taking a half day off." She sighed. "One hour massage, spa pedicure and manicure. It's every woman's fantasy. I'm so glad you added those two women to do nails. If I ever win the lottery, I'm getting one of those massaging spa chairs."

"Well, nothing's too good for my clients," Edward cooed. "Is Jack in?"

"Yep. Go on in." She jerked her head at the door.

Edward rapped once on the door, heard "enter," and went inside.

"Hey, lover," he greeted Jack. Good Lord, every time he saw the man, he got goose bumps and rock hard.

"Hey, baby." Jack looked up from the computer. "Are you sure you can watch him while I go to the police chiefs' meeting in San Antonio this afternoon?" Winston sat by the desk, wiggling in anticipation of greeting his daddy.

"Of course. I told you before I don't mind having Winston with me at work. The clients love him so much they ask for him." Edward knelt and held out his arms. "Come, Winston."

The little bulldog bounded toward him and landed in his lap. Edward scratched his ears, then cooed, "Did you have fun playing police dog? Catch any big, bad criminals?"

Woof.

Jack rolled his eyes. "He was a pain in the butt. Now he barks for me to run the siren whenever we get in the cruiser. And you've got him so spoiled that I'll have to work on his training again this weekend."

"Well, it just goes to show you, a free spirit can never be caged."

"No, it just goes to show you that a little control is never enough." Jack grinned as Edward sat on the edge of his desk. He wore Jack's favorite jeans, the ones with the rips, the ones that gave Jack glimpses of the flesh he loved so much.

"You'll be home later tonight?"

Jack ran his hand over Edward's leg. "Yes. Be ready."

"Oh, I'll be ready all right." Edward leaned over and stroked Jack's bulging erection. "Ready, naked, and oiled up."

"Oh fuck." Jack surged up, catching Edward's mouth with his, pushing his tongue between Edward's lips. Edward melted against Jack. Christ, he loved that.

Jack pulled Edward against him, as they rubbed their cocks together.

"Christ. I need you." Jack moaned. He'd taken Edward's ass this morning, then sucked his lover off, but it felt as if he'd gone days without being inside Edward. Over the last two months, Jack had had more sex than he'd had his entire life.

"Need you too," Edward answered, and with a final caress of Jack's dick through his uniform pants, Edward pulled away.

Jack sighed. He'd never get enough of Edward. Never get tired of loving him and being loved by him. Of the taste of his mouth, his skin, his cock, his sweetly bitter cum.

Edward went to the door, Winston at his heels, then paused and looked over his shoulder. "I love you, Jack."

"I love you, Edward. Unconditionally."

Edward opened the door as if to leave, then leaned back into the office.

"Later, gator." He winked, and he and Winston slipped out the door.

Jack laughed and shook his head.

Yep. Always the last word.

THE END

Lynn Lorenz

Lynn writes a variety of genres besides historicals, including police procedurals, fantasy, paranormal, and contemporary romantic comedy, but enjoys reading suspense and detective stories most of all and wishes more cops would fall in love between their pages.

Born in New Orleans, she has a strong affinity for the South, pralines and po'boys. She's never met food she didn't like, but finds it hard to beat the food she grew up with and constantly craves from N'awlins. Going back occasionally to visit her father who still lives there, her car is often laden with epicurean delights such as Hubig Pies, Barqs in the bottle, Central Groceries' muffalattas and Gambino's pastries.

She has a real job that keeps her busy nine-to-five, but in her spare time she finds it hard to stay away from writing. It keeps her off the streets and out of the bars.

Lynn has two incredible kids, a supportive husband of twenty plus years, and a black lab/Aussie sheep dog mix. She's lived in Katy, Texas, since 1999, where she discovered her love of all things Texan and cowboy, like big hair, boots, and blue jeans. Yeehaw!

Find out more about Lynn by visiting her website: http://www.lynnlorenz.com

Breinigsville, PA USA
05 April 2010
235536BV00001B/84/P